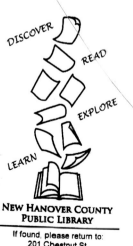

THE CHAOS

THE CHAOS

NALO HOPKINSON

MARGARET K. McELDERRY BOOKS
New York   London   Toronto   Sydney   New Delhi

MARGARET K. McELDERRY BOOKS
An imprint of Simon & Schuster Children's Publishing Division
1230 Avenue of the Americas, New York, New York 10020
MARGARET K. McELDERRY BOOKS is a trademark of Simon & Schuster, Inc.
For information about special discounts for bulk purchases, please
contact Simon & Schuster Special Sales at 1-866-506-1949 or
business@simonandschuster.com.
The Simon & Schuster Speakers Bureau can bring authors to your live
event. For more information or to book an event, contact the Simon &
Schuster Speakers Bureau at 1-866-248-3049 or visit our website at
www.simonspeakers.com.
Book design by Debra Sfetsios-Conover
The text for this book is set in Electra LT Std.
Manufactured in the United States of America
10 9 8 7 6 5 4 3 2 1
Library of Congress Cataloging-in-Publication Data
Hopkinson, Nalo.
The Chaos / Nalo Hopkinson. — 1st ed.
p. cm.
Summary: Toronto sixteen-year-old Scotch may have to acknowledge
her own limitations and come to terms with her mixed Jamaican, white,
and black heritage if she is to stop the Chaos that has claimed her
brother and made much of the world crazy.
ISBN 978-1-4169-5488-0 (hardcover)
ISBN 978-1-4424-0955-2 (eBook)
[1. Interpersonal relations—Fiction. 2. Supernatural—Fiction.
3. Identity—Fiction. 4. Racially mixed people—Fiction.
5. Brothers and sisters—Fiction. 6. Family life—Canada—Fiction.
7. Toronto (Ont.)—Fiction. 8. Canada—Fiction.] I. Title.
PZ7.H778127Ch 2012
[Fic]—dc23
2011018154

Deepest love and thanks to David,
for powering me through the last rough patch of years

ACKNOWLEDGMENTS

My thanks to David C. Findlay for creating the lines of spoken word poetry that Richard recites during the open mike.

This book became stalled when a combination of new and chronic medical conditions overwhelmed my life partner and me, made us both unable to work, and tumbled us into four years of destitution and eventually homelessness. While we were struggling to regain some kind of balance and self-sufficiency, so many people looked after us in one way or another! I still tear up when I think of it. I'm enormously grateful for the wealth of love and support that helped me regain my strength and my ability to write. There are so many people to thank that I'd probably run out of space if I tried to do it here. Just know, each and every single one of you, that you've helped to give me the most precious gift: my life back.

Thank you.

NALO HOPKINSON

"Okay, people," Mrs. Kuwabara called out cheerfully. I'd been back in school barely two weeks since summer break, but I'd already learned that our new English teacher was cheerful about everything. "The bell's going to go in about fifteen minutes. Finish up the questionnaire you have in front of you now, because I have one more for you."

Beside me, Ben sighed and rolled his eyes. "Oh, God," he muttered. "I don't want to know myself this well."

"Yeah," I said. "Don't people go blind that way?"

Ben chuckled. Mrs. Kuwabara had decided that it would be a good idea to spend the first weeks of eleventh grade doing this boring old self-knowledge questionnaire, a little bit every English class. She'd told us that no one was ever going to read them unless we gave them permission, not even her, so we should write whatever we wanted. I ask you, what was the use of doing all that work in school if you couldn't even get a grade for it?

Mrs. Kuwabara handed Jimmy Tidwell a stack of sheets of lavender-colored paper. He blushed. He was all elbows and angles and zits, and he fell over his own feet as often as he walked on them, and he blushed at everything. He was mad good at trig, though. And a decent private tutor, once he got absorbed in the work and stopped blushing and stammering. His face crimson, he stood up and started handing the sheets out to the class. He was cute, in a skinny white boy kinda way. He always tried really hard to talk to my face, not to the front of my sweater. That earned him extra points in my book.

I reread the part of the last questionnaire I'd just spent thirty-five minutes filling in. Mrs. Kuwabara had copied the questionnaire onto sunshine yellow paper. Mrs. Kuwabara was big on colors. At the top of the sheet, printed in swirly black letters surrounded by scrollwork, were the words:

FIVE THINGS THAT MAKE YOU HAPPY

The rest of the sheet had five boxes, made up of more swirly scrollwork, for filling in the answers. I'd written:

1. *Wine Gum jelly candies, but only the black ones. I think they're supposed to be licorice flavored, so I should hate them because I hate licorice, but black Wine Gums don't taste like licorice at all. Wine Gums don't even have any wine in them, either. I know, because when I was little, my parents checked the list of ingredients before they'd let me eat any. Maybe those black ones aren't licorice at all. Maybe they're meant to be black currant, or something. The other colors taste like ass. Can I say that? Oh, right; Mrs. Kuwabara won't be reading this, so I can say whatever I like. Problem is,*

you can't buy a roll of Wine Gums of just one flavor. So I get Glory to buy them and give me the black ones. At least, that's what I used to do back when Glory and I were still friends. Ben doesn't eat candy. He's watching his figure. Really, it's weird how much I love black Wine Gums, seeing as other gummy things freak me out.

2. *Hailstorms in the middle of summer. First time I saw one, I was a little girl. Maybe eight years old. I stepped outside our house in the middle of a boiling hot summer day, and little stinging things were pelting my skin. At least, that's what I thought they were at the time. They lay there, sparkling clear in the green grass, melting even as I watched. I went inside and told my dad that there were diamonds on the ground outside. He's the one who explained hail to me, but I still like to think of it as diamonds falling from the sky.*

3. *Hanging out with my friends Gloria and Ben. At least, I did like that. I still like it now, even though it's only me and Ben any more. We can talk about anything — why boys are so dumb (Ben thinks boys can be dumb, too, even though he is one); why girls are so dumb; whether you should keep your eyes open or closed when you kiss someone, and if you keep your eyes open, how you stop yourself from laughing at how funny someone looks that close up with their pores showing and their eyes crossed from trying to look back at you; whether it's better to have a happy life and die young or to have a miserable life and die old. I met Glory and Ben when I transferred to this school in grade nine. We hang out together, but not like the Thompson Twins. Ben's on*

and off dating this boy named Stephen, and Glory's trying to steal my boyfriend. Okay, he's my ex. But that's why I'm not talking to her anymore, 'cause she turned out to be such a big skank. I used to think that together, me, Ben, and Glory could do anything. Now I think that about just two of us. I mean, right now, it's kind of like a three-legged stool with only two legs, you know? But Ben and me, we'll figure it out. Human beings can walk and run, and we only have two legs. Right? It'll be okay.

4. *Dancing. Even though I've been missing practice lately, and I can't get that new move that stupid ol' Gloria came up with for the life of me, but I'm still the only one on our team that can do that move where you lean backward until your upper body is parallel to the ground. It's because of my thunder thighs. They're strong enough to hold me up, no matter what I do. To me, all kinds of things dance. The words of a poem are a dance. My dad's Jamaican accent is a dance. I can memorize anything, if it dances. That's how I used to be able to make fun of the way my dad speaks, even when I didn't understand all the words. I don't make fun of him anymore, though. There's no fun at all in our house anymore. And it's Dad's and Mum's fault.*

5. *Boys. The geeky, awkward kind that never seem to know where to look, but they always end up staring right at your chest and then they're embarrassed they did that so they try really hard not to but it's like they can't drag their eyes away, and all the time they're going on and on at you about the coefficient of a polynomial or how*

many rare issues of the very first Dolphin Man comic they have, or something else that no one cares about but them. And the first time you kiss them, they think it was an accident, and they always ask you if it was good for you, too, and yeah, that's a total cliché. But they mean it, and I think that's sweet. Don't get me wrong; I like the fine-looking guys too, with their muscles and their baggy jeans and their swagger. But with them, it's like you're seeing a package in a pretty wrapper; you're never sure whether you're going to open it and find the bestest present you ever wanted, or something that totally sucks. The geek boys wear their insides all on the outside, you know? With them, you know what you're getting, because they have no talent for hiding who they are.

Mrs. Kuwabara had said we should keep all the sheets in one place, to review when we'd filled them all out. So I folded the piece of paper and stuffed it into the front pocket of my knapsack, where I'd put "My Five Favorite Colors and Why I Like Them" (one of them is kelly green, because it's the color of that amazing dress that Lil' Bliss wore on the BET Awards this summer) and "Five of the Best Things I Did on My Summer Vacation" (I'd crossed out things one, three, and four because they were all things I'd done with Glory, so now when I thought about them, the happy was spoiled by knowing what a bitch she was being). I pushed the three sheets down to the bottom of the knapsack pocket, ignoring the rustling sound they made when I crumpled them. Jimmy Tidwell held a sheet of paper out to me. I reached for it, but took him by the wrist instead. I swear his face went purple. "Hey," I murmured, "wanna hang out during break?"

"Uh, you mean, like, with you?"

"Yeah, with me. What'd you think?"

"But we already worked on next week's math homework."

"So, what; we can't just hang out?"

From behind me, I heard Gunther Patel snicker. I turned in my seat. He was leering at me.

"What's with you?" I asked, sneering.

He used his tongue to puff out the side of his cheek, twice. He hated it that I laughed whenever he whistled at me in the parking lot. I said, loudly, "You wish." Mrs. Kuwabara heard me, just like I'd planned. She looked up from her desk.

"Is something the matter, Sojourner?"

Gunther scowled. I smiled sweetly at him. "Nothing at all, Miss," I said.

Ben whispered, "Good for you." I grinned my thanks. He'd coached me well.

Gunther mumbled, "What do you know about it, you fag?"

Ben picked his pencil up and started writing on his sheet, but I saw the devilish grin on his face, and I knew that Gunther was going to get it good. "Honey," Ben said, squeezing every ounce of his blackness into that one word and speaking just loud enough for the few people around us to hear, "I'm more man than you will ever be, and more woman than you'll ever get."

Panama whooped. "Lord have mercy! Sorry, Mrs. Kuwabara. I'll behave myself now, Miss."

For the umpteenth time I envied Panama's strong Jamaican accent. Mrs. Kuwabara called out, "Jimmy, now's not the time to be talking with your friends, dear. Please keep handing those sheets out."

Panama looked up in mock alarm. "*Me*, Jimmy's friend? As if."

God, girls can be so mean. Jimmy'd been kinda gaping stupidly at us. He blushed and scurried along on his task. Gunther pressed his lips together and stared furiously down at his paper. Served him right. When boys try to embarrass you like that, it's easy to stop them. So long as the girls don't get into it. Because once the girls decide to turn against you, next thing you know, you're the school slut and everybody's spreading these insane rumors about you blowing the whole basketball team in the locker room, and people are throwing rocks at you when you're trying to walk home from school. I took my sheets out of my knapsack and erased my answer to number five on the "Five Things That Make You Happy" sheet and wrote:

5. *I am thrilled to pieces to not be in my old school any-*
   more.

I looked at the new questionnaire, and groaned under my breath. This one read, "Five Things That Scare You." I sighed and started filling it out. I wrote:

1. *Gunther Patel's haircut. Didn't that bowl cut thing go*
   out in the old days with, like, the Beatles?

2. *Getting someone else's chewed-up wad of gum on me.*
   It really freaks me out. I'm terrified it's going to get into
   my hair. With all these curls I have, I'd never get it out.

3. *Letting my big brother, Rich, down.*

I tugged my right sleeve down over my wrist. Last night's dream had been the usual kind of odd dream I'd been having lately. I was walking in the sun on someone's crop acreage, past beds of spinach, vines of beans climbing wire cones, knee-high eggplant bushes weighed down with shiny purple eggplants. Daddy's voice was murmuring something indistinct in my ear, although I couldn't see him. His happy voice, not the fretful, angry one in which he spoke almost all the time nowadays since we'd moved. But then his voice started getting a little angrier and a little more fretful every second as I trudged past stalks of corn, beds of tomato bushes. And I knew that when I went around the next patch of tomato bushes, there would be something horrible waiting for me. . . .

> 4. *This stupid skin condition I've got. Just when everything*
> *was starting to go great. I thought I'd finally figured out*
> *this school, and Rich was finally back home. And then*
> *this crap started happening. I don't think the ointment*
> *is working.*

What else was I really scared of? I gave the classroom a quick scan. It looked perfectly normal at the moment. Whew. On the lavender sheet, I wrote;

> 5. *None of your damned business.*

If I'd been being honest, I would have written, *People finding out about me.*

The bell rang.

"Thank God," growled Ben. I think the whole class probably felt the same way he did. You could almost hear the relief in how quickly the chairs scraped back as people gathered their things and leapt up. Second to last period of the day! One more class, and then it was hello, weekend.

"Okay, people," said Mrs. Kuwabara. Cheerily. Again. "Hang on to that sheet, and we'll finish filling it out on Monday."

Ben whispered into my ear, "Which 'we' she talking about? She not filling out this blasted questionnaire."

I giggled. "It's teacher speak. You know how it is." As we stepped out into the hallway, we were hit by the deafening noise of hundreds of teenagers laughing, arguing at the tops of their voices, banging locker doors, shouting greetings to each other in the last precious fifteen-minute break of the school day.

Ben asked me, "Did you just invite Jim Tidwell to hang out with us during break?"

"Yeah."

Ben looked incredulous. "But he's such a dork!"

"A sweet dork. Sweet counts for a lot."

Jimmy was standing by one of the water fountains, trying to look casual. I waved at him. "Hey, Jimmy!"

Ben sighed.

Jimmy came over. "Uh, look, I gotta meet my friends. We have this, uh, thing . . ." He stared shyly at the ground.

"That's okay, Jimmy. Next time, all right?" I patted his shoulder. He started, like he didn't expect anyone to touch him.

"Really? That'd be cool. Yeah. Okay. Um . . ."

He wandered off before he'd actually finished his sentence.

"Oh, thank God for Jesus," said Ben once Jimmy was out of earshot. With one hand, he made like he was waving Jimmy away. "Yes, you go meet up with your friends, my love. Go and synchronize your iPhones, or whatever it is you guys do."

I giggled. "Ben!"

A Horseless Head Man zipped past my ear, doing its chittering giggle and being chased by another one. I just managed to turn my flinch into linking my arm through Ben's. "Let's go outside.

It's sunny out." Besides, the Horseless Head Men were harder to see in full light.

We pushed open one of the big glass doors and stepped out into the watery September light. The weather hadn't turned anywhere near cold yet, but the sun didn't seem to rise as high in the sky as it had during the summer, and there was a dampness to the air. Some days were colder than others. Today was a warmish one.

We sat on one of the broad stone stairs that led down to the parking lot. Claudia, Simon, and Mark were scrunched happily together on one of the picnic benches in the school yard. Simon was in the middle. Mark put his hand on Simon's thigh so that he could lean over to say something to Claudia. Claudia and Simon were holding hands.

Glory was hanging out on the sidewalk with Panama and Kavi. Ben smiled and waved. I didn't. I turned sideways so that my back was to Gloria.

Ben had already pulled his cell phone out of his bag and was texting away. He gave a happy sigh. "Stephen says I'm the best boo he's ever had. I love having a boyfriend!"

"You guys on again, then?"

He slid the phone back into his bag. "Yeah. It was just a little fight."

"And your parents are really cool about you dating a guy?" Ben had blossomed since ninth grade. He'd started wearing cute jeans and fancy shirts instead of baggy clothes, and a silver stud in one ear and a cowrie shell on a black leather thong around his neck. His jewelry looked amazing against his brown skin. He walked with more confidence. This summer he'd started dating guys. Stephen was his second boyfriend.

"Dad's still a little freaked out, but Mom says she wasn't

surprised. She's just worried that Stephen's a white guy. She's afraid he might break my heart."

"Your folks are so cool. Mine would lose their shit if they found out I'd been dating Tafari. Or anyone. You know what I keep trying to figure out?"

"What?"

"Are all three of the Thompson Twins sluts, or just Claudia?"

"Obviously, Claudia's the slut! You know how this works. Girls get called sluts."

"And guys who sleep around get called what? Studs?"

He shrugged. "Yeah. And when people call a guy a stud, it's kind of a compliment. But when they call a girl a slut—"

"Then the next step is chewing gum in her hair and talking shit about her on MyFace."

"I know it blows, but that's how it is."

I sighed. "Okay, but check it out." I counted off on my fingers. "So Claudia's dating Simon and Mark. Right?"

"Yeah."

"And Simon's dating Mark and Claudia."

"Yup."

"And—hold on, my head always spins, trying to figure this one out—Mark's dating Claudia and Simon."

"You got it."

"And each of them knows about the other two, and all three of them go on dates together? With each other? At the same time?"

Ben said, "Uh-huh. I saw the three of them at the movies once, all holding hands and snuggling! I don't know how they do it. I'd be too jealous."

Claudia's happy tinkle of a laugh cut through the break-time noise. She leaned over and kissed Mark on the cheek. She never seemed to notice the glares she got from some of the girls in school.

I continued, "Why does everyone call them the Thompson Twins, anyway? There are three of them. And none of them's named Thompson."

He grinned. "Ah. For the answer to that question, my pretty, you need my fairy-certified sparkle dust obsession with pop music. 'The Thompson Twins' was the name of an old eighties band. There were three of them, too."

I shook my head. "If high school's this complicated, how am I ever going to figure out being a grown-up?"

Ben crossed his arms, cocked his head to one side, and looked at me. "Okay, I hate to even ask this, but you're not thinking of hooking up with Jimmy Tidwell, are you?"

Glory and Panama were shrieking happily over something or other. I didn't look over there. "Maybe I am. So what?"

He took my hands. Gently, I pulled the telltale hand away, leaving him holding just the other one. He didn't seem to notice. "Darling, the boy's a total geek!"

"Which means he might actually take me seriously when I say we're going to use rubbers."

"Scotch, for real, what're you thinking?"

"I dunno. I think it might be fun." That was what was so cool about having changed schools. At LeBrun High I'd been the school slut even though I wasn't having sex with anyone. Here I was one of the cool girls and I could do whatever I wanted. I could experiment. So long as my parents didn't find out.

"But you only just broke up with Tafari! Like he really didn't mean anything to you, or what?"

"He did! You know he did. But he's not the only boy in the world."

Ben looked doubtful. "So, are you drowning your sorrows or

whatever by hooking up with some random guy?"

I sighed. "No! At least, it's not because I'm drowning my sorrows. I'm just exploring, okay?" Like I'd been doing before Taf. I hadn't realized how much I'd missed me while I've been dating Taf. I'd known all these guys since grade nine, when they were shy, awkward boy-men with voices still breaking, and I was the new girl with the chest bigger than anyone else's in my class, who was too scared to speak to the boys for fear the girls would get jealous and it would be like LeBrun High all over again. For fear it was something to do with me that had made the harassing and the jeering and spitballs happen.

But pretty soon the other girls' bodies had caught up to mine, and I didn't stand out so much anymore. And Ben had taught me how to stand up for myself. All of us kids, our bodies had filled out and changed, and we were dying to try them out. Take Michel Beaulieu, who'd been short and zitty with that funny, squeaky voice; now he had a sharp trimmed goatee and his voice was all deep and shivery, and his hands had become the size of shovels (I had a thing for hands), and he walked with a swing in his step that he hadn't had before. He was the first boy I ever necked with, no matter what Nancy Poretta at LeBrun had said. Michel had wanted to date me. We did for a while, until I'd figured out that that first taste of Michel had only made me even more curious about other boys. Me and Glory and some of the other girls talked about it all the time. How would it be to sit on chubby Walter Herron's strong, sturdy lap? How would the plumpness of his skin feel under my hands? What did Sanjay Harsha's breath taste like? What would it feel like to run my hands through his hair? Ever since then, I'd been exploring. I wasn't the only one, either. Finally, I was normal. My parents would completely lose it if they ever found out. They wanted me to be good little Sojourner Smith, who always did her homework and came home on time and who was all meek and shit. They wouldn't like to find out that their daughter's school friends called her Scotch Bonnet, the name of a super hot Jamaican pepper, because her moves on her dance team were so hot. My folks wanted me to be safe. They didn't really understand what I'd learned at LeBrun High; being good didn't make me safe. Being popular kinda did, sometimes.

But I didn't tell Ben any of that. Instead I said, "I am sad that Taf and I broke up. Way sad. I think about him every day. But this . . . thing that I do—"

"Thrill of the hunt?" Ben said doubtfully. That's how I'd described it to him once. It had sort of been a joke. Only sort of not.

I smiled. "Yeah, that. I couldn't do it while I was dating Tafari, and I gotta be honest with you; I really wanted to."

Ben drew back. "You're joking, right? You had one of the hottest guys in school, and your eyes were wandering?"

"Uh-huh."

Ben made a *titch* sound. "Well, I guess Mr. Liliefeldt just wasn't doing his job right."

"Oh, he was." I got that sick, lurching feeling in my tummy that I got when I thought about me and Tafari, broken up. "I miss him so much."

He shook his head with an unbelieving smile. "Not hating on you, girl. Just not understanding you. I mean, if a guy's hot, I can totally understand you wanting to get with him. But Jimmy Tidwell?"

The bell rang. Last period. Glory glanced briefly my way, no expression on her face, before heading inside with her friends. Ben stood with a sigh, brushed the seat of his jeans off. "History class. Oh, yay."

"Hey! I like history!" I followed him in as we argued about

whether we were going to ever need history again once we'd graduated. Me, I had geography. I said to Ben, "Come and see me in the gym after dance practice, okay? You gonna be around?"

"You know it. Can't miss our Friday afternoon ritual. Be nice if Glory could be part of it again."

I snapped, "Over my dead body."

"Okay, okay. Just saying."

CHAPTER TWO

So I jumped in too early again, which meant that Jarmilah swept my legs out from under me again, which meant that I tripped her when I stumbled. Again. And we both fell heavily to the school's gym floor. Over the music, I couldn't hear the sound of Jarmilah's breath escaping on impact, but if the thud of landing had been as bad for her as it had been for me, she probably hated me. Hell, I hated me right now. Gloria was probably gloating to see me make another mistake.

A few of the others on our after-school dance team saw what had happened and stopped dancing. The rest kept on going, doggedly. Only five days to the dance-off, and we still didn't quite have that section of our routine down. And I was the one who kept messing us up.

Gloria ran over to the boom box and stopped the music. She was yelling before she even turned around; "God damn it, Scotch, you jump in on the one, not on 'and one'! How many times I have to tell you?"

"I know, I know!" I yelled back. "On the one. I know." Christ, she'd turned into such a bitch over this dance battle thing! More softly, I said to Jarmilah, "Sorry."

"Don't sweat it. Just get off me, okay?" My legs were lying across hers. I moved them, and we both got to our feet. "What's up with you?" she asked. "You're usually the first one to pick up the moves."

Ayumi, who was standing behind us, muttered something. Her friends Jen and Leah snickered. Gloria called out, "What'd you say, Ayumi?" It was her warning voice. Give Glory that; even though she and I weren't being friends anymore, she was on my side when it came to people bad-talking me just 'cause they felt like it.

Ayumi looked to Jen and Leah for support. They'd been smirking at her remark. They wiped the smirks off their faces the minute they saw me looking at them, but Ayumi hadn't noticed. That's probably what gave her the courage to pipe up with, "Maybe those batty riders are cutting off circulation to her brain." The whole team fell out laughing at her joke.

Oh, no, she didn't just say that. There was nothing wrong with my short shorts. She couldn't even say it right. Made it sound like "baddy riders." I bellied up to tiny little Ayumi till my chest was so close to her chin she had to back up or get a sweaty faceful of my girls. She backed up. I followed, my hands on my hips. I wasn't going to touch her. I didn't need to fight, not in this school. "You have something to say to me?" I tried not to listen to my own voice, to how off my accent sounded. Half Jamaican. Pretend Creole. If I didn't watch myself, I turned "batty" into "baddy," too.

Ayumi held her ground, but she didn't answer. She was 'fraid to glare full on at me, but she didn't want to take her eyes off me either, so she did this silly mixture of both, kinda staring up at me with her head lowered and off to one side a little. "You have a problem with the way I dress?" I asked her. Ben had taught me this. If someone's trying to step to you, you just tromp all over them first. With words and out loud, where everyone could hear.

Gloria pushed in between the two of us. "Scotch! Leave her alone!"

"Is she start it! Besides, I'm not doing anything to her."

Jen and Leah pulled Ayumi away. "C'mon girl," said Leah. "It's not worth it."

But I wasn't done with her. "You just jealous 'cause your skinny little legs would look like two dry-up sticks in shorts like these. Chuh. Little piece of half-grown pickney best lef' me alone."

Panama giggled. All right, so my accent wasn't the best. Even Ben and Glory sounded more comfortable than I did when they spoke like their Caribbean parents.

Gloria glared at me, her two eyes meeting mine, making four with my own. "Scotch, stop it now, or you're off the team! For real!"

Everybody fell silent with shock, even me. "But I—I" I stammered. I was the best dancer they had. I looked around. I was surrounded by angry faces. Mocking faces. Girls' faces. And suddenly I was that scared little eleven-year-old again, sitting alone in a crowded assembly while the whisper was passed from mouth to cupped ear, from one sneering student to another: *Sojourner masturbates! Pass it on!* I was back hearing the exclamations of disgust, the hateful laughter as more and more and more kids passed the story on and on, and I just sat there getting more and more alone with my pale brown face going redder and redder and thinking, *But I've never even tried it yet!*

So I backed way off. "All right, all right. Ayumi, I'm really sorry." The other thing Ben had taught me—always be better than the haters, even if that means apologizing to them when you're in the wrong. "I didn't sleep well last night," I told Ayumi. "Bad dreams."

Ayumi's face softened into sympathy. "That's so sad!" she said. "Is it because of Tafari?"

I looked sad, let her think that was it. I mean, it kinda was. I was really down about Tafari. And the part about the nightmare was even true. But breakup blues and bad sleep weren't what had thrown me off just now. One of those things was around. It'd startled me when it had just appeared on top of the gym clock like that, grinning as though it had just discovered teleportation. Made me lose my step. I wasn't even angry at Ayumi, but blowing up at her had helped me let a little bit of the fear go.

Ayumi and I hugged and made up, and I could breathe again. I checked that the sleeve of my sweatshirt was covering my arm all the way down to the wrist, and then took my place beside Jarmilah.

Gloria said, "Okay. Let's try it once more."

Everybody groaned. The thing swooped down and dive-bombed Gloria's head. I flinched, grimacing. Gloria hadn't seen it diving for her. Nobody saw them but me. She noticed me grimace, though. She narrowed her eyes at me. She probably figured I'd made a face at her to give her attitude for threatening to kick me off the team. Whatever. 'Cause I would've done it anyway if I'd thought of it.

The thing went and perched on one of the bleachers, looking from one to the other of us. Our expectant audience. Why didn't they have any bloody legs, or wings, or even bodies? Why were they just tiny, horselike heads, with big, square-toothed, horsey grins?

We were all in place again by the time Gloria had found the beginning of the song. She ran back to her place beside Panama.

The music started. Beat. One. Yes! Sorta got it right this time. Close enough that Jarmilah and I didn't collide.

The rest was like flying. When I'm dancing, the world just feels right, you know? I forgot about the dream, forgot about me and Tafari breaking up. Forgot about feuding with Glory, and the marks on my skin that gave me nightmares every time a new one was about to pop up. Forgot about the skin-teeth grin of the Horseless Head Man on the bleachers. It was like I could feel the rhythm of the world, play with its beats. I was there dead on my mark when Glory had to roll over my back. She stood, turned to me, and pop; our fists brandished, our bodies so close to each other and driving so hard that it looked like we were going to punch each other out. We'd planned it that way together before, when we were still talking to each other. Now, it almost felt like we could do it for real, have it out right there. Instead, scowling, we linked wrists, in time for Sigourney to do her backward flying dive in between us, her arms stretched out above her head. Big trust move, that one. If we weren't going to catch her, she wouldn't see it until her back slammed down onto the floor. We caught her, flipped her back up. She stumbled as she came down. Gloria snapped, "Too high, Scotch!" as she, Jarmilah, and Zoe went down on all fours to make like the wheels of a car. Chuh. Not my fault if Sigourney was so little-bit that I just kept powering her too high out of her dive. Panama and I swung out in front of the people car. Little bit of stripper dance, some attitude, down into the splits like everyone else, bounce, head roll, down flat on our backs, then hit; chest pop so that all our bodies jerked on the final beat.

Gloria leapt up and ran to turn the boom box off. Man, I was winded. Maybe that nasty-tasting medicine from the weird little shop I'd found up on Bathurst was making me short of breath. I lay on the gym floor panting, my arms spread wide, resisting the urge to feel with one hand under the cuff of my hoodie, just to see if the mark was still there. It hadn't gone away in two months of visits to the allergist, of antibiotic skin cream, of whatever treatment I could think of. In fact, it had grown, especially since last night. I knew that when I'd woken up in the morning. I always felt the new marks coming in, even though I might be asleep and dreaming. It wouldn't just magically disappear now.

The others were getting to their feet. Sigourney stood on one foot and experimentally rolled the other foot around at the ankle. She winced. Damn. Gloria went over to her. "You okay?" she asked.

Sigourney nodded. "Little twinge, is all. It'll be fine."

"Ice it when you go home."

Sigourney smiled. "Yes, Mama Glory."

"For reals, girl. Don't want you getting busted up on my watch."

Like hell. She just didn't want to lose one of her dancers five days before the battle. Though I guess it would suck if one of us got too injured to dance.

Then Gloria was towering over me where I was still lying flat. "See how short of breath you are?" she said.

Yeah. Too winded to give her any backchat, in fact. I took in little sips of air and prepared not to listen to her.

"You've missed the last four practices. Miss tomorrow's, and you're off the team."

As if. I'd recovered enough for, "Right. You know you need me." Without me the team was only average, and they all knew it.

The barest flicker of hesitation passed across Gloria's face. Someone who didn't know her wouldn't have seen it. "Yeah, well," she said. "I'll tell you after tomorrow if you're still part of Raw Gyals or not."

Damn, she looked serious. I needed to be at this battle. "Fine, fine. Whatever." I needed my chance at the prize money from the individuals' dance-off. I pushed myself up to a sitting position. "I'll be good, okay?"

"You'd better. And stop throwing Sigourney so high out of the dive."

Leah said, teasingly, "You're just too strong, Scotch."

My heart started pounding. Was she trying to start something? I checked her face. She was smiling indulgently at me. Shakily, I laughed. "Right. And you can't do a simple one-two step."

Panama sucked air through her teeth, mock disgusted. She was grinning, though. It was all right. We were all just kidding around, like we did every practice. "Koo the pot a-backchat to the kettle. After you always missing that one move."

I groaned to my feet. Had I really missed that many practices? "Pot and kettle, huh? You mean you agree with me that Leah have two left foot?"

"Well, now that you mention it—"

Gloria called out, "Okay, people. I have something cool for everyone!" She shone one of her sunshine smiles at us. Leah and Panama stuck their tongues out at me. I stuck mine back out at them. We laughed.

Gloria ran over to the big duffel bag she'd stashed against the wall before practice had started. She unzipped it and started pulling clothing out of it. The Horseless Head Man jittered around the opening to the bag, chirping happily at her. The clothes were all the same colors. Burgundy and gold. Raw Gyals colors. Jarmilah said, "Our outfits!"

We all ran over. Gloria, of course, had a list out with everyone's names and sizes. "Sigourney, you get the weeniest one. Here's yours, Ayumi. Jarmilah, Panama, Leah, these are yours. Scotch, Jen, Zoe, Khadijah; here you go. And this one is mine."

There was all kinds of squealing and exclaiming as we checked them out, holding them up against our bodies. Super short pleated skirts in burgundy with a gold stripe down each side, and burgundy bloomers attached. Jen said, "I thought the name of the team was going to be written on them?"

Gloria grinned. "Flip up the back of the skirt."

I did so with mine. Panama, looking over my shoulder, chuckled. The words "Raw Gyals" were written in gold letters on the backsides of our bloomers. "Sweet," I said, before I could stop myself. Didn't want to do anything to make Glory think we could maybe be friends again. It was too late, though. She'd heard me. She gave me a hesitant smile. I pretended not to notice.

"Our names are on the insides of the T-shirts, too!" said Khadijah. She turned up the bottom hem of hers. The words were written upside down. "But why are they the wrong way up?"

I got it. "It's for that one move," I said. "This one." I did the move where we all faced the crowd and raised our shirts just enough to show off our abs with a body wave.

Gloria looked smug. "Exactly. I came up with the idea of printing the shirts this way, just for that move."

Sigourney was so delighted that she'd already thrown off her sweatshirt and wriggled into her T-shirt. Bet the flash of her in her sports bra had given the guys peeking in a thrill. She flipped the hem of the shirt, rolled her abs like a belly dancer, just like we'd practiced. "These are great, Gloria! How come you didn't tell us you were going to do it?"

"I wanted to surprise you guys. You've been working so hard."

Okay, so sometimes Gloria could be cool. The T-shirts were baby doll hoodies, just like we'd wanted. I thought of something, though. We'd priced our outfits down to the penny and each shared the cost. "Didn't it cost extra to do more printing this way?"

Gloria nodded. "Yeah. Well, it would have, but the printing shop is run by my uncle's second wife's cousin. She gave me a discount."

I was going to look so bitchin' in this outfit, with my stomping boots and my army green socks. Except . . . I got this sick feeling in my stomach. "The sleeves are short," I said.

Gloria replied, "They are, just like you wanted."

"But I can't wear them short like this!"

Panama sighed. "Is you wanted the sleeves short in the first place!"

"I guess." I rubbed at the place on my wrist that my sleeve covered. Glory didn't know about that new spot.

"Okay," she said. "Practice is over."

Leah joined Jen and Khadijah. Panama got her cell phone out and called somebody. In seconds, she was chatting away in a Jamaican so thick I could barely understand it. People wandered off in twos and threes, talking, stretching out sore arm and neck muscles. I headed for my knapsack that was lying against one wall of the gym. "Not you, Scotch," said Gloria. "We're going to work on that move you keep missing."

"But Ben's coming to meet me!"

"He'll just have to wait for half an hour. Come on, let's do this." She switched the music on again. I dragged myself back to the middle of the gym floor. I was sweating and gritty, and there was a muscle twanging in my left thigh. Gloria had worked harder than all of us, but she was barely glowing and she had not a hair out of place. Black Barbie lived.

The right part of the song came. I started dancing. And missed my mark. Gloria raised a perfectly tweezed eyebrow. "Okay, again. I'll do it with you. I really don't want to have to kick you off this team, Scotch. But you know I'll do it if I have to."

"Yeah, yeah. From the top?"

"Uh-huh."

"I'll start the song up." I slouched over to the player, set the song up from the beginning. I did an exaggerated hobble back to join her, but I didn't get any sympathy.

"Four, three, two," she chirped.

I hated her so much. I kinda hit my mark the next two times. But then the Horseless Head Man suddenly decided to start leaping from bleacher to bleacher, whickering softly to itself. And I missed the mark the third time. Ben had come in and was sitting against one wall of the gym, watching us. He raised his eyebrows when I messed up again.

I threw myself down to the floor. "I can't do it, Gloria. I can't do anymore. Not today."

She stopped dancing. We looked at each other for a long moment. I couldn't tell what the expression on her face was. "Ben," she called, "turn that off for me, nuh?" She waited while he did it. Then she stamped her foot and said, "It's so bloody easy for you!"

"Uh-oh," said Ben. "Now it starts."

Gloria ignored him. "That's what makes me nuts!" she told me. "You dance like you were born dancing. I would kill to be like that, Scotch!"

"Wait—what?" I got to my feet, still panting. I was going to stop taking that antibiotic the doctor had given me. Maybe it was making me short of breath. And it wasn't working, anyway.

"You don't practice on your own, right?"

"Girl, you know she doesn't," said Ben.

It was true, I didn't. I shook my head.

Glory threw her hands up. "See what I mean? You barely work on the routine, yet you usually learn the steps first time out. And you remember them."

"So?"

"And every time you come to practice, you're a little tighter than the time before. Except these past few weeks, when you've barely been here at all. What's up with that?"

I pointed at her. "You started acting all high-and-mighty, that's what!"

"Oh, stop it. You don't even think that."

I bit my lip. I wasn't good at lying.

"That's not the real reason you and me are warring."

It wasn't, but I wasn't ready to talk about the real reason yet, so I just crossed my arms and looked away.

Ben chuckled. "And Miss Glory hits a sore spot!"

Irritated, Gloria kissed her teeth. "Fine. So don't answer that one. Is not what we talking about right now, anyway."

Grudgingly, I replied, "So what, then?"

"Scotch, you have all this talent, but you're such a slacker!"

"And another hit!" said Ben.

Glory continued, "I bet you don't say the moves in your head while you're doing them."

"Not once I know the routine." Did she do that? Say the moves over in her head?

"Yeah, and you know it within minutes. I bet you don't have to count the beats."

"No. Well, except for this one entrance," I said sheepishly.

"One! Just one! I have to count off most of them to keep up. I know these damned moves in my head, like a drill! I have them sketched out on a piece of poster board up on my bedroom wall! I go over them every morning. And I still have to recite that drill in my mind every time, every practice."

I goggled. "Really?"

"Really. I'm even going to have to do it during the performance. I'm putting in all this work, and what are you doing?"

"Gloria, cut her some slack, nuh, man?" said Ben.

She rounded on him. "Whose side you on, anyway?"

He held both hands up, like *I surrender.* "Chill, girl. Don't try and drag me into allyou man trouble."

Together, Glory and I blurted out, "We don't have—"

Ben cut in. "Is only one move, right? I will make her practice it. And her solo for the singles battle." He smiled at me. "Every day between now and Wednesday."

Gloria looked from Ben to me, her perfectly straightened hair bobbing perkily as she did. "Okay," she said. She sounded doubtful. "And she best come to every single practice between now and then."

"Every one," Ben reassured her. "If I have to throw her over my shoulder and bring her myself."

"You don't have to talk about me like I'm not here."

Gloria frowned at me. "For the last little while, you haven't been. Even when you're at practice, your mind's not on it."

A second Horseless Head Man popped into the air right in front of my face, then a third. I yelped. Ben raised an eyebrow. Glory just scowled. "See what I mean?" she said. "You're not even listening to me."

"But I can't do extra practice; I have to study for next week's bio test!"

Glory shrugged. "Well, Miss Sojourner, I guess it sucks to be you."

When Gloria called me by my real name, she meant business.

Ben said, "You can't pull that one on Glory. She and I both know you can study and practice and not even break a sweat."

I made a face at him.

"Don't give me that look. I want you to win. I know how important this is to you."

He knew, all right. He and I had figured it out; if my team won, I'd get a portion of that money. If I won the singles battle on top of it, that'd be a bit more cash. Together, it'd be almost enough to make back the money I'd spent instead of saving it for my share of the rental deposit on the apartment my brother Rich and I had our eyes on.

Gloria unplugged the boom box and picked it up. "Start acting like you want to be on the team, Scotch. Or so help me, we going to do it without you. And wear track pants next time. Nobody want to watch you dance with all your business hanging outside." She sighed and headed out the door.

She used to stand up for me and the clothes I wore at school, where my parents couldn't see them. She used to go shopping with me.

Ben laughed. "Don't listen to her, beautiful," he said. "You look amazing in those shorts. Wish I had an ass like that."

"You have a perfectly lovely ass. What? Is not like I haven't noticed."

"Still," he continued, "I think there's too many letters in the word 'shorts' to describe what those are." He cackled at his own joke. The three Horseless Head Men bobbed up and down in time with the sound of his laughter. Gave me the creeps.

I held up my Raw Gyals skirt. "I don't know why she's carrying on like that. This is what we're going to be dancing in."

Ben wolf-whistled. "Wow. That's hot."

"Like you're such an authority on girls looking sexy."

"Gyal pickney, don't give me none of your facetiness." He waved my smart-mouthing away with a flick of his fingers. "I know hot when I see it."

The skirt really was short. "What'm I going to tell my folks?"

"About what?"

"They think I've been rehearsing for some stocious modern dance recital."

He gaped at me, then burst into howls of laughter, staggering around the room and holding his belly. When he stopped for air, I said, "I'm serious, Ben. They want to come and see us dance on Wednesday night."

That only made the laughing worse. He mimed wiping tears from his face. "Girl, why you even told them what you were doing?"

Frustrated, I threw my hands up. "I had to tell them something! You know how they are; they wouldn't have let me stay after school to practice otherwise!"

"Glory know about this?"

"Lord, no."

"So when you going to tell her?"

"I don't know! What'm I going to do? They can't come!" My parents would each bust a blood vessel if they saw me getting buck onstage in a four-inch-long skirt and bloomers. My mom kept saying that she knew the hazing at LeBrun High hadn't been my fault, but she still wanted me to act all modest and shit anyway, "Just so you don't present a target, Sojourner." She didn't know anything.

Finally, Ben looked serious. "Lemme think about it, sweetie. We'll come up with something, okay? Don't fret. What's the top look like?"

Have I mentioned how much I love my friend Ben? I showed him the top. "I'm going to wear a long-sleeved T-shirt underneath, though."

Ben goggled at me. "You? Miss Sojourner Scotch Bonnet 'nobody cyan't make a sweater tight enough for me' Smith? You're going to cover up a part of your precious body?"

For the umpteenth time, I dragged at the sleeve of my sweatshirt to make sure it was covering my arm all the way down to my wrist. Ben's eyes followed the movement. He opened his mouth to say something. I cut him off with, "Let's go. I gotta change." At least I could still show off my legs. For now.

We left the gym. I fought the impulse to look behind me to see whether the Horseless Head Men were following, to shove the door closed so they couldn't follow. Not that that seemed to make a difference. Bloody things were everywhere nowadays. I must really be losing it.

Ben and I headed in the direction of the girls' change room.

When I'd first started seeing the Horseless Head Men, they'd been almost invisible; I'd only been able to see them when the light hit them at certain angles. But every day, they got more solid, more real. Mom might say it was a ha'nt; a ghost. Actually, she'd be more likely to say I was hallucinating and book me into the nuthouse down on Queen Street so one of her colleagues could pry my brain open with a can opener, just like had happened to Auntie Mryss. What was Dad's word for ghosts, again? Oh, yeah; duppies. But if it was a ghost, what the rass was it a ghost of? It looked like a disembodied animal's head, a cross between a dog's and a sea horse's, all covered in short fur. "Hey, Ben; are you a good dancer?"

"Pretty good." He snickered. "Better than Stephen, anyway. Guy dances like somebody Tasered him. Thing is, though," he continued, "I'm good, but Glory's right; you're genius. You dance like . . . well, not an angel. Not with those skanky moves you got going on. But, like, I dunno, like dance is a language, and you were born speaking it."

I did mention that I love Ben, right? "But is it really so hard to do what I do? You just listen to the music, and you move." To demonstrate, I did a slide step into a running man.

"Tell that to Stephen."

CHAPTER THREE

FIVE THINGS ABOUT YOU THAT LOTS OF PEOPLE DON'T KNOW

1. *I like hanging out with my dad's crazy cousin Maryssa. Sometimes I think she sees the Horseless Head Men too, except she can't really be seeing them, because they're not real. They're coming from my brain, but I don't know what they are. Which is weird. After all, they're my hallucination, so you'd think I'd know what my own brain's cooking up, wouldn't you?*

2. *I actually used to think my mom and dad were kinda cool. Not anymore. Nowadays, they're both just harsh. I'm never gonna forgive them for what they did to Rich. They may have ruined his whole life! It's one thing making me wear those old-lady clothes and giving me a curfew, but calling the cops on your own son?*

3. *I'm scared. All the time. I keep waiting for some girl who's cooler than me to start whispering about me behind my back. Then the other girls will start it, and the boys will follow them, and then I'll be so dead.*

4. *I keep having nightmares. And they do things to me.*

5. *I think I may be going crazy.*

"Pangaea," I said to Ben as we walked down the school corridor to the girls' change room, "sounds like it'd be a neat name for a band."

Ben waved a dismissive hand. "Whatever. I just think that's more a geography topic than something for history class, that's all."

"That's 'cause you're failing geography. I keep telling you, you should let me coach you." We walked around Lester Romero, who'd dropped to his knees in front of me, announcing loudly to anyone in earshot that he would work hard and give me all his money, if I would only give him one kiss. I was still wearing my shorts from dance practice. I pretended I hadn't heard him. Lester was the class clown. In school, I guess everyone has their own way of protecting themselves. But I bet that Lester's wasn't getting him a whole lot of play.

Ben said, "Lester would be cute, if he stopped playing the fool like that all the time."

"I think Pangaea is both history and geography. Can you imagine the whole world when it was one giant continent? And there weren't any birds, just pterosaurs, and the seas—well, the sea, there would have only been one—was full of plesiosaurs and mosasaurs? Isn't that cool?"

Ben was still looking back at Lester Romero. "That's just like you, girl. Guy right in front of you here and now, begging for you, and you're on about something that was, like, twenty gazillion years ago."

"Two hundred fifty million years ago. Besides, I smiled at him, didn't I? It's not like I cut him totally dead."

"You, my friend, can be a total geek sometimes. Why do you even know what a mosasaur is? Hey; what's going on?"

We stopped at the small crowd of kids gathered in the hallway just in front of the girls' change room. "Out of the way, please," said a man's voice from behind us, loud and terse.

We stepped back in time to let three paramedics run through, pushing one of those collapsible stretchers on wheels. They yelled for the kids to move aside. As they did, we could see someone lying on the ground, curled into a ball. Ben gasped. "That's Justin! He's in my chem class!"

I grabbed Ben's hand. "Oh, my god! Is he hurt?"

"I don't see any blood or anything."

Justin was rocking back and forth. His friend Jack Chu was kneeling beside him, touching his shoulder and murmuring something. I couldn't hear the words. Jack looked really scared. The ambulance people had reached them. One of them knelt to talk softly to Justin. It looked like one of them was talking to Jack.

A girl beside us said, "We were making posters for our drama club. And he just freaked out. One minute he was kidding around with Jack, and then he just freaked out." She hugged herself. She was in grade twelve. I'd seen her around, but I didn't know her name. "He started yelling all kinds of wacky stuff, dodging and dancing around like something was snapping at his heels."

Ben had his cell out in a hot second. "For real? What was he yelling?"

The girl gave the cell a suspicious look. "Who're you texting?"

"Don't worry, just myself. I'm starting up a school news

zine for my journalism class. You're Mala Something, right?"

I said to Ben, "Now who's a geek?"

"Hush, you."

The girl said, "He was yelling, like, 'Cupcake! Cupcake! No!'"

Ben looked up from his texting. "*Cupcake?*"

"I don't know what it means, either. And yeah, I'm Mala, but I don't want you to use my name, okay?"

"Okay. Confidentiality of sources." He started texting again. "A concerned friend informed us . . ."

Mala considered. "'A concerned friend;' I like that. You're really going to print this? When?"

The paramedics had lowered the stretcher to the ground and lifted Justin onto it. One of them shook Jack's hand. Jack was biting his bottom lip, clearly trying hard not to burst into tears where everybody could see. The paramedics wheeled toward us, leaving Jack standing there, looking lost and frightened. I pulled Ben out of the way. "Come on," I said. "Nothing more to see here, and I gotta go. My folks'll be watching the clock."

"But don't you want to change?"

I still couldn't see the change room door, there were so many people hanging about, talking about the excitement. Principal Maclean was shooing people away, but that'd take a while. "I'm never going to get in there now. I'll just change in the regular washroom."

Ben was watching the paramedics go. "D'you think I should try to talk to them?"

"Nah. Let them do their job. You can ask Justin about it when he comes back."

Mala was still standing beside us. "I don't know how soon he's going to come back," she said. "He freaked out really bad, I tell you. That's, what? The third one since we've been back to school?"

"Fourth," Ben told her. "If you count Nurse Maudella."

Mala shook her head. "No, she just quit to spend a year in the Antarctic."

Ben grimaced. "And you don't think that's insane?"

"It's not the same," I said. "Anyway, Phil Billinger from our class came back. He's okay."

Ben replied, "Concetta wasn't okay, though."

Concetta was a lower-grade kid. Last week she'd told her parents that her morning glass of milk was talking to her. They'd started giving her juice instead. A few days later she jumped from the second floor landing inside the school. She landed on another kid, broke his back. Both of them were still in the hospital. Concetta told her folks her juice had told her to do it. Now the hospital had to watch her when they gave her any liquid to drink at all. That's what Panama had told me. She'd heard it from Khadijah. A few parents had pulled their kids from the school, but Mom says the fact is, kids crack up in schools all the time. She says the adolescent years are the time when anyone who is schizophrenic usually goes nuts for the first time. I'm sure that's true, but the fact is, school is hell on everybody.

We stopped outside the door to the girls' washroom. Mala took the hint and went looking for her friends. Ben grinned at me. I knew why. It was time for the Friday afternoon game. I said, "Back in a sec." I ducked into the girls' washroom. There was one girl doing her hair. I pretended to be looking for a clean stall. In a bit, the girl packed up her things and left. I did a quick check; all the stalls were empty. I poked my head out of the washroom. "Coast's clear," I told Ben. No one's inside." He and I checked up and down the corridor. The fuss over Justin was dying down. Most of the lower-grade kids had already been picked up by their parents. There must have been a football game, or something; there were still a few kids hanging around.

Mandy Grabowski, Sharmini Dhosh, and Prue Smith from my class were shrieking happily at each other about some stupid thing or other, their long, sleek hair swinging as it framed their perfectly made-up faces. A Horseless Head Man was perched on Sharmini's shoulder, facing backward toward me. It winked at me. *I don't see you, I don't see you,* I thought. I wasn't losing it. I wasn't catching whatever Phil and Justin and Concetta had. Wasn't it bad enough that I was growing bits of lumpy black skin overnight? I yanked on my sleeve again. I needed to go talk to Auntie Mryss. She was always on about the manifestations of the Last Days. She knew weird. Weird was her vacation home. "All clear," I said. "We can go now."

"Not yet." Benjamin pointed with his chin. Mike Doucet and his buddies were swaggering down the middle of the hallway, their voices booming deeply as they laughed. Tafari was with them. He glanced at me, and my heart pounded, but he looked away like I hadn't even registered. Ben must have seen my face. "You broke up with him, girl," he said softly.

"I know."

"That was a cold thing to do, Scotch. You know I love you, but that was cold."

"I know."

Tafari was wearing the hoodie I'd given him. Deep moss green, like his eyes, with the Raptors logo across the front. It still looked as good on him as ever. I scratched at the patch of raised skin on my wrist, under my sweatshirt. It had gotten bigger since my last dream.

Ben's eyes followed the movement of my hand. Softly, he said, "Scotch, did Taf hurt you or something?"

For a second I didn't understand. Then I got it. "You mean did he hit me? OMG no, he didn't! What's wrong with you?"

"Jeez. All right. Just asking."

"He'd never do anything like that to me. Look, I just suck, okay? But it was better I make a clean break."

Ben's face went still, like a judge collecting evidence before handing down the verdict. "Why? What did he do that was so awful?"

"It's not like that. It just wasn't going to work out."

Tafari's eyes had a haunted look. And did he startle, just a little bit, when that Horseless Head Man leapt from Sharmini's shoulder and circled round Mrs. Finchley's head?

"I guess." Ben didn't sound completely convinced. Which made sense, since I didn't convince me even one little bit.

The guys had gone past. The hallway was nearly empty, and no one was looking our way. "C'mon," said Ben. "Let's go." He squeezed past me through the open washroom door. I let it shut behind him, joined him at the sinks.

"Fri-DAY eveNING!" he exulted. He did a little victory dance, checked that the counter was dry, then hopped up onto it. I went to one of the sinks, turned on the water, and washed my sweaty face. I slung my T-shirt off and used it to dab at my pits. Ben said, "You gonna change into your good-girl clothes now?"

I stuck my tongue out at him, but I took my knapsack into one of the toilet stalls, wiped the seat off, and perched on the edge of it. My street clothes were inside the knapsack; both sets. My real clothes were on top: Tight white baby doll T-shirt with a sweet scooped neck; long-sleeved, form-fitting dark green Lululemon hoodie with white racing stripes; low-slung Apple Bottoms jeans with my wallet hanging from the chain clipped to the belt loop. I pulled that outfit out and balanced it on my knees while I rummaged for the deadly dull Mom-and-Dad-approved clothes I'd stuffed into the bottom of the knapsack.

Ben called, "What you doing this weekend, Scotch?"

"Me? Whatever the hell I want. Mum and Dad are going to Buffalo for the weekend!"

"No way. You mean, they're taking you and Rich? There's some great shopping in Buffalo."

"As if they'd let me buy anything I'd actually want to wear. It's better than that, though. They're leaving us here! By ourselves!"

"Whoa."

"They say they're trusting Rich to check in with his parole officer."

"Big of them, seeing as they're the ones that got him in trouble in the first place."

"I know. I still haven't forgiven them."

"When're you and Rich going to tell them? About the apartment, I mean?"

"Soon. Maybe when they get back from this trip. Rich only has to check in with his officer once more, and he'll be free and clear."

"And if you wait a few days, you'll have enough money for your half of the deposit."

"Yeah." Oh, man. Dance practice, Tafari, and now this; yet another wave of guilt. Apparently I was going to be swimming in an ocean of it this afternoon. I had to win the one-on-one battle. I had to. I was a couple hundred short of my half of the security deposit money for the apartment my brother Rich and I were going to rent downtown. At the very, very bottom of my knapsack were the new boots that I'd wear with my outfit for the battle. They'd been worth every penny of the two hundred or so I'd paid for them. Right? I would win the one-on-one battle easy.

I stripped down to my underwear and shoved my dance practice clothes and my real clothes back into the knapsack. I pulled on the black polyester parent-approved slacks—God,

I hated that word! Only old farts like my folks wore "slacks" anymore. I yanked the baggy, boring old beige sweater on over my head. When I pulled my head free, there was a Horseless Head Man balancing on the top of the stall door. I yelped.

"Scotch?" called Ben. "What happen? You all right?"

"Yeah, I'm fine. Just tripped on the hem of my pants." I glared at the Horseless Head Man. It just grinned. That's all they ever did. Then it disappeared. Okay; they did that, too. I unclipped my wallet from its chain, slid it into my handbag. When I stepped out of the stall, Ben took one look at me in my good-girl duds and shook his head. "It's like you're two people; Miss Scotch Bonnet 'hot pepper' Smith, and, I dunno, the Virgin Mary, or something."

"Yeah, well, I'll be able to be all Scotch all the time when Richard and I move out."

A toilet flushed. Ben squeaked. He leapt off the countertop and dashed toward the door of the girls' washroom. Before he could make it, though, a stall door opened, and Gloria came out. Oh, great. I'd forgotten to check that last little stall around the corner. Glory looked around, spied Ben. "I thought I heard his voice in here!" she said happily. "No, don't you leave now! You're totally busted."

Ben sighed and came back. "What's your deal? The three of us do this all the time."

"Used to do this all the time," she replied. "Used to be the three of us."

"Is not me who messed that up."

She rounded on him. "And you think I am?"

I opened my mouth to say that of course she was, but Ben cut in with, "Takes two to tango, Missy."

He was ponting at both of us. "Hey!" I said. Ben shrugged.

Glory glared at me, then she peered into the mirror in front of one of the sinks. She took a cosmetics bag out of her gym bag, got a brush out of there, and started brushing her hair. She took her sweet time. The gym bag, the cosmetics bag, and the back of the brush all had the same MAC logo. Perfect Black Barbie, complete with matching accessories. She looked at Ben's reflection in the mirror. "So you're going to be the one who's all responsible, making sure Sojourner practices? Some sleazy guy who hangs out in the girls' washroom?"

I rolled my eyes. "Please. It's Ben."

Glory sniffed. "Don't matter. He's a boy, and he not supposed to be in here."

Ben said, "Come on! Like I'm gonna be peeking up any girls' skirts. Besides, it's not like there's anyone in here."

Glory hissed. "*I'm* here, all right? You trying to tell me I'm not anybody?"

I said, "You know he means nobody else, Glory. Just the three of us."

Softly, she replied, "You really hurt Tafari, you know?"

And there it was. "Well, you seem to be working hard at making him feel better."

Ben muttered, "Two girls fighting over a guy. How original."

Glory kept brushing her hair into a sleek wave. "I told you; he and I have been talking, is all."

I glared at her. "I bet."

She actually looked hurt through the anger. "Time was, you used to trust me."

"Time was, you weren't trying to steal my boyfriend."

She put the brush down and turned to face me. "Which boyfriend, girl? You dumped him, right? So tell me, nah? Is which boyfriend of yours I trying to steal?"

I had nothing to say to that. I looked down at my feet.

"And stop talking about 'steal.' Like a boy is a candy bar you carry around in your purse with no will of him own."

"I'm saying," muttered Ben in agreement. He stepped in between us, a ref keeping two warring prizefighters apart. "Okay, okay, I got it. Here's what you two are gonna do. We'll cut Tafari in half, and you can share him." Glory and I stared openmouthed at Ben. He said, "Only I get his bottom half first. Kind of like a finder's fee."

Glory was the one who broke. She glanced at me. She sputtered out a short laugh. Which got me started laughing, too. Glory's laugh always did. She and I both just fell out giggling. I high-fived Ben, and then Glory and I were hugging.

"Is he all right?" I asked Glory. "Tafari, I mean."

"He will be."

"He's mad at me?"

"He's sad. And hurt, and confused. He really liked you, Scotch."

Ow. "Not anymore, though, right?"

She smiled ruefully. "He's trying not to, but the boy got it bad for you, girl. You should talk to him."

"I—"

The washroom door opened and two girls came in. They eeped in alarm when they saw Ben. "It's all right," he said. "This girl was fainting"—he pointed at Gloria—"and I just helped my friend carry her in here so we could get some cold water on her face. You all right, sweetie?" he asked Gloria. She nodded and fanned herself, trying to look faint while her eyeballs were practically bulging out of her head with the effort of not laughing.

I said to the two surprised girls, "We're going now." I bundled Ben and Glory out of there, the three of us giggling like old times. Friday night! We stopped in the hallway to sort our various knapsacks and bags.

"You guys," said Glory shyly, "I'm going to that patty place in the market. Wanna come?"

Ben replied, "Can't. Gotta screen that new Star Trek movie for GSA on Monday. You could come with me to that."

Glory and I sometimes attended meetings of the school's Gay-Straight Alliance. It was Ben who had persuaded us to give it a try. I shook my head. "Not this time. My folks want us to be home to see them off." I kinda liked the GSA, but they always wanted to talk about politics and demonstrations. Me, I'd rather talk about Katastrophe and Meshell Ndegeocello.

Glory's eyes widened. "Your folks are going away? Without you?"

"Yeah, for the weekend!" I exulted. This felt good, the two of us talking again. I'd never been this angry at Glory before this. It'd hurt to not be her friend. "I gotta run. They're expecting me home. Ben can fill you in."

Ben shouldered his bag. "But I'm going to my movie."

Glory said, "I'll go with you, Ben."

"Cool. Scotch, you sure?"

"I really can't. I'll catch you guys later."

"Say hi to Richard," Gloria told me, blushing. How could I have forgotten? Glory had a thing for my big brother, not for his best friend, Tafari.

It was going to be a great weekend.

CHAPTER FOUR

Dad was in the living room, watching his favorite 100 percent fake reality cop show on the TV. He loved those shows so much.

He caught me glancing at the screen. "No television until after homework, young lady."

"Yes, Dad." As if. Fat chance I'd be I doing any homework this Friday evening. He and Mom would be outta here soon. No way they would know whether I was watching TV or not. I could catch up on my homework on Sunday.

"Come give your daddy a hug." He opened his arms. He got his hug, but then I immediately moved away and sat at the other end of the couch. I ignored how his face fell. That was just the price he paid for what he'd done to Rich. I'd been making him pay it the whole time Rich was in jail, and I wasn't going to stop now.

"When're you and Mom leaving?" I asked him.

He sighed and turned his attention to the TV again. "In about twenty minutes."

All *right*! I only nodded, but inside, I was doing a victory dance.

"I left dinner for you kids in the oven."

"In the UH-ven?" I said, teasingly. He always said it OH-ven, with a long O. Like he said "bowl" so it rhymed with "owl."

He gave me a sideways look. He knew that I'd just made fun of him. I'd better watch it. I asked him, "What'd you make?"

"Oxtail. Peas and rice. Salad. Yellow yam. A plate each for you and Richard. And you going to eat all the yam I put on your plate."

"Yeah. Sure."

He put the remote down on the arm of the couch. "That is sufficient. You will not speak that way to me, young lady."

Crap, now I'd made him tetchy. Better deal with it now. Otherwise the next twenty minutes would be nothing but lecturing about how when he was a small boy, his father would have tanned his behind for speaking to him too familiar, and *Young lady, is this kind of irresponsible behavior that got you into trouble*, yadda, yadda. "I'm sorry, Dad. I promise I'll eat it all."

"That's better." He turned his eyes back to the television. He muttered, almost as if I weren't in the room, "Can't afford to be wasting your mother's hard-earned dollars." He rubbed his twisted leg. Dad ran a construction company. He preferred to do some of the work with his own hands, but his leg hadn't been the same since he'd fallen from scaffolding when I was a little girl.

I heard Mom before I saw her. From the sound of it, she was at the top of the stairs. "Rich! Come down to the living room, please?"

"Please," question mark. Not her usual "please," period. She was sounding a little bit apologetic around Richard nowadays. Good.

"Cutty, is Sojourner down there with you?"

"Yes, darling."

"I'm here, Mom."

"That's good, you're on time. Come and help me with these bags, please."

I, of course, still got "please," period. When they took me out of LeBrun High, they decided that I needed a more "diverse" school, as in a school where I wasn't one of only five black people out of hundreds of students. That meant the big city; Toronto. Mom would never let on how much she'd hated to move all the way here, the long drive to work and back every day. How much she missed the town of Guelph. But ever since then she'd been starchier with me.

"Coming, Mom."

Dad sighed. He shifted grumpily around on the couch, moving his leg to a more comfortable position. Mom had asked me to help her with the bags, not Dad. For all I was mad at him and Mom, I found myself shooting him a sympathetic look. He scowled and looked away.

I took the stairs two at a time, until Dad ordered me to act more ladylike.

Mom stood at the top of the stairs between her big red suitcase and Dad's smaller navy one. She was going over something printed on a couple sheets of paper in her hand. She frowned at the list and shook her head. "I forgot to put down your aunt Maryssa's number in case of any trouble."

"It's in my cell phone, Mom. Don't fret."

"Oh. Is it in Rich's?" Mom had her hair done in that way I liked. She'd pulled it away from her forehead with a snug head wrap, leaving the soft mass of her nappy cloud of hair to poof out the back like a static explosion of pretty.

"I don't know." My hair was a mixture of Mom's and Dad's; it was medium brown and fell in natural ringlets. Lots of girls envied it. "Hey, isn't Auntie Mryss really our cousin?"

"Your dad's cousin. So, your second cousin once removed, or something." She hadn't even looked up from double-checking her blessed list. She was wearing a sensible beige skirt, a plain, sensible cream blouse, with a sensible beige jacket. The wishy-washy beige did exactly that; washed the color from her deeper brown face.

"Wouldn't Dad's cousin just be our second cousin?"

"Whatever she is, just call her 'Auntie,' dear."

"Cecily," Dad called from downstairs. "You wanted to get on the road before the worst of the traffic."

"I'm coming, I'm coming. Rich!"

Almost all her clothes made her look gray. Like I did, when I dressed in the colors she picked out for me.

Rich opened his bedroom door. He didn't make eye contact with her, just came and lifted the bigger suitcase. I got the other one, and he and I thumped them down the stairs with Mom following behind, nattering at us. "I've made three copies of this list. You each get one, and I'll put one on the fridge door."

"Yes, Mom," Rich and I sang in unison.

"Keep your list with you at all times. In your handbag, Scotch. Rich can put his in his wallet."

"Yes, Mom."

Dad was waiting in the hallway, leaning on his cane. He'd barely seen Rich before he snapped, "Richard, how you could make your little sister carry that heavy suitcase down the stairs all by herself?"

Rich boggled at him. "But she can—"

I cut in with, "Mom told me to—"

Mom overruled us all. "Cutty, she's a strapping young woman. Let her do some fetching and carrying. She'll need to be strong in this life." She sighed and plucked a couple of envelopes from the letter slot on the hallway wall. Using the top of her big red suitcase as a table, she folded two of her precious lists into precise thirds and put each one in an envelope. She tucked the flaps inside and handed one to me and one to Rich. "Are you two sure you'll be okay on your own?"

Rich's face hardened. "I was on my own in jail for three months."

Mom drew back a little, like he'd pushed her. "Rich, darling, I—"

I gave him a play slap to the shoulder. "Hey! I came to see you!"

He sighed. "Yeah, you did. You and Tafari."

Dad grunted, a bitter, one-note laugh. "You make your bed, you haffe lie in it. Bring those things out to the car." He turned and limped toward the door.

Mom said sadly, "I'll just put this list on the fridge door." She was darting her eyes everywhere, except in our direction. She bustled into the kitchen.

Rich and I followed Dad outside to the car. Dad yanked on the lid of the trunk. It was locked. Mom had the key. "Chuh," said Dad, frustrated. He used to like driving. Now, his leg wouldn't let him. He leaned against the car, watching our front door for when Mum would come out. He didn't say anything to us. He just stood there, a broad, medium-height white Jamaican man, grimly handsome with short, light brown hair going to gray. That old brown plaid jacket of his was all pills and thin spots, but he wouldn't wear any of his others.

I casually brushed away a Horseless Head Man that had chosen that moment to land on the suitcase I was carrying. And I felt it. Its skin was cool, but it felt alive and muscle-y against the back of my hand. I jerked my hand back. Jesus, now I was thinking I could feel them.

The motion must have caught Rich's eye. "What's with you?"

he asked softly. Mostly we tried not to let our folks hear us talking to each other. A little privacy, you know?

"Nothing. I was just remembering a boa constrictor some Animal Rescue woman brought to our class one time." The Horseless Head Man was looping in cheerful circles around Dad's head.

Rich looked skyward. "You're so weird."

"You're weirder." Not really a snappy comeback. It was the best I could come up with after the shock I'd just had.

Dad started drumming his fingers quietly on the trunk of the car. He was still staring at our front door. "But where your mother is, ee? We supposed to be on the road by now."

We didn't answer. His leg was probably achy from standing this long, but he would never say that. He kept drumming, in a steady syncopation. The Horseless Head Man was gone, heaven knows when or where. They were like that. After a while, Rich started humming, improvising a tune to Dad's beat. Dad said nothing, didn't even look Rich's way. He kept his fingers moving, though. He let the car take a little bit more of his weight. Closed his eyes.

Our front door opened and Mum came out. She took one look at the strain on Dad's face and came bustling over. "Sorry, honey." She unlocked the car doors and got in on the driver's side. She waited while Dad got in and Rich and I loaded up the trunk with their suitcases. She fussed a bit more over whether Rich and I knew how to contact them in an emergency, and reminded Rich about his appointment with his parole officer. "I'm trusting you children," she said.

Just before she rolled up the window on her side, Dad called through it, "And I don't want any of your friends coming to visit while we're away, you hear me?"

We both said, "Yes, Dad."

And finally, the small, neat navy Subaru drove away, taking our millstones with it. We kept waving until Mom rounded the corner out of sight. Even then, although we were grinning like fools at each other, we did a calm, well-behaved walk back into the house. You never knew when nosey Mr. Walter from next door was watching. But the minute the front door was closed, we whooped and hollered and started dancing around the room, crazy Muppet-style. "They're gone!" I yelled, "They're gone! For two whole days, they're gone!"

Rich gave me a high five.

"Freedom for the stallion!" I bellowed. "Or . . . I dunno . . . stallionette?"

Rich grinned at me. "You are such a goof." He mimed holding a mike. "Freedom for the stallion, freedom from the chains, freedom for these young foals, freedom from the pains, t'aint no thing to take this life for a spin . . ."

I wheeled into a spinning running man on the tiles lining our entranceway. I sang counterpoint to Rich's rapping; "T'aint no big thing, to wait for the bell to ring . . ." And *one!* I leapt, dead on time, into the move I'd been struggling to get right at the Raw Gyals practice this afternoon!

Rich watched with that bemused grin he got when his li'l sis acted weird. "You know," he said quietly, "that first day you visited me, I was never so glad to see anybody in my life."

I stopped and stared at him. "But you acted like you didn't care."

He perched on one of the sofa's padded arms. Dad would have had his hide for that. "That first month, I was frightened all the time. Waking, sleeping; always scared." He saw my face. "No, not for the reason everybody always tells you. Wasn't about guys trying to step to me."

I sat on the sofa beside him. "Then why?"

He shook his head. "Girl, you and me, living in this nice, safe house with three squares every day and nobody beating on us, and we have all our teeth and none of them are rotting?"

I made a face. "Eww."

Rich sighed. "We don't know shit, Scotch. Some of the stories I heard from guys in there, some of the things I saw . . . They told me I was rich, that I had it easy. Some of those guys could barely read. Couple of them told me they'd never tasted a vegetable that wasn't out of a can. They all had cell phones, but half of them didn't know which end of a computer was which, made like they were too tough to be bothered with that kind of fairy shit, but the truth is, they were scared to look stupid. They don't know how to Tweet, or Google. They can't walk into a store without security following them everywhere."

"Well, neither can you."

That surprised a bleak laugh from him. "True that."

"You're darker than me. You got that 'breathing while black' thing going on. Makes you instantly suspicious."

"Thing is, they were right. We have it easy. And a lot of them resented me for it. That was the real danger in there; getting ganged up on by a bunch of tough-ass, mean sunnabitches who'd never had what I had and knew they never would. But you know what?"

"What?"

"Not a single one of them had had their parents toss them in jail for having one joint."

"Rich, I—"

"I mean, Doggie, he'd like, beat his dad unconscious. So his moms called the cops on him. But that was different."

"His name was *Doggie*?"

Again with the little smile. "Doug. Dougie. But everybody called him Doggie. His dad had been smacking him and his mom around for years. Doggie only beat his dad up once."

Oh, God. That's where our parents had sent Rich. Into a place like that.

He looked up from the floor. "Jeez, Scotch, don't cry. Or at least go get some tissue. Don't want you near me with snot all running down your face and shit."

I sniffed back the tears. "Bite me."

"Now, that's just wrong." He aimed a play tap at my head. I blocked it and made like I was going to elbow him in the belly. He pushed the elbow away, grabbed my wrist, and then we were both falling out laughing, and everything was okay again, sorta. Except for the hard knot like a rock in my belly.

"Li'l sis, you are such a brat."

"Big bro, you are such a pain. And let go of my wrist. I have a new spot there."

"Don't sweat it," he said airily. "If it was catching, the whole family would have it by now." But he let go. I wished I could be so certain I wasn't contagious.

Rich said, "Hey; wanna come to an open mike with me tonight?"

"You mean it? For real?"

"Yeah, T's meeting me at Bar None. I'm going to sign up to get on the mike."

"Wow." Rich choked up whenever he tried to do any public speaking. I'd heard him spitting his rhymes softly alone in his room, and sometimes he'd do it for me and for Tafari, but he'd never performed on a stage.

"You came to see me when I was in jail. Mom and Dad didn't. Will you come and hang out tonight, too?"

"I dunno. I mean, me and Tafari . . ."

"Yeah. Someday one of you's gonna tell me what the hell's up with all that. Why you guys suddenly broke up, I mean."

He paused so I could answer, but I just crossed my arms and rolled my eyes at him like it was beneath me to even talk about it. Would this scraping feeling in my heart every time someone said Tafari's name ever go away?

Rich shook his head. "Okay, but you're both grown enough to deal with being in the same room at the same time, right?"

I could have said I wouldn't go to the club with him. I should have. But I wanted to prove to him that I was grown enough. I wanted to be a good sister. And I kinda wanted to see Tafari, too. So I said yes. I asked him, "When're you going?"

"Soon as I'm dressed."

"I'll be ready in five minutes. Ten. Hey; can I stash a couple blouses in your closet?"

"I'm running out of space."

"There's only four. Mom and Dad never check your room anymore. Mom's always scoping mine out. Come on, Rich. Please?"

"*Four* new shirts?"

"I think they don't search your room cause they don't want to have a reason to send you to jail again."

"Scotch, did you buy more new clothes? You have enough cash for that and rent?"

"What're you, the twenty questions fairy? Trust me, Bro. Everything's okay."

It would be. I clattered up the stairs to change. I could wear my new boots. This was going to be great!

I sat on the edge of my bed and texted Ben and Glory:

MY BRO'S TAKING ME TO BAR NONE! DOWNTOWN!

In seconds the answer came back:

SRSLY? RICH'S SO COOL!

That was Gloria. I could practically feel the blush over the phone.

AND CUTE!

That second one was from Ben. I texted him back:

TELL U EVERYTHING 2MORROW!

I'd barely hit send when I got back:

YOU'D BETTER!

I smiled and closed my phone. Things were back to normal. It was going to be a good term after all. Now, where the rass had I put that new blouse? "Rich!" I bellowed. "I gotta come get a shirt out of your room!"

CHAPTER FIVE

I waved at the bartender until I caught her eye. She came over. "Yeah?" she yelled over the drum 'n bass pounding out over the speakers.

"Ginger ale and lemon!" I yelled back. No booze for me. If I got caught out in here, at least I could say I hadn't been drinking liquor.

The bartender narrowed her eyes at me. I looked away, playing like I was so old it wouldn't even occur to me that she might think I was underage. She went to get me my drink. Nice tat she had; bear claws on either side of her breastbone, just above the neckline of her T-shirt. I wanted a circlet of briar roses around my left elbow. Soon as I got the lump of black stuff off that elbow. Would probably hurt like hell to get it done, but there's no beauty without pain, right? Mom 'n Dad would just about shit themselves if I so much as mentioned a tattoo, though. I'd start saving up for it tomorrow. Maybe I was diluting that nighttime goop from the naturopath's too much. Tonight I'd start putting it on full strength.

And in a few more weeks I'd be outta my parents' house. I'd be sharing a place with Rich, doing what I wanted to do.

So this was a bar. I could smell decades of beer rising like stale bread dough from the worn carpeting. It wasn't nasty or anything. Just old-smelling. Big tables everywhere, some rectangular, some round. All covered with cheap plastic tablecloths. Heavy, old-looking wooden chairs. The place was filling up with people chatting, drinking. Lots of pitchers of beer on tables. That's it. Except for the booze, it was nothing special. I'd kind of expected it to feel more, I dunno, *illicit*. Wicked, even.

The stage was near the entrance, with a big picture window behind it. There were a couple of mikes up there. The spotlight was on center stage. Rich'd be standing in that light soon. I'd love to be in that light, dancing, with all eyes on me. I could hardly wait for Raw Gyals to make our debut.

Bar None was right at the foot of the city. The window looked out onto Lake Ontario. Which, seeing as it was night, meant that the only thing I could see out the window was mostly blackness, pierced here and there with the running lights of small planes landing at the Toronto Island Airport, and the lights from those party boats you could rent so you could have your office party on the lake, complete with DJ and dancing.

Somewhere out there in the darkness was the string of small islands in the lake. It'd be so wicked cool to live on Toronto Island and have to take a ferry to and from Toronto every day to go to school. But Dad said that people who had those homes never gave them up, just passed them on to family or friends. Ward's Island was out there. And Centre Island. I hadn't been to the mini amusement park on Centre Island since I was a kid. Maybe Ben, Glory, and I could do that thing we'd planned to do this summer before things with

Tafari blew up. We were going to take the short ferry trip out to the island, go to the amusement park, and take a swan boat ride, just like we were six-year-olds again. The swan boats were so hokey; small, white fiberglass boats in the shape of a swan. They could seat about six people. Only they didn't really float, and they weren't even on the lake. They were in an artificial pond inside the amusement park. They were attached to a track below the water. There was a pedal on the floor of the boat. You pedaled the boat out along the track, and there was someone in the boathouse timing how long you'd been out on the pond. When it was time for you to bring your boat back, you'd hear this tinny voice on a cheap speaker system call out, *"Swan number twelve, come back to the deck!"* I loved that part. It'd be a scream for the three of us to do that. When I'd suggested it back in June, Tafari hadn't wanted to go. Said it was kid stuff. Didn't he realize it was only kid stuff if you were still an actual kid? If you weren't, it was, I dunno, retro, or something.

The bartender brought my drink back. I paid her. She had only stuck one lemon wedge on the rim of my glass. I love lemon wedges. I tried to call her back, but she was busy at the other end of the bar and didn't hear me over the music. But there was a little bowl of lemon and lime wedges right there on the bar, just one stool over from me. Was I allowed to take from it? I looked around the bar. There were two more bowls just like it; one at the middle, one at the other end. But they might belong to people. People who liked lemon wedges even more than I did. I sipped at my drink and considered; try to sneak a couple of the wedges, maybe piss somebody off, or ask the guy beside me whether anybody could take them? And look like a real newbie. As if.

A girl came up to the bar, took a wedge, plopped it into her drink, and walked away. Cool. I touched the shoulder of the guy beside me to get his attention. I leaned over and said, near his ear, "Can you pass me that bowl, please?"

"Of course. My pleasure." He handed me the bowl, trying to make like he wasn't noticing my cleavage.

"Thank you." I loved it when guys tried to pretend like that. It was so sweet. It was only gross if they made a big deal of it, staring at your chest as if they wanted you and resented you at the same time.

The guy asked me, "You here for the show later? That poetry thing?"

"The spoken word open mike? Uh-huh. You?" I took a casual sip of my drink, as though I spent every Friday night in downtown bars talking to older guys. He was kinda cute. Looked white, maybe about twenty-two. Pretty hazel eyes, brown hair shaved just a little bit above his ears so it showed off the full cap of it above. His green sweatshirt was bulky, but not too bulky. Not so tight that he looked gay, but it didn't hide how he had broad shoulders. Loose black jeans, rolled up neatly at the cuffs. Nice runners.

He said, "Not me. I didn't know there was a show on. Just came in for a quiet drink after a long week at work, you know?"

"Uh-huh, I know what you mean." I didn't, but I would pretty soon. Mom and Dad were going to flip when I told them I was taking a couple of years off before going to university.

The guy looked doubtfully at the stage at the front of the bar. "I may leave before it starts. I'm not the poetry type."

"Oh, it's not like that! It's not guys in berets with a bongo drum playing in the background."

He chuckled. "No? What's it like, then?"

"When it's good, it's like rap, it's like freestyling."

"I dunno. I can't really get into that if there's no music."

"The words and the rhythms are music. You should stick around, you'll see what I mean."

Now he was noticing more than just my breasts. "Wow," he said. "Maybe I will stick around. Especially now that there's a beautiful, intelligent woman to tell me all about it."

Oo, nice. "I'm sitting over there." I pointed to where Rich had found us a table, about halfway between the bar and the stage. "But I could come and hang out with you a little bit."

He looked where I was pointing. His face got wary. "So, that guy's your boyfriend?"

I laughed. "Naw, he's my brother." I was testing him now, though I bet he couldn't tell.

He looked at Rich. He looked back at me. He said, "You're kidding me, right? You're just trying to pretend he isn't your boyfriend."

Oh, he was skating on thin ice. "No, for real, he's my big brother. You can go ask him."

He got this look of hopeful comprehension. "Oh! So he's your half brother, or something? Or one of you is adopted?"

Yikes. He could still pull this one out of the hole he was digging for himself, but the signs weren't good. But his was a reasonable question, right? I didn't have to be so trigger-happy. Still, my voice came out a few hundred degrees cooler than before. "We both have the same parents. One black, one white. Can't you see how much we resemble each other? I came out lighter and Rich came out darker, is all."

"Wow." He visually compared me and Rich again. "I never thought it could happen that way. I just figured the kids would all come out, I guess light brown, you know?"

"Uh-huh . . ." *Our champion only has one more chance for a comeback! Can he do it?*

"I think it's so neat that you're each a different mix. You're both unique."

Okay, a step in the right direction. I gave him a little smile.

Again he tried to hide how hard he was checking me out. I knew this blouse would rock with these jeans! Totally worth the price I'd paid for it.

He leaned forward and said, "But you know what's really cool?"

"What?"

"You don't look like you're half black. I mean, you could be almost anything at all, you know?"

And, he's down. Down AND out. My smile froze on my face. *Nothing left but the shouting, folks.* "I could, huh?"

"Yeah! You could be Jewish, or Arabic, or Persian. I had a Persian girlfriend once. You could even—"

"Pass for white?"

He stopped, a confused frown on his face. "Well, yeah, if you wanted to. But you don't have to be black or white. You're, like, a child of the world!" He smiled, threw his arms out to punctuate his not-the-least-bit-triumphant conclusion.

I slid off my stool, picked up my drink. "Yup, that's me. Child of the world, daughter to none. I'm going back to my table now."

"Oh. Well, can I come and sit with you guys?" He was halfway off his own stool.

"No, you can't."

He stopped midslide, one foot frozen in midair, the other on the floor. "What? You really mean that?"

"I really do."

"What's wrong? Did I say something?"

"Oh, you said plenty." He genuinely had no clue. They never did. I was seething as I walked back to our table. I could be anything. Right. I could pretend to be Jewish, maybe from one of those old Montreal families. Invent a whole different set of parents, of relatives. Disown my brother, maybe, so no one would see him and wonder about me. Disown my mum, too.

Or I could hint at some "exotic" Middle Eastern heritage. Or Greek, or Gypsy. I could be anything but what I actually was; the daughter of a white Jamaican and a black American. Yeah, that would be so freaking cool, to have no people, no culture.

I threw myself into one of the empty chairs at our table. "People can be so stupid," I told Rich.

He didn't look up from the sheet of paper in his hand. "Who was it? That guy you were talking to?"

"Yeah."

"Which kind of stupid was it? He say something sleazy, something dumb, or something racist?"

Fake brightly, I chirped, "I'll pick numbers two and three, please!"

He smiled a little, shook his head. "Yeah, well it be's like that some days. Most days, actually." He tore his eyes away from the piece of paper. "Hey; you okay? He didn't do anything creepy, did he?"

I shook my head. "Naw. He was just trying to be friendly. In a thoughtless kind of way."

Rich made he-man muscles with his arms. "You want me to go over there and kick his ass?"

I giggled. "It's okay."

"Cool." His eyes were back on the wrinkled piece of paper.

"I don't know how you can even see your handwriting in this dark room."

"Shush. I'm trying to concentrate."

"Yuh bumbo."

"You know Dad would ground you for a week if he heard you say that."

"Yuh bumbo."

"After he got done laughing at your accent, that is. Just let me concentrate for a few minutes, nuh?"

I sighed. Rich could be so irritating. One minute he'd talk to me like an adult, and the next he'd be going all older brother on me, trying to tell me what to do. "You should already know your stuff by heart."

His shoulders slumped. "I did when I came in here."

That's when I realized just how nervous he was. I leaned over and lightly cuffed his shoulder. "You'll knock 'em dead," I said. "Don't fret."

"Yeah, okay." Then he was back to whispering at his piece of paper, like a wizard's apprentice muttering a spell he was unsure of.

"Hey," said a voice from beside our table. My heart leapt in recognition at the voice before I even looked up to see who it was. Sure enough, it was Tafari. He scowled at me.

Rich looked up from his piece of paper, saw Tafari, and leapt to his feet. "Bro!" They gave each other that shoulder-bump hug-to-the-side thing that straight black guys do. Tafari pointed at me with his thumb and hissed, "What's she doing here, man? She could get the place shut down."

I glared at him. "I will not! Why're you talking to me like I'm some kid?"

He ignored me. "Rich, if your parole officer finds out you snuck a minor into a bar . . ."

"Scotch is all right. She'll be cool."

I stuck my tongue out at Tafari. Okay, so now I was acting like some kid, but whatever. It was the best I could come up with while fighting the urge to get up and kiss him, tell him I was sorry, take him to a quiet table where I could explain everything. About the marks on me. About the Horseless Head Men. And then he'd look at me like I was some freak, and first his eyes would get far away, and then the rest of him. I could be magic like that.

Tafari said, "But she's got a drink!"

As though he'd never snuck me a vodka tonic or two when we were on dates.

Rich's eyes were all for the empty stage. He darted a quick glance at my glass. "Bet you she doesn't."

He hadn't even asked me first. He just trusted that I wouldn't do anything stupid. I loved my brother so much right then, I could barely stand it. Smirking, I held my glass out to Tafari. "It's ginger ale. Here, smell."

He waved it away, shaking his head. "If the place gets busted, I've never seen you before in my life."

That hurt.

Rich was so jittery; tapping his fingers on the rickety round table, looking around every which way.

"Still nervous?" I asked him.

He smiled. "Yeah."

"When do you go on?"

"There's an opening act. Some chick. Open mike starts after that."

"And?"

"I'm the first one up."

"Wow. No pressure there, huh?"

Rich didn't look as though he appreciated the joke. I tried again. "But that's good, right? That way, you get it over with quickly."

"Put it like that, I guess so." He didn't seem reassured.

Tafari clapped him on the shoulder. Rich jumped nearly a foot. "You're gonna kick butt," said Tafari. "Serious poetry slam butt."

Over by the bar, the guy I'd dissed was talking to someone else; an olive-skinned girl with long, wavy black hair. Her background was even harder to place than mine. Maybe he had a thing for that. Maybe he'd be smart enough to try a different line on her.

Tafari and Rich had their heads together. Looked like Rich was repeating his pieces and Tafari was coaching him. He could, too; like me, he'd heard those rhymes till he could recite them in his sleep. Kinda weird, being jealous of your own brother's friendship with your boyfriend. Your ex-boyfriend. While Tafari and I were still dating, it hadn't bothered me that he and Rich were best buddies. It was just one more thing we had in common. But now I was on the outs, but Rich could still call Taf up for a chat, go hang with him at the mall, and do stuff together.

Oh, I was such a shit. How could I begrudge Rich having a friend to hang with? Three months ago, he hadn't been able to go anywhere, with anyone.

My wrist was itching. I slipped the other hand under the sleeve of my blouse and scratched the slightly raised place. If this kept up, pretty soon, I'd be nothing but one big, sticky blob. A real, live tar baby.

I checked out Mr. Be-Everyone-But-Yourself again. He and that other girl had progressed to laughing at each other's jokes, occasionally giving each other a light touch on the knee or shoulder.

He hadn't been able to tell I was black. Was I really looking that pale? My skin did tend to fade to a more yellowy brown in the winter, but it was only mid-September.

There was another guy eyeing me, from one of the tables over by the wall. He was sitting with three other guys, all of them excited, yakking at the tops of their voices. He was cute.

"Soon come," I said to Rich and Tafari. I stood up and gave the guy a quick eye flash. You know; the kind where they're not exactly sure they've caught you looking? Then I looked down demurely, like I was too shy to keep looking. I'd wander back his way after I'd checked on my makeup. Tafari saw what I was doing, and scowled. It was pretty much the same way I'd caught his attention, those first few times at school. I looked away from him. It's not like I was trying to hurt him. It was just better if we both moved on.

I had that ointment in my purse. Not the nighttime mixture from the naturopath; the other stuff, the one that Mom and Dad didn't know about. The guy who'd sold it to me had said I could put it on anytime I wanted, as many times a day as I felt like. "Be right back," I said to Taf and Rich. Taf's scowl deepened.

I found the signs to the women's washroom and headed where they pointed. Down narrow stairs, brick walls with about an inch of latex paint layered on. So tacky.

CHAPTER SIX

Why did bathrooms in public places always smell so weird? It's like the ghost of rotting cabbage from fifty years ago had seeped into the walls and was slowly leaking out. And talk about cold. I didn't notice that the toilet seat was metal until I sat my naked butt down on it. Yow! My bladder cinched up so tight, it was like the shock had made it forget how to pee. Not quite, though. I peed, washed my hands in water as hot as I could make it. So then I had warm hands, which made the rest of me shiver even more. I got the ointment out of my purse. It was in one of those tiny eight-sided jars, clearly a Tiger Balm jar that someone had soaked the label off and glued a hand-made paper label onto. The label used to read, in wavery, badly photocopied black pen, YONKER GENE'S NATURAL REMEDY FOR BLISTERS AND BLEMISHES. The tin screw-on lid had the same message glued onto it, also written on cheap white paper. Both labels had mostly worn away through weeks of my handling the jar with damp hands. The Tiger Balm logo on the tin lid was showing through. I screwed the lid off. My nose wrinkled at the weird sulfur-mint smell of the muddy green ointment inside.

I pushed the sleeve of my blouse up. The new patch of tar on my wrist was like the others; black, weirdly shiny, slightly raised, a teeny bit sticky. I rubbed the ointment into it. It tingled, probably from the peppermint oil the guy in the little shop behind the market had told me was in it. He'd been kinda vague about what else was in it. I rubbed and rubbed until the ointment had all soaked in. I resisted the urge to scrape at the patch of skin. It'd only hurt if I did; I'd found that out long ago. I stopped rubbing, peered at it. Had it spread since last night? Was it edging up onto my hand a little? They did grow. The one on my shoulder had started out as a quarter-sized patch. Now it was bigger than my hand, edging its way around to my armpit, with a little piece of it, like a tributary, heading toward my collarbone. I could never have let Tafari see me like this.

No one knew what was causing my skin condition. My parents had taken me to doctors, skin specialists, allergy specialists, a nutritionist, even a psychologist. I'd been given antibiotics, antihistamines, injections, special diets. I'd been scanned, biopsied, had an MRI. All negative. And none of the treatments worked. Okay, so sometimes I'd cheated on the diets a little. It just wasn't fair to have to put apple cider vinegar on your popcorn instead of butter and salt.

Whatever we did, the marks just kept on coming. There were three streaks of black on my tummy, from my left side almost all the way to my belly button. The oval patch on my right shoulder blade. I hadn't told Mum or Dad about it, but I'd found a patch on my scalp, hidden by my hair.

When the conventional pills and potions hadn't worked out, I'd started hunting down the other kind. The zit treatments advertised in the ads on my MyFace page. Handwritten cure-all notices taped to telephone poles, the kind of notes that had scrappy tear-off fingers with telephone numbers written on them. Business cards thumbtacked to the notice board in the grocery store. Glory'd been after me to check out this botanica place that she knew about. I'd had to look up what a botanica was. My mom would have sneered at it and forbidden me to ever set foot in an "establishment that pandered to superstition." That's what she called churches, tabloids, CNN. Bet you Dad wouldn't have been so dismissive. When his great aunt had died back in Jamaica last summer, he'd stuck a ton of blue glass bottles upside down over all the branches he could reach on our old crab apple tree out back. To keep her duppy from coming to haunt him. "That woman was mean in life," he'd told me. "Wouldn't surprise me if she was vengeful in death, too."

As my blemishes got bigger, I'd stopped talking to Glory about them. I'd let her think they were fading.

Botanicas didn't sound so dumb to me. Mom didn't have any trouble trusting in the herbal tinctures from the nutritionist, or in the vitamin and mineral supplements from the drugstore. Looked like botanicas just did the same kind of thing, with a little bit of faith healing thrown in. Mom even believed in the placebo effect. Said it was the marvelous power of the human mind at work. But I just knew the major shit fit she would throw if I suggested a visit to Seer Angel's Healing Palace, or whatever it was called. That was the kind of thing that got on my last nerve about my parents. The hypocrisy.

If I concentrated on the marks, I could feel them itch ever so slightly. I mostly didn't feel them unless I was really quiet and thought about it. But at night, when I was sleeping, I could sense the new ones as they were coming in. Gave me nightmares, and when I woke up, sure enough, there'd be a new one. Mom and Dad didn't believe me that they showed up overnight. They were sure the marks came in slowly, and I just didn't notice until they were way obvious. "You young people," Dad would say with a mocking smile he meant to be a gentle one. "Heads so full up of yourselves that you can't see your own nose to spite your face. You think I forget what it was like to be young?" That was another thing that drove me nuts about the 'rents. It was like they didn't trust the report cards I brought home. All those As and Bs. I worked hard for those! But they thought I was too stupid to notice when new marks showed up on my very own body.

Maybe now that Glory and I were talking again, I'd get her to remind me where that place was. Could hardly be worse than rubbing some greasy goo that smelled of peppermint-flavored rotten eggs into my skin every day and swallowing drops of some other gunk in tepid water every night.

I checked my face out in the mirror. Damn; three zits on my cheek. 'Bout time I outgrew the acne stage. I dabbed some foundation on over them, blended it in with my fingers. It was a shade darker than the little chart on the back of the bottle said I should wear for my skin tone. Made me look healthier, that's all. More like my nice summer brown. Then some lip gloss to finish it off. All of My Purple Life lipglass; my favorite.

The toilet in the next stall flushed, and the stall door opened. I quickly shoved my sleeve back down.

Someone came out of the stall. Legs bent at odd angles, walking with aluminum crutches. Sorta thick-bodied. At first I thought it was a guy, and I was about to tell him off for being in the women's washroom. But no, she was a girl, just handsome in a guy kinda way. She looked Sri Lankan, or something, maybe. Dark skin, half her head shaved, the other half black spiky hair, gelled, with the tips dyed green. Eyeliner giving her raccoon eyes. Tight, torn black jeans and a black sweatshirt that read NO

ONE IS ILLEGAL. She wedged her crutches under her armpits and started washing her hands at the sink next to mine.

"I like your hair," I said to her. She kind of grunted at me, scrubbed her hands dry on her jeans, and headed for the door. I held it open for her. She didn't even say thanks. Whatever.

Upstairs, on the way back to my table, I passed by the cute guy. He was leaning over the table, making some earnest point to his buddies. They saw me coming, and their eyes widened. He had his back to me. I touched his shoulder. He turned, looked up, realized that I was the girl he'd been looking at. I bent and whispered into his ear, "Those guys over there with me? They're my brothers." Then I walked away before he could respond. Ball was in his court now. I mightn't be able to let anyone see my awful skin, but at least I could get my flirt on. Behind me, I could hear his buddies laughing. At me?

Rich had gotten himself a beer. I sat down. "Gimme a taste of that?" I asked.

He handed it over. Tafari looked at us with alarmed eyes, but he kept his mouth shut. I took a gulp of the beer. Yeah, still tasted like soap, like the first time Dad had let me have a teeny sip of his. I made a face and gave it back. "Why d'you like that stuff?" I shouted through a thumping swell of Beyoncé's latest song. Maybe there'd be dancing later.

He grinned. "It's cheap. Why d'you like that guy?"

Because it was bugging Tafari. I shrugged. "Looks like he's checking for me. And he's cute."

"He's gotta be almost thirty!"

I glanced over at the table my guy was at. He was deep in conversation again. "You think so?"

"At least. What, you into old men now?"

"Uh . . ." Shit. There was a Horseless Head Man, sitting right on the edge of the stage. Well, more like bobbing, actually, with its goofy sea horse grin. Damn. I'd been hoping I wouldn't see any tonight.

"Scotch?" said Richard. "You all right?"

I nodded. He turned to look at where I was staring, and a girl hopped up onto the stage right there, about an inch away from the Horseless Head Man. It floated politely out of her way. They had manners, I'd give them that much. There it hung, about two feet in the air above the stage, invisible to everyone but me.

The girl tapped on the mike a few times. The music went down. She was a tiny-waisted black girl, about Richard's age, with straightened and bobbed hair. "Good evening, good evening," she said. "Thank you all for coming out."

If Dad were here, he'd have boomed out a cheery "Good evening" back at her, West Indies style. Thank God Dad wasn't here.

"I know you're all dying to get to the open mike portion of the evening," she said. Rich groaned.

"Nah, don't be front'n, I know how y'all are." The American slang didn't quite fit with her north Toronto accent. Girlfriend thought she was on BET. If she started going on about how much she missed Biggie, as if he'd been her next-door neighbor or something, I was going to puke. Betcha none of those U.S. rappers even knew that Drake was Canadian.

"I mean," she continued, "who in here *isn't* a poet?" She looked around. Not a hand had gone up. She gave a smug smile. "See that? So it's gonna be an evening of playing to the choir, nah'm saying? Y'all'll be talking amongst yourselves, poet to poet, so y'all'll know if somebody's flow is stank, right?"

She got a smattering of applause for that. She launched into her thank-yous for everyone who'd sponsored the event. I tuned her out. I looked around for the Horseless Head Man. It'd disappeared. I had to stop using so much styling gel. The fumes were making me see things.

"Oh, God," muttered Richard. He was mangling his sheet of paper in his hands. "Ill just walked in."

"Holy crap!" said Tafari. "What's he doing here?"

The guy who'd just come in the door of the club looked pretty average to me. Medium height, medium handsome guy with a head of perfect, salon-twisted dreads, wearing an oh-so-cool Nike sweater. Other guys started rushing up to him, doing the two-handed handshake and the sideways hug thing, knocking themselves out to, I dunno, touch the hem of his raiment, or something. I pointed in his direction. "Him?"

Richard nodded miserably. "He just put out his third album. Guy's stuff kicks. I can't screw up in front of him. I just can't."

"Better stop getting fear sweat all over your lyrics, then."

Rich gave a horrified look at the wad of paper in his hands, started smoothing it out to go over it *again*.

Tafari scowled. "Stop teasing him, Scotch."

I scowled back. Ill had that shine on him that people get when they spend a lot of their time performing for an audience. But take that away, and he was just regular. "What's his real name?" I asked Rich.

"Huh? Christ, I can't put my mind on that now, Scotch. What difference does it make?"

"Just try to remember what it is."

"Marlon," said Tafari. "His real name is Keven Marlon Jones. Keven with two *E*s, no *I*."

I shook my head. "Keven Marlon Jones? That's for real? Not Keven Marlon Jones the third, esquire? Not Keven Marlon Jones the High Supreme King of Everything? Or maybe it's Keven Marlon Jones the Greatest Poet in the World, Before Whom Everyone Else Must Bow Down?"

Though he tried not to, Tafari was already laughing by the time I was halfway through. Richard started smiling too. It was a weak grin, but it was a grin. He straightened his shoulders, neatly folded the piece of paper, and put it down on the table. Tafari gave me that look he got when he and I were sharing the best joke ever. It was like old times, except it hurt like hell. We both stopped smiling.

All this time, the MC had been working her way through the list of people to thank for making the event happen. Now she said, "Now, people, I'd like y'all to give it up for Punum!" She started us off clapping, then went to the side of the stage, where the stairs were. Someone in black with spiky hair wheeled herself over to the stage in a wheelchair. It was the rude chick from the bathroom! She took an electric guitar off her lap and handed it up to the MC. The crowd waited in uncomfortable silence while Punum levered herself up out of the chair, took her crutches from the back of it, and made her way up the stairs onto the stage. There was a low stool waiting there for her. She put her crutches down beside it. The MC went to help her sit down, but Punum shook her head, a little irritably. She sat on the stool, adjusted the mike to the height she needed. She held her hands out for her guitar. With an awkward smile, the MC gave it to her and got off the stage. Punum kicked that thing on the floor that electric guitars have. The guitar shrieked, and she grabbed the mike and snarled . . . something into it. Sounded like, *"This shit's gotta stop!"*

Rich did his suave one-eyebrow-raised thing. Tafari outright sniggered. "Is what kinda spoken word that?" he said, louder than he really needed to.

"Hush up, nuh?" I told him. "I want to hear her."

"She's right, guy," Rich whispered. He put a finger to his lips. "Shh." I preened at Tafari. My bro had backed me up over his best friend. Tafari scowled at me, but he stopped his nonsense.

Didn't stop other people in the audience from doing the same kind of thing. This crowd had its own idea about what was spoken word and what was not. They were polite about her using a wheelchair because they had to be. They could have put up with her being Sri Lankan instead of black or Caribbean if she'd done her piece innna black people stylee. But she was doing her own thing. Sweet. I didn't business with the haters. I paid attention to the stage.

Her performance was a poem, I guess. She did lots of almost shouting into the mike while she played this wicked hot guitar riff, kinda like old-style Prince. She said stuff about wars going on around the world; Sri Lanka, Africa, Palestine. She said something about Canada, too, about how we mistreated Aboriginal people. Stuff about injustice to women, children, queers. And every so often, the chorus *"This shit's gotta stop!"*

When she screamed the word "queer" at the crowd, a guy shoved his chair back and stood up. He strode to the bar and bellowed, "Gimme a Heineken!" The chick playing up onstage caught all that, I know she did, because her eyes followed him. But she didn't falter once. Her stylings weren't my kinda thing either, and I didn't understand half of what she was on about, but I gave her mad props for having the guts to get up there and do it. Plus there was that cool hair. The loud guy leaned on the bar and glowered the whole time. She did a set of three songs, or poems; they were a little bit of both. She got some polite clapping from the audience.

When she stopped performing, her face shut in on itself. Suddenly, she looked really shy. She put her guitar on the floor, picked her crutches up. The MC was so flustered by all this that she nearly stepped on the guitar when she came back onstage. Punum had to tell her to watch where she was walking.

Endless seconds later, Punum was down off the stage, back in her wheelchair with her guitar on her lap. The MC raised the mike to her height and said, "Okay. Next up, from uptown, is Richard Smith."

Richard jumped to his feet, knocking his chair over. With the dark bar and the sound of the clapping, I bet that almost no one noticed. But Richard's face was like death as he and Tafari put the chair upright. I tried to pat his arm to reassure him as he rushed by me to the stage, but he was going so quickly I barely grazed him.

He'd left his notes on the table! I grabbed up the crumpled sheet to take it to him, but Tafari grabbed my wrist. The marked wrist. I yanked my arm away from him. "What?" I barked.

He pulled back. He covered the hurt look with a sneer. "Rich can't be reading from a piece of paper up there, like he's in English class!" he said. "You want to make him look like a fool?"

"Oh." I sat back in my chair. My face was hot with embarrassment. I took a sip from my ginger ale.

Rich muttered, "Ah, um . . . this first one's called 'Jail Time.'"

Someone from the crowd shouted, "Talk into the mike!"

Rich looked at the mike as though it were the head of a spitting cobra. He leaned a micro-inch closer to it. God, this was going to be agonizing.

> "Rolled up late, pissed off, exhausted
> Couldn't stop my friends from gettin' arrested
> Notice it's always the darkest brother who gets tested
> Again, and again, and again . . .
> Uh . . ."

He'd forgotten the next line. It *was* agonizing. Rich choked his way through two poems. Twice he forgot the words for long seconds. Tafari and I were whispering Rich's lines along with him; *"The charges won't stick 'cause they're little white lies / but the message is / 'We're afraid of your size / We're afraid of your youth and your time and your blackness.'"* It was all I could do not to shout out the ones he was blanking on. He kinda sorta came up with words to fill in for the ones he'd forgotten, so that was something. But we could barely hear him. None of the passion of the way he spat when he was doing it for just me and Tafari to hear; none of the fire. Just fear, choking out his talent. Every so often, someone in the audience would say, "Louder!" He'd said he was going to do three pieces, but after he'd mumbled his way to the end of the second, he just stuttered, "Th-thank you," and all but ran off the stage. The applause was even more lackluster than it had been for the chick who'd gone before him. Worse yet, that Ill guy was shaking his head. Rich rushed past us in the dark, headed for the stairs to the washrooms.

Tafari blew out a breath. "Ouch," he said.

"Yeah."

"I'll make sure he's all right." He took off. The MC announced a five-minute break.

A voice behind me said, "That seat free?"

It's not like I wanted company, but Mom and Dad had me raised so bloody polite that I was saying yes even as I was looking round to see who it was. Damn. It was Snarling Chick Punum. Or Rude Chick. Same diff.

She wheeled herself over, took a bottle of beer from where she had it clamped between her knees. "Fuck, I'm glad that's over with," she said. She swigged back a good third of the bottle before she set it down on the table.

"That must have been hard, huh? First time you're performing?"

She leaned back in her chair, gave me a knowing look. "No, I've been doing it for years. Places I can get my chair into, anyway. Why would you think it's my first time?"

Shit. Busted.

She grinned nastily. "And don't try to tell me it's because I sucked, because I know I didn't."

"No, you were great. It's just, well, it's not the kind of thing you see every day."

"You mean a chick doing spoken word, or a crip doing it?"

"Um, both, actually. But I never said you were, you know—"

"A crip? No, I said it. But you'd better not."

"Actually, I get that."

Her look changed. "You do?"

"Yeah. It's like me being black. There's names we can call ourselves that other people better not."

"Oh. Okay." For a second, she didn't seem to know what to say. What she didn't say was, "But you're not black." Maybe she wasn't so bad after all.

She had another swig of her beer. "Anyway, I'm always sick with nerves before I play. You saw me in the bathroom. I was throwing up. Hey, I wasn't rude to you, was I? I'm so scared before I go on, I barely notice who I'm talking to."

"Oh. That's why you were being so weird. Why d'you do it, then?"

She grinned. "Why do I perform? You kidding? I fuck'n love it! It's a high, like skydiving. You stand on the edge, looking out at a long, long drop, and you're so scared, you're practically peeing yourself. You're scared because you know you're going to throw yourself off that edge, and either you'll make it, or you won't." She toasted me with her bottle. "Better than sex." She took another swig of beer.

"What's that mean on your shirt; 'No One Is Illegal'?"

She rolled her eyes, shook her head. Little smug smile. "You're from Scarborough or Mississauga or someplace like that, right? Come downtown for a bit of the rough tonight?"

"Eglinton West, actually." I wanted to slap the smile off her face. Bit of the rough . . . ?

She shrugged. "Same thing. So, how old are you? Fifteen?"

Whoops. I tried to act all haughty. And old. "What d'you mean? I'm nineteen!"

She gave a sarcastic little laugh, shook her head. "Doubt it." She gestured at my face. "The makeup gives you away. You're trying too hard. Got it caked on like icing."

Now it was my turn to roll my eyes. "Please. You think I should look all mannish like you?" I mean, I liked her hair and all, but yikes.

She looked down at her knees, but it didn't quite hide her bashful smile. "Naw. I kinda like how you look. I just mean you don't have to work to make yourself pretty." She took a breath. "Please tell me you're at least seventeen."

Her eyes met mine again, and I felt my face flush. Great. I had a big old dyke stepping to me. Or wheeling to me. As if. "Uh—"

Richard scraped his chair back, threw himself into it. "I suck," he said. He put his head in his hands.

"Naw, bruh," said Tafari, sitting beside him. "It wasn't that bad."

He was lying through his teeth, and we all knew it.

"You don't suck, you know," said Punum. Didn't even give me a chance to talk to my own brother. "You just need a little more experience up there onstage."

Rich turned his head just enough so he could see her. "Yeah, right. You don't have to be nice to me. I'm not gonna get any better that way."

She smiled. "See? You got some stones. You're already talking about doing that again. That's the kinda balls you need to get up in front of a crowd night after night and tell them things they don't wanna hear. Now you just need more experience in front of the mike, more of the courage of your convictions."

"I dunno . . ." But he was sitting up, paying attention to her, not hiding his face.

She leaned a little closer to him. "Next time," she said, "don't announce the name of the piece. Not unless it's really cool, you know? Not unless it's almost a line of poetry itself."

"What, then?"

"Just get right into it, dude! Come strong!"

Huh. That's what I needed to do with that dance move I kept missing. Never mind all that bloody counting. It was messing me up. Just hit the stage hard with my left foot, *one!* Leap right in. I grinned.

The Horseless Head Man was back, floating a little above our table. It was staring into my glass of ginger ale. I saw its nostrils flare. Was it *smelling* my drink? Euw. "Shoo," I told it.

"Fly in your drink?" asked Rich.

There was another one, sitting on Punum's head. I half-stood, went to brush it away. Bloody things were everywhere now: floating in the air; perched on people's shoulders. One materialized in front of my face, grinning its goofy grin. I stood up the whole way. "Get out of here," I whispered. "Leave me alone." And here it was. That psychotic break my mum was always on about. I was totally losing my shit right here, in public. I was going full-on crazy.

Punum, Rich, and Tafari were all staring at me. At least, I think Tafari was. There was a Horseless Head Man blocking my view of him. Could I brazen my way through this? "Oh, nothing's wrong," I said, casually trying to wave the Horseless

Head Man away. But it was like trying to wave my hand through thick honey; it slowed my swing down. "Yuck!" I cried out. The others looked at me like I was nuts, and who could blame them?

Now there was an iridescence in the corner of my vision. It was coming from under the stage. I pointed at it. "What's that?" Shit. Shouldn't have done that. What if no one else saw that, either? It looked like a gigantic bubble, lit from within, all rainbow colors. But kinda smoky. I couldn't see through it.

"The hell?" said Tafari.

I asked him, "You see it, too? Like a big balloon?"

He nodded, staring at the bubble. Other people were noticing now. They were standing and pointing, because the bubble was growing. It bulged and swelled out from under the stage. The bouncy girl MC leapt off the other side of the stage. I heard her thunk down onto the floor. Horseless Head Men were gathered in the air all around the bubble. They all had the same happy, goofy grin on their weird unicorn faces, like that dumb dragon in that never-ending movie.

The bubble swelled really quickly. It was almost touching distance from our table before I knew it. I heard the scrape of chairs across the floor as the others stood up and backed away. Richard grabbed my hand. "Scotch, get out of the way!"

I shook his hand off. What was it with him and Tafari, trying to shove me around all the time? The bubble was only inches away from me. It was maybe twice my height, a glowing, opaque white. Soft colors inside it. Some of them colors without names. And the smell coming from it! Almost too faint to detect over the odor of stale beer coming off the barroom floor, but it was there. Like the memory of how last summer's lilacs smelled. Like a Jamaican beef patty, hot from the oven. The kind with more meat in it than cornstarch thickener. Like your dad's cologne the last time he hugged you. I reached my hand out toward it.

Punum was beside me. She slapped my hand away. "Are you mad? Stop that!" God, people were so bloody handsy tonight! But she didn't move away from the bubble, either. She stared at it. It swelled a little more, and got longer, like, a pseudopod, or something. A big, fat, wiggly arm, only with no hand, no fingers. Or bones. We moved back.

I glanced to my other side. Richard was still beside me, Tafari only a little farther away. I craved to touch the arm of the thing the way I'd longed for the boots I was wearing, going to Marcus Shoes in the mall every day at lunch break for a month and just staring at them in the shop window. Standing in front of that thing was like staring in that shop window, and knowing that to have it, you would give up something you couldn't afford to give up. "Dare you to touch it, Rich," I said.

He stepped a little closer to me, to the bubble. "What is it?"

"You not going to find out by just standing there looking at it."

"Why you don't touch it, then?" His eyes never left the bubble.

God, I wanted to. Wanted to get to that thing I knew I could never really have. Because the truth was, I'd wasted my chance at moving out of our parents' place and I was going to lose Rich's trust, too, when he found out about the boots. I put my hand on his shoulder. Had to reach up to do it. "You touch it," I replied. "You're the one who wants to know what it is."

Punum swore. Tafari muttered, low, as though the bubble might hear him, "Don't do it, Rich. Let's go, man."

I didn't think he'd actually do it. Rich was the sensible one. Saved his money, looked before he crossed the street. Always giving me shade for one thing or another. I didn't think he'd listen to me! But he flashed me that big, rare grin of his, said, "Tag; you're it!" and slapped his hand up against the bubble, just as it swelled toward us. A painful buzzing zipped from my hand on his shoulder, up my arm, zapped the rest of me.

And then, the weirdest thing; the picture window lit up. From outside it, the world *flashed* for a second. That's the only way I can describe it. Like the whole earth became a lightning strike, only without the lightning. It made my back teeth sing with pain. I looked out the window just in time to see a cone of blackness even blacker than the surrounding night shoot up from the surface of Lake Ontario. A red fireball shot out the top of it, with the loudest bang I'd ever heard. My hand flopped from where Rich's shoulder had been. It hung, jangling, at my side. People were screaming, chairs scraping back. I kinda went weak with the surprise of it all. And dumb. I just stood there while that thing reached out toward me, Punum, and Tafari. At least Punum hadn't lost her mind. She took hold of my useless arm—her touch made the pins-and-needles feeling almost unbearable—and pulled me out of the thing's way. I stumbled, grabbed on to the table for balance, but it was dancing across the shifting floor; the ground was shaking. As the table skidded, I lost my balance and fell onto Punum's chair. It tipped and we fell off, her half on top of me. I heard the *whuf* of the wind being knocked out of her. Through our clothes, her breasts mashed against my own. Her face bounced against mine. Her breath was sweetish from the beer, her eyes surprised. I'd never been this close to another female, not unless you count my mom nursing me when I was a baby, I guess. With only one working arm, I struggled to sit up. Punum used her arms to pull herself off me. "You okay?" I asked her.

"I think so."

Rich and the bubble were both gone. I couldn't believe it. "Rich!" I yelled. "Where are you?"

The old chandeliers were swaying. One of the ugly

fluorescent bulbs broke free with a crack, crashed down onto a table and exploded, spraying broken glass. The people at that table screamed and jumped out of the way.

"Rich!" I yelled. I couldn't see him anywhere in the bar. The Horseless Head Men were buzzing, darting about everywhere, like flies on shit.

Punum pointed. "Holy shit." The stage was gone, too. And with it, the whole wall of the bar to which it had been attached. The bar was open to the outside. Lake Shore Boulevard was covered in fog so thick you could only see the glow of streetlights and lit signs. Cool air blew into my face. There was a neat, scooped-out hole in the ground where the stage—and my brother—had been. Its edge was a hair away from my foot.

I got down on my knees and peered into the hole. It was dark down there. Is that where Rich was? "Rich!"

No answer. Tafari pulled me to my feet. "What the fuck'd you make Rich do that for!" he yelled. "Why were you even here, anyway?"

Punum said, "Leave her alone. It's not like she forced him to touch it. And will someone please help me up, already?" Taf and I each took an arm and helped her back into her chair.

Commotion all around us. People streaming out the door. Others punching at the keys on their cell phones. Cells weren't working, apparently. A big old guy with an apron on came hurtling out from the back of the bar. "Terrorists!" He shouted. "Everybody downstairs! Go!" People started barreling over each other to get to the basement stairs. The guy whose friends had laughed at me went rushing by, his face blank with panic.

Tafari pulled me by the hand. "Let's go! It's not safe here!"

I yanked the other way, threw the full strength of my thighs into it. "Rich is down there!" I yelled into the hole, "Rich!"

Then, from somewhere far away, there was another bang as

loud as the whole, wide world. The whole building shifted to one side, then back again. People lost their balance. Chairs and tables fell over. Bottles and glasses tumbled to the floor. I saw a girl get hit in the small of the back by another table skidding across the floor. There must have been more screaming, but it was as though someone had stuffed cotton wool into my ears. Punum was shouting something at me. I couldn't hear her. She was struggling to stand, using her hand on my shoulder for leverage.

And just like that, I was away.

CHAPTER SEVEN

It felt like I was in a subway train. I was sitting in something that was rushing forward really quickly. That is, I think it was forward. I felt really not right, like my limbs were hung on in the wrong order. Which part of me was the front? For all I knew, I could have been sitting on my ear. And my eyes appeared to be in my elbow. Both of them in one elbow, except I could see just fine.

There were other people, also seated in rows of seats. If you could call them "people." A few looked human, except for the bandicoot heads. And the arms made of smoke. And the fact that you could see through their chests and they each had three hearts beating inside. And the jointed metal legs. Okay, they didn't look like people at all. But way more so than the ones that looked like a cross between a melty, burning wax candle and the color three, or the ones that tasted like yesterday and whistled like empty brains. It smelled weird in there. Lilac-y, if lilacs were to be nightmares soaked in regrets. Where were we headed? What in the world had just happened? Had I hit my

head back in the bar? Maybe this was a concussion or something. Maybe I was dying. I should have been way more freaked
than I was, but my stomach was all twisted up inside with worry
about Rich. Had it been a bomb, back there in the bar? Had
Rich maybe gotten on someone's wrong side while he'd been in
jail? Maybe somebody'd showed up at the reading to blow him
up, or something? But then, what was that thing we'd seen outside the window before I'd gone away? Shooting up into the sky?
That hadn't been in the bar. That hadn't even been on land. It'd
looked as though it were out in the lake.

The walls of the train thingie were wet and flexing. My
perverse brain immediately thought of intestinal smooth muscle,
and I felt even more weirded out than I already was. Damn that
surprise bio quiz that Mr. Butler had sprung on us today. I didn't
even know what smooth intestinal muscle looked liked for real,
though I could draw a diagram of it.

Something else about me felt wrong. Yeah, I know; under-
statement. I looked down at my legs. "Oh, God," I whimpered.

My seatmate, a purple triangle with an elephant's trunk,
twitched. "Scotch?" it said. "Holy crap, is that you?"

"*Punum?*"

"Am I in a coma?" the triangle replied. She sounded
miserable. "Am I dying?"

"I don't know what the hell is going on," I said. "What was
that thing coming out of the lake? Did you see that?"

"Yeah. It exploded. That was freaky."

"No, that was just weird," I replied. "This right here is freaky.
Where are we?"

She was all outlined in gold. Me, I was . . . I stared down at
my legs, all eleven of them. Or maybe only nine, since two of
them seemed to be Punum's as well. "Wait; are you holding my
hand?"

"I grabbed your wrist when shit started to go weird. Now, I don't know what part of you I'm holding. Feels like your ankle. Both ankles."

"Let go of me," I said. "You're not my type."

"I can't," wailed the purple triangle. "I'm stuck."

"Oh, goody." My ear stung. I knew that was bad for some reason. Nine legs or eleven, all of my legs looked like half-melted black rubber. They were some busy legs, too. I was sharing two of them with some mouthy punk chick I didn't like, and two more of them were intertwined with each other, with puffy-looking bulges where they touched. Where had I seen something like that before? Oh, crap. Earthworms. In that video we saw in bio class. Were my legs trying to *mate* with each other? Probably explained why I'd been feeling this tickling sensation, well, in places I didn't want to think about right then. Could give Punum the wrong idea.

"Whatever I'm tripping on," said Punum, "I don't like it."

I didn't answer her, though, because right then, one of the puffy places on my mating legs bulged a little more—it felt as though my leg was yawning—and spat out a tiny version of the floppy-legged thing I'd become. "Holy shit!" I said. I managed to catch the baby before it rolled off me onto the floor of the train, or whatever we were in. It immediately wound sticky legs around the place on my wrist where that weird patch of skin had appeared the last time.

Some of the other beings in there with us started clapping; those that had hands, that is.

Punum the purple triangle looked at the baby; don't ask me how I could tell she was looking. Not like she had eyes, or anything. She went all jangly around her gold-lined edges. "Jesus. What is that thing?"

"I think I just gave myself a baby." The kid kind of had my

face, only with a beak. The irises of its eyes were yellow, shading inward to bright green pupils. It stared calmly at me with them. It only had nine floppy little legs. I guess the two mating ones came in when it got its first period, or had its first wet dream, or both, or something. It'd need to be a hermaphrodite to fertilize itself, right? I think maybe. Its legs weren't as sticky as mine. And not black, either. Kind of a tortoiseshell brown, almost see-through.

The baby whipped some of its scary legs toward my face. I yelped and ducked my head, but I was too slow. The baby didn't hurt me, though. It just started tapping on my chin.

"What's it doing that for?" asked Punum.

I felt like I was going to upchuck. I felt like I was *supposed* to upchuck. "I think it's hungry," I said. And I was supposed to feed it my own stomach contents, like birds did. But there was no way I was going to hurl in public, even if this was really a coma, with people—well, things—watching me, much less spit it all into a baby's mouth. But the feeling was getting stronger, moving upward into my chest. I wouldn't, I wouldn't. It could starve for all I cared, or learn to drink formula. I clamped my mouth tightly shut and held my breath, willing the upchuck feeling to go away. It didn't work, and I was going to spit up any second. In panic, I reached deep inside myself and *pushed*. That's the only way I could describe it.

We began to fade out. Thank heaven. Anywhere but here. But as we were leaving the dream, I heard, in a really big voice but weak and from far away, "Scotch! Oh, God, you gotta help me! It hurts so bad!"

Richard! He was here! I didn't dare open my mouth to answer, for fear of spewing. Instead I tried to, I dunno, unfade us back into the dream. *Richard!*

■ ■ ■

. . . but Punum and I were sprawled on the ground on Lake Shore Boulevard now, outside Bar None with its torn-open front. Punum's chair was on its side. Its wheels were spinning, as though it'd only just fallen over. Her crutches were lying nearby. We were in a puddle. "You okay?" I asked her.

Her face was blank with confusion, but she replied, "Yeah. Damn, I get tired of people asking me that. Fix my chair, would you?"

I did. She pulled herself over to it and clambered into it. "Hey," I said, "were we in . . . Did we just . . . Was I out just now? How'd we get outside? How come it's light out?"

It wasn't all that light. More like early morning. Kinda dark, and the world was a mess. Buildings with smashed windows. An ambulance careening the wrong way up the street, its siren blaring. People standing outside buildings, clutching injured arms and legs. People crying. Shit lying in the road; desks, a smashed-up refrigerator that looked as though it'd fallen from an upper story. Power lines torn loose and lying on the sidewalk and the road. Way too many people huddled at the nearest streetcar stop, like the streetcar hadn't shown up in ages. Punum took it all in, then turned to me. "I don't know what to tell you," she said. "That was seriously weird. Do you remember anything at all?"

Someone had stretched yellow police tape in an "X" across what used to be the glass front of the bar. We hadn't been lying in a puddle. The whole street was wet. "You were a purple triangle."

"For real? I could have sworn I was a hat stand."

"Did you see me?"

"Yeah. You were a big bowl of licorice Jell-O."

"Gross."

"And you had a baby."

"Well, at least you got that part right."

Punum was looking all around, her mouth open in amazement, her eyelashes golden.

Wait. What?

She said, "Scotch, I don't think it was just the bar."

"Uh-huh, I figured that. Wow. Some crazy shit must have gone down last night." There were cops everywhere. People sitting on curbs crying. Crashed cars. One of those half-pint smart cars was in the middle of the street with some kind of thick hose wrapped around it. Hard to make stuff out with all this smog everywhere, sucking in the daylight and making my eyes water. Above us was the sound of helicopters, though how they were flying in this smog, who knew? I coughed as acrid air hit the back of my throat. "What smells like that? Like burning brick? And why's it so foggy?" I'd been close enough to hear my brother calling my name, asking for my help, and I'd left him behind. And it had felt like more than a dream. My ear was still burning, but I didn't reach to touch it. I wasn't ready yet. Too much else to deal with right here, right now.

"Scotch," said Punum, pointing to the lake.

Her voice was quiet, the kind of quiet you get when you're trying to tell someone that the guy with the knives for hands who comes for you in your dreams is standing right behind you, grinning.

I turned to see what she was pointing at. I gasped. "No way!"

There was a volcano in Lake Ontario. I could see it through the billows of gray cloud. In fact, it was the reason for the gray clouds. A full-on freaking volcano, complete with spouting flame, glowing orange lava flowing down its sides, and steam rising in dirty gouts when the hot lava hit the water. It was pumping out a thick, boiling mushroom cloud that was getting bigger every second. Punum stared up at it as though she were seeing God. "That's why it's so dark," she said. "All that smoke."

"But how'd it get there?"

"You saw it last night, same as me."

The scared little rabbit inside of me cowered at the memory of the massive cone, blacker than blackness, that I'd half-glimpsed thrusting forth from Lake Ontario last night, just before the world blew up. "No," I said, "that's not right. Volcanoes don't just shoot up in seconds."

A woman's voice said, "They're calling it Animikika." She said it like Ah-nee-mee-KAY-ka. "On the news, I mean. That woman on Citytv's been calling it Animikika. She says it's Algonquin for 'It is thundering.' I think that's what she's saying, anyway. Sometimes her lips are forming different sounds than the words that're coming out of the TV."

Punum asked her, "Come again?"

She looked surprised. "Haven't you noticed? Though I guess TV's the least of everyone's worries right now. I'm looking for my son. He was hanging out with friends last night, and I haven't heard from him." She was already looking past us, wanting to continue her search.

"Uh, okay," I said. "Good luck or whatever." Then I felt like a dork. Who says "whatever" after wishing somebody good luck finding their son?

"Thanks," she replied. "You girls take care."

"I gotta find my bro," I told Punum. Though I had the awful feeling I knew where he was. Not where, exactly. He wasn't here, you know? Not in this world, insane as that seemed.

"Do you know where he was last night?" Punum asked.

"You talked to him. He was the guy who had the mike after you. The other guy at our table was my . . . brother's friend, Tafari. Shit. My folks will be calling any minute to check up on us. And Rich has to check in with his parole officer today."

Punum raised an eyebrow, but only said, "Maybe someone in the bar saw him. I'll come with you." Then she gasped and felt around the back of her chair. "My axe! Where's my axe?"

"Your what?"

"My guitar! Oh my god, I can't lose that! I'll never be able to replace it."

"Maybe it's in the bar?"

"You think so?"

"Yeah."

There was such panic on her face. "It's probably fine," I reassured her. "Let's go over there. We can check for my bro and get your guitar."

"Okay."

"Want me to push?"

But she was way ahead of me, practically halfway across the street already. I made to follow her. I felt it as soon as I took a step forward; that tightness pulling at my skin. That's how new blemishes felt when they came in! It was my right calf. And did the boot on that foot feel just a little bit tighter? Oh my God, not my whole lower leg all at once. I'd never had one that big before. And I could have sworn that while I'd been dreaming last night, or whatever it was I'd been doing, the one I'd felt show up was on my ear.

Fear welled up in the back of my throat. The burning on my ear had faded to a tingling. I touched that ear. Oh, crap. Right there on the top edge of the ear was another blemish. I could feel its slightly raised edges, the tiny hint of stickiness. My ear *and* my leg? I couldn't have gotten two at the same time, I just couldn't. That had never happened before.

Punum was across the street. She whipped her chair around. "Hey! You coming, or what?"

I waited for an ambulance to rush, keening, past me. Then

I ran across the road. I had to sidestep smashed concrete and broken glass. And at least five dead salmon. WTF? As I ran, I untied my hair, which I'd bound up on top of my head. I didn't know for sure that I had new blemishes. I hadn't seen them, right? I'd felt the one on my ear, but that was probably the only one. My hair would cover it.

I caught up with Punum. Inside the bar, the older man I figured was the owner was sitting at one of his tables. He was the one who'd tried to get everyone down into the basement when the front window of the bar blew out. His plaid shirt had a long rip in one sleeve and the front of his white apron was smeared with what looked like soot. He had his chin in one hand, propping sorrow. He was rubbing his other hand in fretful circles over his balding head. A Horseless Head Man floated just above him, watching his circling hand in fascination. A couple of cops, a woman and a man, sat with him, asking him questions and taking notes. Okay, so I'd ask them about Rich. If I had to, I would make up some story to cover up that I'd been in there last night even though I was underage; tell the police I'd been at the movies with Gloria, tell them I'd heard what happened from Tafari . . .

Punum and I made our way past overturned tables and chairs, and for some reason, one of those almost life-sized singing Santas. I went over to the hole that'd been blown into the floor, hoping in a crazy way that I'd find Rich in there, whole and healthy.

The hole was like it had been last night; a jagged gash in the ground. Dirt and broken bricks lined its edges. Bits of rusty rebar poked through here and there. If one of those had stabbed Rich—

"Something I can do for you two young ladies?" said the woman cop, in a tone that let you know she wasn't asking, that she wanted an answer from you and she wanted it now.

I rushed over there, ignoring the pulling in my leg. "Did you find him? My brother? He fell into that hole there last night."

Wheeling up behind me, Punum said, "I'm just here looking for my guitar. I left it behind the bar."

Great. My world was falling apart, and all she could think about was her stupid guitar.

"It's over here," said the bartender with the bear claw tattoos. "I grabbed it and put it under the bar for you."

The worry lifted from Punum's brow. "Hey, great!" The bartender brought the guitar over. It was in a black and gold soft case with a sturdy carry strap. The bartender went back to sweeping up broken bottles and mopping booze up off the floor. The place smelled like Mr. Lane's breath in ten a.m. geography class. Euw.

The woman cop said to me, "What's your name, Miss?"

"Sojourner Carol Smith." I was so dang obedient, I answered without thinking. But then, was I going to refuse to answer a cop's question? I didn't want trouble.

"Address?" As she wrote, she fanned a Horseless Head Man away from her face. I guess everyone could see them now.

I said, "I just want to know if anyone's seen Rich. My brother. He fell in that hole over there last night. Did he get taken to a hospital, maybe?"

The owner said, "Miss, we didn't find anyone in the hole. Thank God, or my insurance would go through the roof." My gunmetal gray bomber jacket was hanging on the back of his chair. I took it and put it on.

Suddenly, to the tune of "Jingle Bells," someone started bellowing, "Stock markets fell/The volcano smells/Everything's gone to hell." It was the singing Santa. It lit up from the inside as it sang, its suit glowing a cheery red. It rocked back and forth and shook its tambourine. Then it went silent and dark again.

"What in the world?" I said.

The owner shrugged. "It used to be one of the bar televisions. I think it's still trying to report the news, only it comes out in song. I can't make it stop." He sighed. "All the others turned into giant clown faces and just rolled out the door. I ask you, how do you write that up on an insurance claim? Fifteen years I've been running this place, nothing like this has ever happened. It's those bloody terrorists."

The two cops glanced out the broken picture window, to where an active volcano was spewing lava. The male cop shook his head. "Yeah, I don't know about terrorists, but I don't think anything like this has ever happened anywhere in Toronto." His voice shook a little. The quaver made him sound a little bit young, and a little bit scared.

The woman cop said, "Miss, I think you'd better start checking the local hospitals. It's going to take you a while, I'm afraid. Does your brother have a cell phone?"

I nodded. What I wanted was to cry.

"Try giving him a call. Maybe he's just fine."

The cops gave the bar owner their cards, shook hands with him, and went out the door. In the gloom, it looked as though there was a small, sexless face in the back of the woman cop's neck. A pretty face, and young, like a baby's. It smiled at me. I took a couple of steps backward, and then her head was in the shadows again, and I wasn't sure what I'd seen.

I called Rich's number. The phone rang and rang. Just as I was about to hang up, there was a click and it went silent. But not the disconnected silent. This was that kind of hollow silence that you sometimes get before the person on the other end speaks.

"Rich? Hello?"

The sound that came out of the receiver made the little hairs on my arms stand up. It sounded big, as though it were way huger than the phone could contain, so only a little portion of it squeezed through. If there were words in it, I couldn't tell. It sounded like a million people screaming in pain.

I dropped the phone. With shaking fingers, I picked it up again. I put it to my ear. The sound hadn't changed. "Rich?" I said, my voice cracking.

The phone went dead. I called the number again, but only got a recorded voice saying that the caller was out of range.

Punum came over. "Hey. You okay?"

"No, I'm not okay." I sounded whiny and scared, like a little kid who'd gotten lost in the mall. "He's supposed to check in with his parole officer this morning, and something really weird is going on with his phone, and—"

"Come," she said. "Let's go get some breakfast. I'm starving."

"Are you insane? I have to find my brother. Plus I don't have a lot of money."

"I'll treat you," she said gently. "You'll do a better job of searching for him if you're not hungry."

I thought about it. She was right. "Okay, then. Hey; did you have golden lashes last night?"

"What? No, I don't do that kind of foofy stuff."

"Huh. 'Cause you have them this morning."

"You're messing with me."

"Nope. You have them, for real. And they don't look fake. They look really good on you."

She swore under her breath. She went over to the mirror above the bar. Or to what was left of it, anyway. Looked as though something heavy had crashed into it last night; it was mostly spiderwebs of broken glass, some of them falling out of the frame. Punum peered at her own reflection. She tugged gently at the lashes on one eyelid. "Wow."

The bartender stopped sweeping up broken glass long enough to say, "They look really cool."

I shoved gently at Punum's shoulder. "Told you so. It goes with your guitar case."

"Not," the bartender continued, "the kind of look I'd usually expect to see on a butch. But on you, it so works."

OMG, was she *flirting* with Punum? I'd never seen anyone come on to someone in a wheelchair before.

"Ho-ho-ho," chortled the Santa Claus. He was lit up and rocking again. "The hospitals/Are overflowing/Only emergencies, please." It didn't really fit into the rhythm of "Jingle Bells," but he did his best. Then he started bellowing "Oh Carolina." The rude version; "Oh, Carolina/Kiss mih rass/ Bumboclaat."

Punum stared at it. "It's like I did too many tabs of acid."

The bartender said, "More like the world did."

Punum shook her head. "Well, I'm outta here. Catch you later, Kathy." She turned a full-strength devilish grin on the bartender, who twinkled back.

"See ya," she said. "Call me, okay? When things get back to normal?"

Punum said, "Coming, Scotch? Eggs are on me."

I went with her. When we got outside, she said, "Her name's Kathy. Isn't she cute? I think she likes me."

"I guess she's cute. Kinda chunky, though." I stepped over another dead salmon.

Punum smiled a little. "You jealous?"

"Me? No!"

Her smirk got even broader. "Sorry to disappoint you. It's just that I don't do jailbait."

"I'm not a little girl!" The street wasn't just wet; it was flooding in places.

She laughed, shook her head. "Caked-on foundation, remember?"

Absentmindedly, I said, "She seems to be really digging on you." Was that *algae* festooning that stop sign?

"Uh-huh. And just exactly why do you sound so surprised about that?"

Busted again. I blew out a breath. "I guess I just have a lot to learn," I replied. My ankle was kinda itchy now. I needed to get to somewhere private so I could look at it.

"You bet you do."

The number of people hanging around the streetcar stop had grown bigger than the shelter could hold. They spilled out of it, filling the sidewalk. They were watching five guys wrestling some kind of animal into an animal rescue truck. It really didn't want to go, whatever it was. I glimpsed it between the bodies of the men. A beautiful iridescent pattern in green and yellow slithered along the length of it. A snake? It'd have to be massive.

The smart car I'd passed on the way here was squeezed in the middle. Maybe that hadn't been a fire hose I'd seen wrapped around it. I shuddered. Whatever was going into that truck, I didn't want to know.

Punum tried to check out her eyelashes again in the clear Lucite of the stop's shelter. Great. She comes back with gold eyelashes, but I come back with a skin condition.

I asked her, "What's with all the dead fish?"

"Beats me."

CHAPTER EIGHT

Everywhere we walked, things were a mess. People were sweeping debris out of their businesses and homes. Ambulances, cop cars, and fire trucks were dashing about. There were telephone poles cracked in half; we had to pick our way around the fallen electricity lines. Cars piled up in the street. Some of them had crashed and were busted up so badly that I didn't see how anyone in them could have survived. And there were Horseless Head Men; hundreds more than I'd seen before. I pointed at one. "Can you see that?" I asked Punum.

"Yeah, why? What is it?"

"I don't know, but I was seeing them for a few weeks before all this started."

"Really?"

"The difference is, now other people can see them, too."

"So," said Punum, "what'd you come back with from our little jaunt?"

"Nothing," I lied.

"Are you limping?"

"Little bit. Stone in my shoe."

She stopped. "Stop and take it out, then."

"Uh, no. It's a boot, see? All those laces, it'd be a pain. I'll do it when we get to the restaurant."

"Suit yourself."

A thought pulled me up short. "Hey; in your dream, did you see what happened to the baby? The one I gave birth to?"

"I hadn't thought of it that way! Tiny kind of octopus kid?"

"Yeah, out of my leg. It had a beak."

Softly, she said, "You pregnant?"

I felt a lurch of fright for a second. But . . . "No, I just had my period. I can't be pregnant if I had a period, can I?"

"Don't ask me. I only date chicks. It's not the kind of thing I ever have to worry about."

"Oh. Right."

I called Rich's cell a few times. Kept getting the message that his phone was out of range.

We had to dodge around pieces of buildings that were lying in the street. The fire department was trying to put out a blaze in a row of three two-story buildings. Punum whistled. "That must have been some earthquake."

"This was more than just an earthquake."

Her face got serious. "I know. I'm trying to deal with one thing at a time."

I nodded. "Okay, gotcha."

"I just hope my place is okay."

She and I compared notes about our dreams as we went. Some of the things we'd dreamt were the same, and some were so not. She asked, "And were we sitting inside some kind of giant snake thing, only it was also a subway car? With, like, spirochetes or something along the sides?"

"Spiracles."

The more we talked, the more freaked out I got. Punum was, too, but she also seemed excited about it. "Whaddya figure put us both to sleep like that? And how did we get outside the bar?"

I dunno. I'm not so sure we were unconscious."

She considered that. "Whoa. Too weird. Give me a hand here, will ya?"

I pushed her chair over a tree branch that was lying on the sidewalk. She asked me, "So where do you think we were?"

"I don't know! I just know there was an earthquake and my brother fell into a big hole in the ground." The sick fear feeling washed over me again. "Oh, God." I sat down right there on the cold ground rather than fall down. Now that I'd said it, it was like it had suddenly become real. "I can't," I said, my breath coming in gasps as I found it harder and harder to breathe. "I can't . . ." I didn't know what I couldn't, just that everything was finally too much.

Punum leaned over me. "Whoa. Take it easy, Scotch. Deep breaths, okay? But slow ones. Come on, breathe with me, now."

And I did, imitating the rhythm and depth of her breathing until the light-headedness had faded a little. "My parents aren't coming home," I told her. "I mean, not until Sunday night. And I can't find my brother. He isn't answering his cell, I don't know what to do, I don't know who can help me."

"Stand up. You can't stay on the pavement like that. You're getting your ass wet."

A homeless guy sitting on a milk carton with his back against the wall of the bank said, "Tell me about it." He looked like he was about my age. "I don't suppose you ladies have the price of a cup of coffee on you?"

Punum said, "Hang on a bit." She fished around in a pocket kind of thing slung under one arm of her chair. She took some change out and handed it to me. "Give this to him, please."

I raised an eyebrow, but only said, "Okay." I went over to the homeless guy and put the money into the used coffee cup he was using to collect change from passersby.

"Right on," he said, smiling at Punum.

"Yeah. You take care, okay?"

He tipped his cap to her. "Doing my best."

Then, no lie, a Sasquatch pushed between us. The homeless guy yelped and dragged his dog out of the way. But the dog went apeshit, snarling and barking at the Sasquatch while the homeless guy struggled to keep hold of the dog's collar. "Farley, down!" he yelled.

The Sasquatch stopped, turned, and eyed Farley. It was maybe six feet tall, but wider than two people. Its eyes were huge. I could see the little bloodshot veins in them. And it smelled. Sweat-stink, really strong, like, I-haven't-bathed-for-a-thousand-days strong. There was a wildness to the smell, like fermented cat piss. That smell was almost strong enough to be a sound. The Sasquatch smiled or snarled, and I came out all over goose bumps. Its fangs were yellowed at the tips, and there was food caught in between them. Farley bravely kept on barking, but a more tentative bark than before. Even he was thinking better of tackling something like that.

The Sasquatch scratched its flank with a black-clawed paw. Dandruff flaked out of its heavy black fur. Then it just stumped away. Passersby skipped out of its way. Some of them squeaked in alarm. Some of them just looked irritated.

Punum's mouth was still hanging open. The guy with the dog looked at us and said, "Interesting times, huh?"

"Tell me that was a costume," said Punum.

I shook my head. "If you're standing close enough, you know when someone's wearing a costume. That thing blinked. Gorilla suits don't blink. That thing was real. Oh, God. It was real." And all the weirdness I was trying to hold back came crashing down on me again: the glowing bubble in the bar; Richard disappearing; riding inside a giant worm, not to mention being stuck with barely five bucks in my purse in a downtown Toronto that looked like someone had picked it up and shaken it. And then there was that volcano, filling the sky with ash and muffling the warmth and light of the sun. I tried to flip my cell phone open, but my hands were trembling so much that it took me three tries. "Gotta call someone," I said. "Gloria. Ben. Someone has to come and get me out of here." Before I thought about what I was doing, I punched the first number on my call list. Shit. My parents. But you know, right then, I didn't care how much shit I was in, didn't care that they would ground me forever, didn't care how angry they would be. I just wanted them to come and get me out of this mess.

There was only static on the line. "Something's wrong," I said.

"Maybe with your phone," Punum replied. "I've been texting with my friends just fine."

"Try another number," suggested the homeless guy.

"Okay. Maybe that's it."

"You take care, dude," Punum said to him as we moved on. We went in silence for about a minute. Then Punum said, "I'm sorry about your brother."

"It's okay." It really wasn't, but she probably knew that.

The first diner we got to was closed. The second one was open, but Punum said, "Not this one."

"How come?"

She pointed. You had to walk up three steps to get inside it.

"But can't you use your crutches?"

"Yeah. But my friend Jeremy couldn't, and my ex Sharmini

couldn't. I just don't go into places like this anymore if I don't have to. Won't give them my money."

"Don't you think that's kinda harsh?"

"No, I don't. Let's go."

There was a Tim Hortons doughnut shop a little farther on that looked open. There were a ton of customers inside. And it had a ramp. But the door was locked. We had to bang on the glass door a few times before one of the employees came out from behind the counter and opened it a crack. "You guys real?"

"Yeah," I replied. "I'm not bigfoot, and neither is she."

"You're not going to turn into a pile of jelly beans on me? Last guy did that. Well, his clothes did, anyway. And his little dog. And the jelly beans had teeth." She looked us up and down. "Hell, who can tell? You look okay. Come on in."

It was weird in there. People were quiet, all huddled over their coffees and doughnuts, staring up at the televisions mounted near the ceiling. A few people were crying. Punum and I tried to get sandwiches, but they only had doughnuts left. "Didn't get our morning delivery," explained the woman at the counter.

Punum got a cinnamon bun and a coffee. She bought me a grape pop and a couple of those vanilla glazed doughnuts with the little multicolored sprinkles on them. I put it all on a tray for us. I grabbed us a table, but Punum couldn't pull her chair up to it; all the tables in there were the kind with the seats bolted down to the floor. Punum sighed, levered herself up out of her chair, and slid into one of the seats. I put our tray on the table and hung my jacket on the back of one of the seats.

"Gotta pee," I told Punum. "I'll be right back." Not looking at me, she nodded. She had her cell phone out and was punching in numbers.

I found the women's washroom and looked in the scratched

mirror there. Yup, I had a new blemish on my left ear. A tiny one, thank heaven. I could tell people it was a mole.

I went into the stall. I perched on the seat, took my boot and sock off, looked at my leg, and started to cry. The blemish covered my foot and ankle and went all the way up to just below my knee. It was like someone had dipped my right leg in some kind of dull, lumpy black rubber. And worse yet; as I watched, a small spot popped up out of the skin on my knee, about the size of a pinhead. Slowly, the skin all around it began to blacken and bubble. It didn't hurt. It was the slightest tingle. If I hadn't been looking right at it as it happened, I wouldn't have known I'd grown another spot. "Out, spot," I whispered, trying to make a joke of it. That only made me cry all the harder. Pretty soon, this stuff was going to be covering my whole body. My shoes wouldn't fit, or most of my clothes. And now there was no way I could take part in Wednesday night's battle; not looking like this! Which meant I wouldn't have the money to give to Rich after all, and I'd be stuck living with my folks. Assuming Rich made it home alive sometime soon. Assuming my parents did. Assuming the world wasn't coming to an end.

I got my ointment out of my purse. The nasty smell of it was the least of my problems right now. I rubbed ointment all over my foot and the lower part of my leg. It started to sting right away. I used up all the cream that was in the jar.

Someone knocked on the door. "Just a second!" I yelled. I sniffed the tears back as best as I could, jammed my sock and boot back on, stuffed the empty jar back into my purse. I left the stall so the next person could use it. She was wearing a scarf, but I caught a glimpse of vines peeking out from under it. I tried washing my hands, but the stuff coming out of the faucet looked weird. It was fizzy. I leaned in close and took a sniff of it. Then

I put a fingertip in and tasted it. Diet Sprite, not water. That was going to get old quickly.

When I got back to our table, Punum was talking on the phone, half in Tamil, half in English. In between the words I couldn't understand, I caught, "No, Mom," and "Why did you do that?" and "It's okay." Then she said, "I gotta go now, Mom. What? No. With a friend. No, not another girlfriend. I'll come by later, okay? Okay." She closed the phone. "Finally got through to my folks. They've been on the phone to Sri Lanka since last night, checking in on relatives and friends."

"Are they in Toronto?"

"My folks? Yeah. Some stuff fell off the wall in their apartment and broke when the ground started shaking, but they had too many ceramic figurines of English shepherdesses, anyway."

"Your folks know you date girls?"

"Yup. That's why I don't live there anymore. My dad kicked me out."

Confused, I said, "But you're going to visit them later?"

"They're still my folks! Besides, my mom would kill my dad if he tried to stop me from visiting her."

Her voice sounded funny; kind of far away. I looked closely at her. Her face was gray. "Someone's bombing Sri Lanka and India. Direct hits to Colombo and Delhi," she said.

I nearly choked on my doughnut. "How bad?"

"Bad. No one can reach my uncle and his family. They live in Colombo."

"Oh, God, Punum. I'm so sorry."

We watched the news. The chaos was all over the world; a combination of things that couldn't exist and things that shouldn't have happened. Sri Lanka had experienced heavy casualties. The country was accusing Pakistan of an act of war. Sri Lanka would have been retaliating, except that all their soldiers' uniforms seemed to have turned into flocks of green geese that roared like lions instead of honking. The geese appeared to be made of garbage bags. Meanwhile, Pakistan was asking for emergency aid; something was the matter with their food supply, but they weren't saying what. They had no electricity at all, and even backup generators weren't working reliably. A lot of people on life support in hospitals had died when the power had suddenly gone out.

"The same thing happened here!" wailed a man standing in front of one of the televisions. He turned to the people nearest him. "My brother died in the hospital this morning. He died!" He started sobbing; that racking, awful sobbing that comes from people who don't let themselves cry often. It got me crying, too. An old lady took a tissue out of her purse and handed it to him.

Punum and I had one of those uncomfortable silences you get when two people don't know each other well. Then she said, "Power's gone out in the subway. News announcer just said a bunch of trains are stuck in between stations. There are people trapped in the trains! In the dark!"

An older man sitting near us said, "They'll get them out of there, sonny. Don't you worry."

I guess he was talking to Punum. He smiled reassuringly. Punum just nodded. "Anyway," she said to me, "unless you can afford a cab, you aren't going home to North Yuck in a hurry."

"I don't live all the way up there, all right? Besides, me and my bro are moving into an apartment downtown on the first of the month." I took another bite of my doughnut. "Hey; if the trains stay closed all day, I won't have to go into work this evening!" It'd be nice to have one Saturday where I didn't spend Saturday evening wearing a paper hat and scooping fries into paper cones.

"But then people would be stuck in the trains for hours," Punum replied.

"Yeah. I didn't think of that." I took a sip of my pop. The shop that sold my skin ointment was open on Saturdays. But it was too far to walk, and I sure didn't have money for a cab. I sent Ben a text. I was so relieved when he texted back almost right away. Stephen had sprained his ankle. Ben was okay. I asked, HEARD FR GLORIA?

YEAH BUT SHE GOT CUT OFF.

Oh, man. This was all making me sick with worry. WHERE R YOU?

COLL & YONGE.

College and Yonge. I texted him the cross streets where the Tim Hortons was. COME OVER IF U WANT. I hoped he would. It'd be nice to see at least one of the people I cared about, to see that he was okay with my very own eyes.

"He call you yet?" Punum asked. "Your brother?"

"No. And if he doesn't report to his parole officer by ten a.m., they're gonna put him in jail again. What'd they make this doughnut from, sand?" It tasted awful.

"Hey," said Punum, "what about that other guy who was at your table? Heard from him?"

I sat upright. "Oh, crap. Tafari! How could I forget about Tafari?" I'd thought about everyone else before him, even my parents.

I called him. I was using up a lot of my minutes today. "He's my ex," I told Punum. Then I realized that now she was thinking I'd told her that so she would know I was single. Sure enough, she grinned her butter-melting grin at me. I pretended I hadn't seen. Tafari didn't answer his phone. I got the mechanical voice that said, *"The customer you are calling is out of range."* Yikes. Was he trapped in the subway with those other people?

Punum was working her phone hard, checking in on friends, friends checking in on her by text and by voice. At one point I heard her say, "Yeah. Snapped in half, right in the middle of the neck. Something fell on it, someone stepped on it, I guess. I dunno, man. No, I can't afford to fix it!"

She talked a little longer, then got off the phone. She looked pretty glum. I asked her, "Why didn't you tell me your guitar was broken?"

She shrugged. "You have your own problems."

"Can I see it?"

She shrugged again, but there were tears in her golden-lashed eyes. She picked her guitar case up off the floor, and put it on the table. She unzipped it.

The body of the guitar was fine. The rest looked like an accident in a tackle box; wires in a tangle, splintered wood. "Holy," I said.

She quickly closed the guitar bag back up. Her lips were pressed close together. "There goes my singing career for a while."

"Can't you just get it fixed?"

She shook her head, with that look someone gives you when they think you're too dumb to live. "Kids," she said. "I work three days a week, for minimum wage. Best job I could get. Took me six years just to save up for that axe." She put it back beneath the table. I didn't know what to tell her.

On the television, a news announcer was saying that in London, Big Ben was now blowing giant soap bubbles and chanting dirty seventeenth-century drinking songs. There appeared to be a new island off the coast of Jamaica, and it seemed to be made of gumdrops. Bet my dad would love to see that. One news channel had given a name to all the bizarre, scary stuff that was going on. They were calling it "the Chaos." Some big preacher guy in the U.S. was saying that God hated homosexuality, and that was why he'd given every Pomeranian in that country pink fur overnight. Punum grinned. "He thinks pink Pomeranians are because God *hates* homos? I know about a hundred fags who'd give their eyeteeth for a pink Pomeranian!"

The thought made me smile a little. "Seriously, though," I said, "what do you think's going on?"

A lady at a nearby table piped up, "It's terrorists. You aren't safe anywhere nowadays."

A man reading a newspaper snapped it extra hard to stop the top half of it from flopping over. He kept his face hidden behind the paper, but I knew that gesture. I leaned over and whispered to Punum, "That was Torontonian for, '*Lady, you are so full of shit. Shut up and go away.*'" Punum grinned. Her smile helped a little bit. Just knowing that I could make someone smile, even though everything was so messed up.

"Maybe this is the end," said a young white girl with what looked like a steel mohawk. "We've poisoned the environment, and now Nature is getting back at us."

Her hawk was real metal. Bet that was new. Newspaper guy rustled his paper, which was Torontonian for, "*Keep quiet, all of you. Can't you see I'm reading?*"

Two policemen in bulletproof jackets ran by the window we were sitting by, then one more. One of them had a long, swishy tail poking out the back hem of her jacket, like a horse's. She tripped over it and fell. She got up and kept going. Another came running out of a side street. They all pulled out their billy clubs and surrounded a man in a wheelchair who'd been trying to get across the street. People inside the doughnut shop exclaimed and crowded around us at the window. I heard the same lady ask, "What is it? Is it a terrorist?"

The cops were blocking my view of what they were doing around the guy. And the girl with the steel mohawk was sticking my shoulder with one of its points. "Ow!"

"Sorry. Woke up with it like this this morning. Not used to it yet."

The ring of cops suddenly tightened. They all seemed to be flailing away with their clubs.

"What's happening?" asked the man who'd thought Punum was a guy. "Are they beating up that poor man?"

"He must have done something to ask for it," said another voice.

Someone else replied, "Come to think of it, I thought he looked suspicious when he was in here just now."

"Like hell you did!" yelled Punum.

"What? Who's saying that? I'm just saying I know what I saw."

"Maybe he's turning into some kind of monster!" said an eager child's voice. "Maybe a dinosaur!"

"Hush, Ashok."

"I'd like to be a dinosaur," said Ashok.

The knot of police thinned, and we could see the man again. He wasn't in his wheelchair anymore. He was on his stomach with his hands behind him, handcuffed. His face was turned towards us. He looked terrified. He was screaming something; I couldn't hear what through the heavy glass window. He had cuts on his face; I could see the blood. One of the cops had a foot on the man's head, holding him down.

"Oh, my god," said someone. "I wonder what he did."

"Maybe nothing. But they have to be sure. They have to find out."

"These are horrible times. Just horrible."

Punum had tears in her eyes. "Fuckers." I wasn't sure whether she was talking about the cops or about the other people in the doughnut shop.

Two policemen picked the man up. His legs flopped out of the grip of the cop at his feet. The other cop almost dropped him. He didn't, but he started yelling at the disabled man. He dragged him into the back of a cop car. He tried to sit him up, but the man fell over. Punum made an outraged noise. The cop's buddy came over and the two of them kind of stuffed the man into the back seat, lying down. They got into the car and drove away. The wheelchair stayed there for a second, in the middle of the road. Then a car hit it and knocked it up against the sidewalk. It landed on its side. One wheel fell off. Punum said, "Christ." She yanked her chair closer to her and pulled herself into it.

"What're you going to do?" I asked her.

"I'm going to try very hard to not go postal. Come and open the door for me."

She wheeled her chair about and bellowed, "Coming through!" Bit by bit people cleared the way. As I opened the door, she said to me, "Stay here."

"Are you sure?" I asked her, relieved.

"I'm sure." Just before the door closed, I heard her yell, "Hey!" in the direction of the remaining policemen. They turned toward her. Was she insane?

People in the doughnut shop wandered away from the window. A woman asked me, "Is your friend okay on her own like that?"

"She told me not to go with her."

The woman looked concerned. "But can she be on her own? I mean, does she understand what she's doing?"

A cold anger bubbled up through me and out my mouth. "You know what?" I said. "I understand what you're saying, and you need to check yourself."

"Oh!" she said, all offended. "Young lady, I was just—"

"You were just making assumptions, and now you're going to just mind your own business. Right?"

Her face went red. She turned her back on me. "So rude," she muttered as she walked away.

The serving people went back behind the counter and started working again. The lights flickered. People gasped. The lights became steady again. I sat there, tense, as Punum talked to two more of the cops. She was gesturing at the guy's wheelchair.

Oh. She was coming back. Behind her, one of the cops righted the guy's wheelchair and started clumsily trying to fold it.

I let her back in. She was fuming. She gestured for her coffee. I handed it to her. She stared at the writing on her cup as though she were trying to memorize it. "Bastards." She fussed and shifted around for a second. Then she handed her cup back to me and turned her chair around again.

"What're you doing?" I asked her.

"I can't stay here, feeling useless. Some of my friends are down at the Convention Centre, helping to put out cots and stuff for people rescued from Toronto Island. You wanna come?"

Jeez, I couldn't look after her and try to get my life back in order. "Uh, well, Ben might be meeting me here, and I still haven't found Rich, or Tafari . . ."

"I get that, but while you're calling around to try to find them, you could be helping some people who've lost everything."

She saw the look on my face. "Fine. Suit yourself. It's been real. Well, no, it hasn't. Nothing's real today. But you know what I mean. Put my guitar on the back of my chair."

"But you can't just . . . Don't you want me to come with you? How're you going to get there?"

Teeth gritted, she said, "Yes, I can just, and no I don't bloody want you to come with me." Her smile was all edges. "And as for how I'm going to get there, it's all downhill from here. Like the whole world is going. Or hadn't you noticed?"

I picked her guitar up. "You don't have to be so mean," I

said. Where did she get off, being so high-and-mighty? I'd just defended her to some lady! She should have been grateful I even wanted to give her a hand getting around. I slung the strap of the guitar case over the two push handles at the back of her wheelchair. The broken guitar made a jangling noise as it swung against the back of her chair. Then I sat back down, scowling. No way I was going to open the door for her now.

She didn't even ask. She just said, "See you, Li'l Miss Mississauga."

"North Toronto, I told you. What are you, deaf?"

"No, I'm a different kind of crip."

"Hey, I didn't mean it like that." Now I felt like an idiot. "I mean, it's just an expression. Here, let me get the door for you."

"Stay the fuck away from me."

Stung, I stepped back. Punum wheeled over to the exit. An old guy opened the door for her. I watched her go down the street. She looked determined. Like she knew where to go, what to do. Like a grown-up.

My cell rang. My ring tone was the theme from the latest Bratz movie. At the time, it'd seemed like this cool, ironic joke. I mean, it's not like I even went to see it; imagine me and a cinema full of nine-year-olds and their parents? But now, the tinny tune coming from my phone just made me feel childish. "Hello?"

"*I was frightened all the time . . .*"

The voice was whispery, almost familiar. Behind it I could hear the awful screaming I'd heard the last time, but muted. "Who is this?" Maybe my phone was haunted.

"*I'm running out of space. I was frightened all the time. I was frightened all the time. I'm running out—*"

The phone went dead. But I'd recognized the voice, remembered who'd said some of those words to me. My brother, just before we left for the bar last night. Frantically, I hit redial, but the phone hadn't picked up the number where the call had come from. I called Rich's number.

"The customer you are calling is out of range."

My hands were shaking as I flipped the phone shut. I grabbed up my jacket and got out of there.

CHAPTER NINE

I wandered around the city for I don't know how long. Harbord Street seemed to have turned into a loop. It used to be a straight line, I swear. I walked around and around it about three times before I figured out what must have happened to it. I took an alleyway. At the end of it was a small side street, the usual Toronto street with tall trees on either side, and those old houses with the big front porches. It looked normal, if you ignored the downed power lines and the occasional broken window.

A little boy was on his tippy toes on the sidewalk outside his house. He was about five years old. He was reaching into the mailbox. He was probably Japanese, wearing a striped navy and white baseball cap with jeans and a green T-shirt. He pulled out a wad of mail and yelled, "Ba-chan!" He held the mail out to show it to an old lady who was sitting on the front porch of the house. Her hair was pulled up into a bun. She and the little boy looked alike; same shape to the head, same mouth. Maybe she was his grandma.

The little boy thumped up the short set of stairs to the house. She smiled at him as she took the mail from him and gave him a hug. She put her knitting down and opened a big plastic cooler that was on the table beside the green Muskoka chair in which she was reclining. She pulled out an ice cream bar and gave it to him. She said something to him I couldn't understand, straightening his cap as she did. She beamed at him so full of love I could almost feel the glow from it. He went and sat on the stairs to watch the spectacle going by out on the main road. He pointed and called something out to her in his piping boy's voice.

He'd dropped a letter on the sidewalk. I picked it up. It was addressed to a Yachiyo Momono.

I took it to the old lady. "Thank you," she said. She looked at the envelope and smiled. "For me. From my grandson Joey." She jerked her chin in the general direction of the outside world. "Better than the TV today, right?" I chuckled. She picked her knitting up again. "You be careful, okay?"

"I will!" Wow. Was there some kind of grandma gene that every old lady had? For a second, thinking of it like that made me feel safe and comforted. The feeling only lasted until I got onto a main street. It was a zoo. People were mobbing the banks, groceries, and corner stores, clamoring to get in although they were already full inside. I went to buy a bottled water from a drugstore, and my bank card wouldn't work.

"Most people's cards aren't working today," said the girl behind the counter. Buying the water used up a third of the cash I had on me. What would I do when I ran out of the rest? It wasn't even enough to buy a sandwich in most places. Electricity kept going on and off. I heard someone say that Garrison Creek had resurfaced and was flooding the whole area that had been the riverbed before they'd paved it and made it into a sewer.

I called a couple of hospitals to see whether Rich was in any of them, but they all put me on hold for so long that I gave up. I hadn't brought my phone charger with me. I still couldn't get through to my folks, and they hadn't tried to call me. People were stocking up on water, groceries. I saw a handwritten sign in a convenience store window; NO MORE WATER.

A tendril of smog from the volcano snaked its way through the air, about head height. A man walked right through it. When he came out the other side, his brown hair had gone white, and he had no mouth. Like, nothing there, as though he'd never had a mouth. His eyes got humongous. I could hear him trying to scream. He looked across the street to where I was, but I was so creeped out that I kept walking. I mean, he could breathe, right? So he'd be okay until he got to where someone could help him? Right? Funny thing is, that volcano smog was everywhere, and I saw all kinds of people walk through it, and nothing happened to them. After that I avoided the stuff, though.

Rich hadn't called back.

I found a public library and waited for a free computer. The wait was taking longer than usual because the terminals kept turning into traffic lights while people were using them, so then they had to get extra time because the minutes during which their computer was a traffic light didn't count. I finally got to one. I poked about online for a bit, but everything I saw just made me feel worse. Horrible stuff was happening all over the world. Well, that's not true. Some of it was good stuff; like every homeless person in San Fernando, Trinidad waking up inside a brand-new house. But some guy had blown up an LGBT bookstore because he said God was displeased with gays, like Reverend Whatsisface said, and they needed to be purged from the earth if we were going to be free of this scourge. Twenty people inside the bookstore had died, and six more had been injured. Two weren't expected to recover. One of the dead was a lady's two-month-old baby. Some town in I think Indiana was having a plague of lemon-and-green-striped plastic frogs that were swarming everywhere, yelling everyone's secrets out loud. The people in the town were killing frogs as quickly as they could, but more kept coming. How did you kill a plastic frog, anyway? And this guy over in Petawawa? He went wandering around down by the train tracks. Only there was something haunting over there. On LJ, people were saying that it made a noise like the rattle of meat locker chains, and if you were getting close to it, you would know by the taste of rotting mint leaves in the back of your throat. It sounded to me like those fright spam posts that people will make on ViewTube. You know, "Post this message to twelve thousand of your friends in the next hour, otherwise you'll lose both your hands"? Only it was for real. The guy ran into the thing haunting the railway tracks. Nobody knew what really happened to him, and he couldn't say, because now when he spoke, his words came out in a high-pitched, warbly banshee wail that broke windows and spooked dogs. There was a clip on ViewTube of him on the news this morning. They wouldn't let him talk, though, because he would have broken all their cameras. His hair had gone white. He was seventeen years old. He'd been a redhead yesterday when he went down by the tracks.

I wrote Mom an e-mail. Dad had an e-mail address, but only because I'd gotten him one. He never used it. He didn't really like using computers. He was happier deciphering a roll of blueprints. In the e-mail to Mom, I said, *Mom, I'm okay. I haven't seen Rich yet. I'm trying to find him. It's scary here. Please come home soon. I hope you and Dad are all right. Love, Sojourner.* I remembered the name of the conference my mom had been going to. I found a website for it, but there wasn't anything useful on it. I did find the schedule. My mom was supposed to deliver her paper tomorrow. It was called, "Violent Ideation in Prepubescent Girls." It sounded so normal, so Mom. She was writing about the shit that had happened to me in my last school, telling other psychologists about it, hoping they could find a way to make sure it never happened to another girl ever again. And she hadn't even told me. I could feel the tears rolling down my face. I didn't care. I wasn't the only one crying while they sat at a computer, trying to find the people they loved.

My computer flashed a bright red stoplight in my eye. "Fine," I told it. I let the next person have it, even though my time wasn't up yet. Oh, and the blemish had worked all the way up one leg, and there was another one starting on the other leg. Our family doctor wasn't answering her phone. I didn't even bother trying a hospital emergency room. People who had been hurt really badly were having to wait for treatment, so why would the hospital pay me any attention? Nothing was broken and I wasn't dying.

Oh, God, I hoped I wasn't dying. What would happen if that black stuff grew all the way up to my face? I didn't know what to do about anything. I just kept walking. Then I realized that someone was walking along beside me. "Tafari!" That was his favorite trick; sneaking up on you quietly like that and waiting until you noticed. He was smiling that warm, gentle smile he smiled when he knew someone would be glad to see him. I leapt at him and gave him a big hug. It felt so good to be holding him again. "I have never been so glad to see anyone in my life! Where've you been? Were you stuck in the subway?"

He laughed. "Yeah, I suppose. But I'm here now."

He was, and he looked so good! I could have just eaten him up with my eyes alone. "Where's Rich? Is he with you?"

He frowned. "No."

"Taf, I'm so scared. Things are all creepy everywhere, and

people are even dying, and I can't find Mom and Dad or Rich. Are your folks okay?"

"They're okay. Don't worry, they're just fine."

"And I have this, like, skin disease, and I'm so sorry I didn't tell you about it before, when we were dating, but I was afraid you'd think I was gross."

He took me into his arms again. "I could never think that!"

"Well, I hope not." I was blubbering now. "Because it's spreading, and pretty soon it'll probably be all over me, and everything's just a mess!"

He held me, kissing the top of my head every so often. Not a lot of boys could do that. Not when we were standing up, at least. "Don't be scared," he said. "It makes me feel so bad to see you like this."

After a while I calmed down a little. Tafari said, "I gotta go."

"What? Why? Can I come with you?"

He shook his head. "Something I gotta do, right now. I'll come back."

"Promise? You'll call me and tell me where to meet you?"

He nodded. "I'll call you."

I'd just turned onto University Avenue at Queen when an enormous, clawed foot crashed onto the sidewalk, a few feet from where I was standing. It looked like I imagined a dinosaur's foot would. I yelped. A second foot crashed down on the other side of me. People were scattering, cars and bicycles swerving out of the way. The feet were attached to ginormous drumsticks, which were attached to ginormouser thighs, all covered in big red and black feathers. With my eyes, I followed them upward, maybe twenty feet above, to where they disappeared into the volcano smog.

At first I thought a house was falling on me. I flinched. But it turned out it was just the body attached to the legs, leaning down and peering between those legs to get a good look below. And the body was a house. I mean a for-real house, with four walls and a door and windows and a roof and everything. I could see all that from underneath it because it had tilted down at a steep angle so it could see me better. I mean, I think it was looking. The house part cocked itself sideways so that one of its windows was facing me. I swear, the window blinked, its pane slamming open and shut like a big, square, startled eye. I was standing underneath a house that walked on two humongous, feathered dinosaur legs. Then the house gave a startled squawk. And in case I'd had any doubts about the walking part, it lifted one of its legs and stomped.

I ran, screaming, out from under it. The house thing ran too, continuing its tromp northward up University Avenue, careening every so often against one of the big bronze statues of old, dead white guys they had in the narrow paved strips that ran down the middle of the wide avenue. It even managed to crack one of the statues on its marble base. Horns were honking, brakes screeching. There were a ton of near misses and a few rear-enders. A squat brown UPS delivery van ran up onto the sidewalk and crashed into the cast-iron railings around the Osgoode law buildings. A lavender hippopotamus wearing a party hat shouldered its way out of the back of the van, rushed to the open driver's side door, and gently tugged the groggy driver out onto the sidewalk by the back of his brown-uniformed collar. It knelt beside him. "Minh?" it said. "Minh? Talk to me!" Its party hat on an elastic string around its neck had shifted to the side of its head. The driver opened his eyes to see a talking hippopotamus in a tiny hat kneeling over him. He screamed and crab-walked backward.

There was an abandoned bicycle lying near me. I picked it up. It looked a little shorter than my leg length.

Minh peered at the hippopotamus and said, "Loopy-Lou? Is that you? How did you turn real?"

I got on the bike to follow the running house. I mean, what else did I have to do?

Behind me, I heard the hippopotamus say, "Well, who d'you think it is, dummy? You okay?"

Out of the corner of my eye, I saw something small and black darting in my direction, but it ran behind a Dumpster before I could see it properly. Blasted volcano smog.

I caught up to the leggy house a couple minutes later. It was being herded by a couple of cop cars. Dunno whether "herded" is the right word, since the cars seemed to be doing more dodging out of the way of those huge feet than they were doing any chasing. Just as I rode up, the house did an alarmed hop out of the intersection of Dundas and University and hightailed it west. Two cop cars followed it. Out of a side street ahead of it shot a third cop car and two ambulances. The house was boxed in for now. It stopped its headlong run, began dithering around in circles, right in front of the 52 Division police station. A crowd had already gathered on the sidewalks and was halfway to a flash mob, seeing how many of them were punching away on cell phones, which would probably bring more people. Yay, text messaging. I got off the bike. Someone tapped me on the shoulder. I turned. "Ben!" I gave him a big hug. "How'd you know where to find me?"

"I didn't. I was on the way to you in a cab when that thing showed up. You know I had to come see that." He tried on a grin, but it looked fake.

"You okay? You don't look so good."

He didn't answer me. He was looking over his shoulder.

"Ben?"

"No, I—" He turned back to face me. "What'd you say?"

I repeated the question. He shrugged.

"It's just all this," he said.

He gestured to where bystanders were pulling a screaming man out of the way. The house had just stepped on his foot. There was blood seeping through his shoe. I gulped. "Jesus." I'd never seen someone in that much pain. Watching him was actually making me feel kinda sick to my stomach, because I knew I couldn't help.

"It's kinda getting to me," said Ben. "You know?" He darted a glance to one side, wrenched his attention back to me.

"Yeah. I know."

Something tumbled out of the underside of the house. Like a big, white ball or something. It crashed down onto one of the police cars, crushing it flat. People in the crowd shouted. Shit. I hoped nobody'd been in that car. Yesterday, I would have said that the crash had made the loudest sound in the world, but that was before the roar last night of Animikika bursting out of the lake.

The big white ball connected with the cop car and burst open. Huge pieces of hard, curved white material flew everywhere. I saw one piece slice across a part of the crowd, heard the screams. A bunch of us ducked as another piece crashed to the ground near us. It fragmented into splinters. Shrapnel flew. Some of it scraped across my cheek.

he ball cracked open, a wash of clear goo bloomed upward in a crown shape, like you see in those slo-mo videos of raindrops. It splashed down over all the cop cars, the cops, and the nearby gawkers, as far as the sidewalk on both sides of the street. It left a big globby bubble of rich yellow in its center, that stretched over the cop car, then collapsed with a wet plop.

Ben gasped. "Holy crap! It's a giant egg! That house just laid an egg!"

People were shouting for help from parts of the crowd. Others were screaming or moaning in pain. There were people lying on the ground. There was more blood. I saw a woman giving CPR to a guy lying on his back on the ground. He was big, but she'd somehow managed to straddle him so she could pump on his rib cage. A guy was on the ground next to them, holding his wadded-up scarf to the big guy's neck. The big guy's side was covered in blood. Dunno what good all that heart pumping would be, if all she was doing was pumping the blood out of a large hole in him. Something ran down into my eye. I blinked, and saw red. I put my hand to my forehead. It was bleeding from where the shrapnel had grazed me. Ben murmured, "Don't be afraid," almost like he wasn't talking to me.

"Too late," I said.

The two-legged house was still running in circles. Just like it was stepping on an empty pop can, it crushed the back end of another cop car with one of its splayed, scaly feet. There was a piece of shell the size of a sewer cover lying near my feet. I gave Ben the bike to hold. I bent and looked at the bit of shell. It was curved like a potato chip, sitting concave side up, like a bowl. It was more ivory than white. And translucent. Even the gloomy volcano light gave it a bit of a glow. Mom had some mother-of-pearl earrings that gleamed like that. I reached out and touched it. It rocked a little. It was warm and smooth. There was a little bit of the clear liquid left in it. I dipped a pinkie finger in. Yup, slippery. It was egg white, all right. I picked the piece of shell up. It was way lighter than I'd expected it to be. I turned it over. It took me a second to realize that the greenish-brown smear I saw there was probably house poop. "Euw." I dropped it and wiped my hands off against my jeans.

The house-bird thing slipped in the egg white and slid, legs flailing, in our direction. People scattered out of the way. Ben said, "Come on!" Together, he and I dragged the bike over to the sidewalk. Some of the cops tried to make a human cordon around the house as it struggled to its feet, but most of them were too busy wiping egg white out of their eyes to be any use. So some of them pulled out guns.

"What're they doing?" said a woman near me. "They're going to hit innocent people!"

For the first time in my life, I heard the pop of real guns firing. Funny how harmless it sounds, like popguns.

Where were the bullets landing? I couldn't see anyone being hit. Someone was firing fruit at the house, though. Must have been at rifle speed, too, 'cause I only saw blurs before produce began to splat, pulverized into mush, against the side of the house. I only knew what the splats were because the banana and grapefruit peels didn't go mushy. The police were looking at their guns in amazement. One of the guns turned into a hanging lamp. The officer holding it dropped it.

Ambulances and fire trucks were beginning to arrive. There were wheeled stretchers everywhere. The house just stood there, covered in slime, its sides heaving. Under the racket of the crowd, the helicopters overhead, and the sirens, I could hear it making sad cheeping noises. "Poor thing," I said. "It looks upset."

Ben said, "We need to get out of here before the police start using sound cannons, or something. I don't want my eardrums busted."

"Okay, but look." I pointed into the sky. Dodging a couple of copters, another giant egg was swooping down. Well, half an egg. Half an eggshell. And it wasn't falling out of control; it was flying somehow. There was someone standing inside it, waving a big stick around. I think the person may have been yelling at the house, but I couldn't hear for sure over all the noise.

The big eggshell landed in the intersection, right in front of the house. More popgun noises, more fruit splattering, this time against the side of the eggshell, staining its ivory surface with smeared fruit mush. The person standing inside the eggshell was an old woman wearing a sack of a black dress. She had a red and yellow paisley scarf tied over her head and knotted under her chin, inna old-fashioned stylee. I mean, even my mom didn't wear her scarves like that. The old lady was definitely carrying a big stick. Kinda like a baseball bat, only almost as tall as she was. She brandished it at the cops and yelled at them in a language I didn't recognize. She was protecting the house! A policeman with a bullhorn ordered the old lady to step away from it. She looked around for the source of his voice, yelled something back at him. Whatever she was saying, it didn't sound polite.

In her excitement, the woman dropped her stick. I don't really know why I ran out into the intersection toward her. I guess because my parents always told me to help little old ladies. Behind me, I heard Ben yell my name, but I didn't stop. I picked the old lady's stick up. It was thick around and seriously heavy. Twice my length, too, but I managed to wrestle the end of it up until it touched the edge of her eggshell ride. "Here," I said.

She took the bat from me like it weighed nothing at all. "I leave her for a second to go shopping, and she gets into trouble." She swung her stick, cracked a cop over the head who was trying to climb into her eggshell. "Eggs, eggs," she said. "That's all my dacha Izbouchka gives me, is eggs. No pullets, just empty eggs. I ask you; how many of her eggs can one old woman eat? And the shells; thin as paper! That one she just laid should never have cracked. Her eggs used to be so sturdy." To demonstrate, she rapped her knuckles against the side of her eggshell. "And then, there's all the stress of, well, you know." She jerked her head in the general direction of the police, the volcano. "The fright won't be good for her laying, it won't."

"Do you know what's going on?" I asked her. "Why is everything crazy?"

She used the end of her stick to ram some more cops off her eggshell. Another officer leapt for the windowsill that was one of her house's eyelids. She swatted him away. "Crazy on the inside, crazy on the outside," she said. She leaned out of her eggshell. She reached out to me. Her arm seemed to stretch longer than it should have been able to. She took my arm by the wrist. "Izbouchka needs bones to strengthen her eggshells. The bones of men are best. And women." She held my arm up and considered it with the kind of look in her eye that Dad got when he was picking out lamb chops in the supermarket. "You look like a nice, big-boned girl."

"Let go!" I tried to pull away from her, but her fingers held me in a barbed-wire grip. She smiled. Her teeth were too sharp, and all snaggly.

"Ah, dyevuchka; prikrasnaya mulatk," she cooed, "budesh li tee fkusnaya? Karichnyevaya ee fkusnaya?"

She yanked my wrist close to her nose and sniffed my skin, like you smell a cantaloupe in the market to see whether it's ripe. I saw the flare of her nostrils, the stiff black hairs peeking out from them, and I lost it. Using her grip on my wrist for leverage, I rammed the heel of my boot against the side of her eggshell chariot with all my strength, trying to break her hold. It didn't work. "But if I truss you up and roast you in my oven," she mused, "I'd have all the trouble of boiling your bones clean afterward. Can't have any flesh on them, because it upsets my dacha's delicate stomach, doesn't it, Izbouchka?"

The house gave a chirrup of agreement. The old lady nodded and let go of my wrist. "I'll find another way, then. But if I change my mind, dyevuchka, I can find you wherever you are."

Her smile was terrifying. I didn't wait to see what she would do next. I hightailed it back to the crowd, over by where Ben was standing. His lips were moving. When I reached him, he pulled me into a hug. "Jesus, Scotch, you okay?"

He could probably feel that I was trembling through and through, but I said, "Yeah."

"Why'd you even go over there?"

"She dropped her stick. She's an old lady. I wanted to help her." At least it'd been something I could do to help.

"It's a pestle, not a stick. And she wondered whether you would be tasty," said a man standing near us. He looked about my dad's age. He was wearing jeans and a heavy tweed jacket. He had a gash over one eye. When he spoke, the words came out in dialogue bubbles, like he was a cartoon character. They floated over his head long enough for you to read them, then popped and disappeared.

Ben made a face. "Tasty? Euw."

I shoved his shoulder. "What, you think I wouldn't be?" I tried not to think of what kind of rump roast I would have made.

"What language was that?" Ben asked the man.

"Russian." His face was full of wonder. "You got away from her. You're a lucky girl." Then he blushed. "I think she's kinda racist. She called you a mulatto."

"Yeah, and she's an old mother hen."

The old lady said something that sounded like, "Dacha maya, idti syuda." Her house shook the egg slime off itself like a dog shaking off water, spraying more cops with goo as it did so. It waddled over to the old lady. On either side of the house, a thick paned window flapped its shutters open. The shutters snapped out and out and out, extending until the wings of the house were fully unfurled. People screamed, cowered.

"Damn," I muttered, "her dacha can do the wave."

The house gave a quick flap of its window-wings. They

clacked like the tumbling of large bones. It took a flapping run—
its first step crushed a streetcar stop into Lucite smithereens—
then leapt into the air. The old lady led the way in her eggshell
flying saucer. Airborne, the house tucked its bird legs up under
itself and flew after its owner. A few of the cops shot fruit at
them.

We watched the eggshell chariot and the flying house
disappear into the distance.

"Let's get out of here," I said to Ben. Christ. Getting eaten
by an old lady and her house wasn't as scary to me as trying to
help some poor guy who'd just had his foot crushed. What kind
of loser was I?

"We'll be right behind you," Ben replied.

I looked at him. "We?"

He gave a weak laugh. "Royal we. Trying for some humor.
Where do you wanna go?"

"Down to the Convention Centre." I picked up the bike.
"Come on. I'll double you."

"You'd better not drop me off onto the dirty road, girl."

He was sounding a little more normal again. He straddled
the back of the bike, put his hands on my shoulders. "Ready."

Something black poked its nose out from behind a car that
had wrapped itself around a lamppost. The something was about
the size of a big dog, but the three paws that were in view looked
almost like hands. As soon as it saw me looking, it shyly pulled
its head back behind the car to where I couldn't see it. I guess
if a person could be turned into a cartoon today, they could be
turned into anything. "Let's hurry," I said to Ben. The blemish
on my body was spreading. I didn't know how much time I had.

CHAPTER TEN

"Here you go," said Ben, handing a couple of water bottles to a scared-looking man who'd been flooded out of his home last night.

"You can wash your hands at one of the sanitation stations over there." He pointed to where the temporary green carousels of hand sanitizers had been set up.

"Thank you," said the man.

"Don't clean your face with that stuff, though," Ben told him. "It's murder on your skin."

The man nodded and wandered dazedly over to where Ben had pointed, picking his way through the crowds of people trying to settle down until God knew when on the flimsy green cots that volunteers like us were setting up as quickly as we could.

The great hall of the Convention Centre was a sight. Hundreds of cots in straggly rows. People's belongings piled next to the cots. Some people had tried to build teetering privacy walls with the things they'd rescued from their homes. Every so often a pile of coats or something would topple to the floor. Volunteers kept asking them not to pile their stuff up like that, but there were always new people to tell. There were kids running everywhere. There were adults yelling at their kids who were running everywhere. Kids crying. Adults crying. People yelling at the volunteers. Volunteers yelling at the people. People yelling at each other. Did I mention the crying? People curled up on their cots, quietly or loudly sobbing. People on their cell phones, trying to locate people who had gone missing, or to let their friends and their relatives know they were okay. Volunteers trying to hand out sandwiches. Lines for the Johnny on the Spot portable toilets. The main Convention Centre toilets had all overflowed, and a couple of stalls had become tall, thin clock towers that played the *Sesame Street* theme song over and over. Out of sync. The floor was still wet in spots from the flooding last night. The whole place smelled of unhappy, and the hubbub was deafening.

Gloria used the sleeve of her green hoodie to wipe the sweat off her brow. "If I have to bend over again to pull one more bottled water out of this box, I think my back is just going to break in two!"

I grinned at her. "Good practice for the battle."

I grabbed two of the bottles from the box underneath the folding cafeteria table we were working at, and handed them to the little boy waiting there. "Here you go."

"Thank you."

Maybe it was silly to be thinking about a dance competition now. But maybe the world would get back to normal soon. Maybe if we hung on to our memories of what it used to be just a few short hours ago, we could go back to that place. Not that I'd be taking part in the competition now. Not with my skin the way it was.

Glory stared blankly at me. "Battle?" Then her face cleared.

"Oh! For a second, I had no idea what you were talking about. That seems like a lifetime ago." She started to bend again.

"Here," said Punum, "take one of mine." Wheelchair or no wheelchair, it was like she'd come out of nowhere. Two of the volunteers, Bo Yih and Jim, were with her. Punum had a case of bottled water on her lap. She handed one of the bottles to Gloria.

When I'd gotten to the Convention Centre, I'd apologized to Punum for being such a shit. She'd shrugged. "At least you're here to help," she'd said. I didn't feel forgiven, just . . . tolerated. She and Glory had only met each other hours before, with the other volunteers, but they were carrying on like they were already best friends. Every time I tried to talk to Glory, she'd be all like, "Did you know Punum writes her own lyrics?" or "Punum says . . ." Yadda, yadda, yadda.

Glory beamed at Punum. "Thank you," she said shyly, as she took the bottle.

"No problem at all." Hard to tell beneath that deep brown skin, but it looked like Punum was blushing. "I'm your relief," she said, her cheeks flushing even more. "I mean, we are. Jim and Bo Yih and me. For all of you. Lunch break." She stuttered to a halt with a goofy grin on her face.

"Yeah," said Bo Yih. "Go before there're no more sandwiches." She and Jim and Punum took our places.

The little boy I'd given the two water bottles to was still standing there. He said to Jim, "Mom says to say she needs milk for my baby sister. The water came into our house and the wall came down and Mom grabbed my sister and my dad grabbed me, but nobody grabbed the milk, and now Emily's hungry."

As the three of us walked away, I heard Jim asking, "Where's your mom, son? The lady in the green dress? That's your mom?"

"God," said Ben, "I can't even imagine what this is like for little kids."

I shivered, suddenly chilly. A bedraggled woman carrying a wide-eyed brown tabby in her arms had pushed open one of the big glass doors to the Convention Centre, and a bit of cool air had blown in. Had she brought her dog, too? A black shadow had come in with them. It dashed into a dark corner between some lockers and was gone. The woman looked around, a lost look on her face. I'd seen that look a lot today. I was probably wearing it, too. She saw the bunch of cafeteria-style folding tables laid out end to end. Someone had handwritten NEED HELP? in black marker on a big sheet of paper and taped it so that it hung off the front edge of the tables. The woman headed that way. She was limping.

The clock tower toilet stalls bellowed, "SUNNY DAYS . . . ," one right after the other, like they were singing a round. Ben winced.

Glory said, "This is all so nuts. On the way over here, while my mom's car was stopped at a red light, I saw a tiny cow with wings. It flew over our car and pooped right on the windshield. Then this little thing that looked like Tinker Bell, only with fangs, flew down, scooped the poop up, and flew around throwing it at people's heads and laughing an insane little Tinker Bell laugh."

Ben burst out laughing. He'd stopped acting all weird and suspicious. I was relieved. People get nervous if black guys act too twitchy. There were all these tweets online about mobs beating up anyone who acted funny, like they might be one of the monsters roaming around.

We went over to the closest of the hand sanitizer stations that had been set up all over the main hall of the Convention Centre. Shane, the guy supervising our team of volunteers, had told us to clean our hands often. "Last thing we want is some kind of infection spreading through this crowd," he'd said.

Was this thing growing on me contagious? The doctors had said no. But that's when it'd been just a little spot here and there, a lifetime ago in a world before this one, where things that had been harmless the day before could come alive and kill you today. Man, if I could go back to then and all I had to worry about was a spot or two, that would be so nice. I wouldn't freak out whenever a new one showed up. I'd just get it lasered away.

Well, I could at least keep my hands clean. I let the cool sanitizer gel glop onto my hands and rubbed them together until it evaporated. It was drying my hands out. Ordinarily, the itchiness of dry hands made me crazy. But here, with blankets to hand out and cots to set up and lost children to help find their families, it really wasn't bugging me much at all. If I just concentrated on doing the job in front of me, I could keep my mind off everything else, just for a little while. I bet my folks would be home soon. I wouldn't have to tell them I'd gone with Rich to a bar. They'd find him, wherever he was. My mom would make a few calls, and probably he'd be unconscious in a hospital somewhere, and they'd fix him up, and everything would be fine.

Me, I was looking forward to taking the weight off my feet, even for a few minutes. The blemish had spread to my left foot and leg all the way to my hips. Both my boots were too tight now. The blemish was continuing to move up my body, too. It was almost at my navel. It was making my tight jeans even tighter. I was chafing like you wouldn't believe. Ah, well. Think about something else. "So what's with you and Punum?" I asked Glory.

Too casually, she flicked her hair out of her eyes, pulled it back, and refastened her ponytail. "I don't know what you mean."

Like hell she didn't. I knew her too well.

Ben chortled, "You can't hide anything from me and Scotch! You two are totally flirting with each other."

"We are not! She's just, you know, sweet. And she's really interesting to talk to."

That stung. "I'm interesting to talk to!"

"Yeah, about some things. Not about everything."

I sighed and rolled my eyes; one of my trusty comebacks for when I didn't know what to say. "You don't even like girls. So don't play her, okay?"

"Jeez, I won't! Just leave it alone, already!"

"Wow, okay! Sorry I asked."

Glory looked contrite. "I didn't mean to snap at you. I'm just tired."

Ben and I had gotten to the Convention Centre and discovered that Glory and her folks were there volunteering. They'd all been in bed and asleep when the world had gone insane. They hadn't even felt the tremors much up where they lived. The first thing they'd known about it was when they'd woken up this morning to find that their lawn was now made of cheese. Gloria thought maybe it was Havarti, but her sister Joey was sure it was Edam. Her dad said he was just thankful it wasn't blue cheese.

I smiled at Glory. "Apology accepted." I caught a glimpse of a shadow disappearing behind a Johnny on the Spot. Somebody'd better get that lady's dog into a cage. It could bite someone. "So, Ben."

He raised an eyebrow at me. "My turn now, I see."

"You feeling better?"

"Yeah," he said, sticking his hands under a pump, "I'm kinda getting used to it."

Glory asked, "To everything that's going on?"

"No. Stuff's still freaking me out, big-time. I mean, my cousin's family in Bolton are probably all dead! No, I'm getting used to Junior here." With his chin, he pointed to his side. He smiled down at empty air. "Aren't I, you little brat?"

The skin of my scalp prickled. Glory and I exchanged looks.

"Ben," I said, "there's no one there."

He was rubbing his hands dry. "You're right," he replied cheerfully, "there isn't. Only there kinda is something there. I can sorta glimpse it, only not with my eyes, exactly. It tastes like candlelight and looks like the day after next Tuesday. It's feeling sad, but sometimes I can make it smile like lemon drops. It's been following me since the world went crazy."

Glory was looking at Ben like he'd grown another nose. "You're creeping me out," she said.

"Don't worry, he's only little, whatever he is. I think he's scared. I told him he could stick around with me for a while. You guys coming to eat?"

We followed him as he headed for the volunteers' room. "But shouldn't you tell someone?" I asked him. "Someone adult?"

He cut his eyes at me. "You the same Scotch who's always telling me she's grown-up now, right? I'm gonna deal with this on my own."

Glory grabbed his arm to stop him. "She's right! Something could be wrong with you."

I said, "You might be going crazy."

Glory said, "Some kind of super poison gas might have gotten released by accident. You might have breathed it in."

"Or maybe you are going to turn into some kind of monster thing, and there's a way to stop it."

Gloria blurted out, "It might be aliens!"

Ben folded his arms and looked at us.

"I haven't the faintest idea what it is. But poison gas doesn't make a volcano grow overnight, and that volcano is real. Just ask all these people whose homes are underwater. And Gloria, don't even get me started on that 'aliens' business."

I asked him, "How about the thing where you might be going nuts, then?"

Four Horseless Head Men swirled past us, giggling. Ben watched them go, then turned back to me. "Look around you, girl. Everything is nuts. I always carry on like I have an audience watching every move I make, and now"—he blew a kiss at the invisible thing at his side—"I do. Glory's always going on about how boring her family is, and now they have a lawn made of cheese. And you; I bet you some weird secret desire of yours turned into something real. You going to tell us about it?"

That did it. "So Rich always wanted to fall into a hole and disappear? Or maybe I wanted him gone? Is that you trying to tell me?"

"Uh, I didn't mean—"

"All these people here always wanted to lose everything they own? That guy on that cot over there always wanted to turn into a giant cockroach in his sleep? Never mind, maybe he did. But you really telling me that your cousin's family always wanted what happened to them?"

His face fell. "I don't know! I'm just saying, people are crazy. We make the world a crazy place. Maybe some of it is that our crazy isn't invisible anymore."

We were not going to talk about my crazy again. "Let's just go eat," I said coldly. "We only have half an hour."

In the volunteers' room, people moved over at one of the tables so that we could all sit together. Tafari came over and joined us. I blew a kiss down the table at him. There were a couple of cardboard flats on the table, already half-emptied of sandwiches.

"Two kinds," said the woman beside me. She was kinda old, white, with short pink hair and piercings. I think her name was

Helen. "Ham on whole wheat, and cheese on white. That's as vegetarian as it gets. And be careful; some of them bite."

She was right; the first sandwich I took the plastic wrap off opened like a mouth at me and tried to nip at my fingers. The group around the table laughed when they saw my face. Helen said, "They aren't all like that. If you don't want that one, just keep opening them till you find one that's just a sandwich."

"Is it cheese?" asked Lenny from across the table.

I nodded.

Lenny held a hand out. "Give it here." Lenny was short and muscular with olive skin, an amazing nose, and short, straight black hair with a streak of silver in it, even though Lenny didn't look old enough to be going gray. I hadn't decided whether Lenny was a girl or a boy. I was waiting to hear someone use either a "he" or a "she" to talk about Lenny.

I handed the mouth sandwich over. Lenny made a kissy face at it. Its sandwich-crust lips made a growling motion back. Lenny bit into it. I eeped in alarm. Through a mouthful of sandwich, Lenny said, "What? It's not like they really bite. They're soft and they don't have teeth. I already ate one. Two, in fact. And I'm fine. Except for, you know, eating dairy."

"You should be careful, Lenny." That was Sita, a tall, plump dark woman with a long ponytail of straight black hair. "You don't know what's in them, what effect they might have on you later."

"Please. Have you looked around you? As of today, I don't know what effect my next breath will have on me. None of us does. You can't count on anything being the way it used to be."

"Whatever," said Glory. "I'm hungry." She grabbed a sandwich and unwrapped it without looking at it. She took vicious little bites out of it as she ate.

Those sandwiches were the closest thing I'd had to a meal

since the doughnut and juice Punum had bought me this morning. I ate the one I had unwrapped. Then another. Then I started on a third one. I was ignoring Ben. I was still feeling hurt by the stuff he'd said. Glory and Helen were talking about the best kind of bread for open-face toasted cheese sandwiches. Hidden by the table, I slipped my fingers under the bottom of my blouse and touched my stomach. I could feel the blemish, raised and ever so slightly sticky. It had filled in my belly button. I didn't even have a freaking belly button anymore. I kept breathing. In. Out. Kept on doing it, at normal speed. Things would be all right. Maybe tomorrow the hospitals wouldn't be as busy, and someone would be able to see me. They probably had some killer app you couldn't just go and buy in a store, right? Some kind of major blemish dissolver/exfoliant ray, or something. T'aint no big thing, I kept telling myself, like Mom would say. T'aint no big thing.

"Scotch, what're you doing?" Gloria's voice cut through the chatter at the table. Everyone turned to look at me. Guiltily, I pulled my hand out of my blouse. But Glory was looking at the table in front of me.

I'd eaten most of the plastic wrap that had been around my sandwiches. It'd tasted good, too. Kinda like fruit leather, only stretchier. "Uh . . ." I said, trying to think up an explanation.

Bo Yih ran in through the doorway. "Somebody come quick! Some guy's cot just turned into a giant feather duster and attacked him!"

While everyone was rushing to take care of that, I snuck quietly out of the lunchroom and found a quiet alcove. I called Rich's line. The metallic lady voice said, "There is no one here to answer your call at this moment. Please leave a message after the tone." Then there was a beep.

"Rich? I guess you're not around. I really hope you're okay."

I took a deep breath. "So here's the thing, Bro; I was the one who tattled on you to Mom and Dad. I told them you had weed in your room. Mom and Dad had been making me crazy, hounding me because my grades had slipped. But anybody's grades would slip, if their lives were like mine! I was slowly being covered in sticky black blemishes, and you were pissed at me because you'd had to move to our new school too, even though you hadn't been the one in trouble. Though maybe if you had stood up for me at LeBrun, we wouldn't have had to move, you know? You ever think about that? Then to make it worse, a guy I used to know from LeBrun High had just been transferred to our school, and I just knew that Tafari, who was always mad at me anyway because I didn't dare tell our folks we were dating, was going to hear from the new guy that everyone used to call me a skank at LeBrun High, and then Tafari would get that sneery look and he'd stop hanging out with me and he'd start spreading lies about me around this school, too, and pretty soon people would be sneaking rotten sandwiches into my knapsack again. Because, Rich, once people decide you're the school slut, it sticks. It gets tangled up in you like the chewed-up gum in your hair. It's like you're wearing a big S on your forehead, and no matter how much foundation you put on over it, eventually it shows through. Eventually somebody'll look at you a certain way, or a bunch of girls will laugh as they walk past you, and even if that look doesn't mean anything and those girls aren't laughing at you, in your mind you'll be the school slut all over again, with girls calling you skank and saying that you stole their boyfriends. In your mind you'll be sure that it's going to happen again. You'll be sure that a bunch of girls will corner you in the parking lot after school one day and hold you down and scream names at you and spit on you and take the gum they've been chewing all day just so they could have it for this out of their mouths and smoosh so much of it into your hair that your mom will have to cut all your hair off with a pair of scissors and your dad will be mad and say that you must have done something to deserve this, that girls are gentle and wouldn't do something this awful unless you'd done something to make them mad.

So Mom and Dad were on my case, and I was jumpy at school all the time and snapping at Tafari even though I wasn't mad at him, I just wanted him to break up with me and get it over with. And I wanted to take some of the pressure off at home. I wanted to show Mom and Dad that I was still their good little girl. So I told them about you, and they freaked out and called the cops. And then I kinda went nuts, but all inside, where no one else could see it. I told Tafari I wanted to stop seeing him. I got tired of always being scared that he was going to break up with me, so I did it first. And you were in jail and everything had gone to shit and it was all my fault. And Rich, I'm so, so sorry. I really suck. But please be okay. Please come back, even if you never talk to me again. You shouldn't ever talk to me again. I wouldn't."

I hung up.

"SWEEPING THE CLOUDS AWAY . . ." bellowed the clock towers. Clearing the air seemed like a good idea. There was more weird going on than I could deal with all at once. Best not to think about how plastic wrap suddenly was tasting good. There were boxes of donations at the loading dock; blankets and clothing waiting to be carried upstairs, sorted, and distributed to people who needed them. I could keep busy. I grabbed a box and started climbing the stairs to the level above. It was safer than taking the escalator, which had developed a habit of asking people who rode on it riddles about quantum physics, and if they gave the wrong answer, it would loop them round and round like in an Escher drawing, never reaching the top or the bottom, until they got dizzy and fell off. Made you dizzy to look at, too. The laws of physics just weren't supposed to work like that.

Tafari came up the stairs beside me. He was carrying two cardboard boxes of donations. "I could have carried that for you, you know."

"What, and carry yours at the same time?"

He nodded. "I could do it."

"You know I like to do things like this myself if I can. If something's too heavy for me, I'll ask you, okay?"

He nodded agreeably. Well, that was a change. Tafari was the arguingest guy I knew. He'd fought with me for days over the breakup, trying to convince me of all the reasons it made more sense to stay with him. Now it looked like he'd finally accepted it. I had something to accept, too.

The room where we were doing the sorting was full of people chattering away and separating the stuff into clean and dirty, usable and unusable. "Come with me," I told Taf. "Bring the boxes." *This is a test*, I thought.

"Okay." He followed me, no argument.

I walked around the upper level. It was empty of refugees for now, but more people kept pouring into the Convention Centre. There'd probably be cots up here soon. Taf and I wandered until I found a quiet alcove where no one could see us. I turned to Taf. "Okay, you can put them down for a second."

He did.

"No," I said. "Upside down is better."

He didn't bat an eyelid. He just stacked the boxes one atop the other, turning each one upside down as he went.

I held both his hands. They were warm and solid in my grip. Big hands. I couldn't have carried three boxes up those stairs, but he could. I sighed. I looked down at his hands in mine. They were perfect. The real Tafari had this thing called syndactyly. His two middle fingers on one hand were fused together, and all the other fingers were crooked. He'd been born that way. And he sure as hell had never been the type to just do anything I said without questioning it. "You're not really Tafari, are you?"

He smiled. It was Tafari's smile, every detail, and it made my heart ache. "I dunno. Aren't I?"

I'd realized that he didn't mention anybody by name unless I did so first. He showed up out of nowhere, and went away again with no warning. He didn't argue. "Do other people see you, too?" I asked him. "Or is it just me?"

"What other people?"

Oh, crap. "Okay, now you're creeping me out."

Tafari's smile wavered a little. "Scotch, what's wrong? We should get back to work."

"Are you a ghost?" I couldn't make myself ask, "Are you Tafari's ghost?"

He frowned. "Maybe? Do you think I could be?"

I took a deep breath. Ben had his solution to his ha'nt, and I had mine. "You need to stop coming to me." I prayed that it would do as I said, whatever it was. "You made things easier for a little while, and I thank you for that. But you have to stop coming to me now."

He nodded. He took my hand with his five straight, unfused fingers, and kissed my palm. "Okay, then." He picked my box up, turned it upside down, and put it on top of his two. I followed him as he carried them all the way back to the sorting area. I waited outside the door while he took them inside for me. When he came back out, he gave me that Taf grin and went over to the stairs. He stopped at the top and said, "Oh; and you're welcome."

The noise from the convention hall below was a constant roar, so I couldn't hear his footsteps as he went down the stairs, or even whether they made any sound at all. When I looked down the stairway a second later, there was no one there. I couldn't have carried all three boxes. I didn't know who or what had. All I knew was that it felt like I'd just broken up with Tafari for the second time. And even worse; now I knew that the real Tafari was missing, too.

I put my fingertips under my blouse, touched my skin. Still there. Apparently, I hadn't gotten rid of all my crazinesses.

"FRIENDLY NEIGHBORS THERE/ THAT'S WHERE WE MEET . . . ," sang the clock towers.

I was downstairs, by the rows of lockers for the volunteers, when I saw the black shape again. It had just slipped out from under one of the cots. It was heading my way. It didn't look exactly like a dog. I couldn't tell how many legs it had, for one thing. Sometimes it seemed to be loping along on two, and sometimes galloping on . . . five? Eleven? Looked like it had more of a face than a snout. Not that I could be sure of that. It was maddeningly twitchy. Wouldn't hold still for a second.

Who did it belong to? It shouldn't be loose like that. This was a scary situation for an animal to be in. It might get startled and bite someone.

It ducked between two rows of lockers. I followed. Maybe it would lead me to its owner.

It was shaded in the alley between the lockers. I couldn't see the dog, but I did see Glory and Punum. They were hugging. I stopped right there. They hadn't seen me yet. Glory was sitting in Punum's chair, on her lap with her arms around Punum's neck. They were hugging; no big deal, right? My friends and I hugged each other all the time. But as I watched, they kissed. Full-on tongue and everything. Holy. I went flushed all over from the surprise of it, from stumbling into their secret moment.

I waited for Glory to pull away, to say that that wasn't what she'd meant, something. Nope. When Punum moved her head away for a sec, Glory pulled her back into the kiss again. "Yo," I said, "get a room." They both started and turned to look at me. Gloria jerked out of Punum's arms, but Punum kept her arms around her neck.

Gloria gave me a hesitant smile. I pasted on a grin. I could do this. I could play this cool. I moved closer to them. Glory licked her lips, looked sideways at Punum, and burst into a breathless giggle. She turned to Punum. "I kissed a girl!"

Punum preened. "Yeah, you did."

"I've been wanting to do that for so long!"

"You have?" I asked. "You never told me."

Punum asked, her voice hesitant, "You think you might want to do that again? No, wait; not right now!" she said as Gloria lunged for her. They went into a clinch, and then they were both laughing. "I guess I have my answer," said Punum.

"Again and again and again! Only—" Gloria turned to me. "Scotch, please don't tell anyone yet, okay?"

"Sure. Not even Ben." Mock-challenging, I said to Punum, "I thought you didn't do jailbait?" Whoa. That came out harsher-sounding than I'd meant it to.

Glory's smile faded a little. Then she waved a dismissive hand. "Like that's a problem, when Punum's only seventeen herself."

Punum said, "Uh—"

"Wait; you're seventeen? I thought you were years and years older than me?"

"Yeah? How old did you figure I was?"

"I dunno, maybe twenty five or something."

She looked gratified. "Cool. That's about how old I want to look."

"But why?"

Gloria answered, "She wouldn't be able to work in bars if they knew she was underage."

"Huh. Punum, you live on your own, right?"

She nodded. "Couple years now. My dad really freaked when I came out. Took me forever to get out of there and get my own place. He tried to have me declared mentally incompetent!"

"Shit." Still, if she could live on her own, it was probably going to be a piece of cake for me. I mean, I had a job.

Glory and Punum were beaming at each other bashfully again. I couldn't stand it. "Glory, you can't be gay!" I wailed. "I'll be all alone!"

"Oh, Scotch, I wouldn't stop hanging out with you just because—"

"Don't you see? I'll be the only normal one of the three of us!"

Too late I heard the words that had just fallen out of my mouth. "Oh, *incandescent* shit." How to describe the look on Punum's face? Half sneer, all pity.

Glory crossed her arms and glared at me. "The only normal one, huh? So that's what you think of Ben? That's what you think of me?"

"I—"

"I need your support right now, and that's what you give me? You're a piece of work, you know that? Everything is you, you, you. I'm beginning to think you did Tafari a favor by breaking up with him."

"But I—"

"Go away," she said. "Just walk away from us, right now. I don't want to talk to you."

"Okay, fine! See if I care!"

I stalked away from them. Who did Miss Glory think she was, talking to me that way? I scratched my itchy tummy through my shirt.

"Oh, God, I don't want to know myself this well."
"Yeah, don't people go blind that way?"

Suddenly, I couldn't stand to be around all this stuff anymore; the noise, the misery, the bad food, the yelling kids, the barking dogs, the clock towers. "Later for this," I muttered. I stomped in the direction of the exit. I barely noticed the shadow trotting along beside me, almost behind me, in my peripheral vision.

"You better stay away from my boyfriend, skank."

Anyway, I didn't regret what I'd said to Glory. I'd told her what I really felt.

She stamped her foot. "It's so bloody easy for you!"

Hey, that lady's dog was bigger than I'd thought at first. Why were people pointing at me? And what was that growling, clanking noise? I turned my head to get a full-on look at the thing beside me.

"Well, Miss Sojourner, I guess it sucks to be you."

You ever step in melted asphalt on the road on a blistering hot day? What does it feel like? Yeah, you know what I'm talking about. Like you've just gotten all the chewed-up, discarded wads of sticky, gross gum stuck to the bottom of your shoe.

The thing that had been pacing beside me was no dog. It looked like a hip-high pile of half-melted asphalt. Matte black that swallowed light. Gooey-looking. Its shape wouldn't stay still. It undulated as it stood there, on three-five-seven-eleven goopy legs that were slowly spreading their ooze along the concrete floor. Kinda smelled like asphalt, too; that horrible boiling sulfur smell. I got a brief impression of chains wrapped around it any which way. Angry yellow eyes. Its mouth was more like a maw, wetly grinding away as it growled. It was pissed. It bristled and stalked toward me, stiff-legged. Loops of its chains rattled against each other and dragged along the ground.

"Get it away from me!" I screamed. My voice was swallowed up in the general cacophony.

One woman near by did hear me. She squinted in the direction of the monster, then said, "Oh, what a sweet little kitty! You can't be afraid of that tiny thing."

The "sweet little kitty" was big enough to swallow me whole. It growled and rushed me. I dashed toward the door, away from it. Step by step, it chivvied me out into the chaos that the streets of Toronto had become. Every time I slowed down, it threw its sticky self in my direction. It herded me along Lake Shore Boulevard. And I ran . . .

CHAPTER ELEVEN

The thing leapt at me. I screamed, "Go away!" It spat a gob of blacker-than-blackness at me. I dodged it. The gunk kept arcing through the air, and landed *zot* on a plant by the side of the road. The plant withered instantly. I fled, all the way to the Harbourfront Community Centre buildings.

I yanked on one of the glass double doors. It was locked. So was the other. My breathing had become a soft, terrified whimpering. I couldn't help it. I ran lakeward down the length of the building, looking for anything. Some shelter. The second doors were locked too. I crouched behind a squat cement garbage container, the right leg of my jeans straining against my itchy, tainted skin. I slid my cell phone out of my back pocket. I punched quick dial.

Please, please. One ring. Two. Please answer.

Someone picked up on the other end!

"Sojourner?"

"Mom!" I whispered. God, she sounded so scared. Almost as

scared as I was. I scanned all around me as I talked. "Mom, you gotta—"

"Sojourner, where are you?"

"Down by the lake. Mom, listen! You gotta help me!"

Her voice came back garbled, then it faded out entirely. Two beeps came from the phone before it fell silent. I was totally out of minutes.

"Oh, God. Oh, God." I was sobbing now. I stood. The tarry monster was bounding toward me. Its feet had picked up so much city debris that they weren't sticking to the ground any longer. It galumphed along on tatty slippers made of discarded hot dog wrappers, used condoms, and fallen maple leaves. The clanking loops of its chains bounced from side to side as it ran, or whirled, or whatever. The sight would've been a riot if I hadn't been rigid with fright. Then it was in front of me, growling. I tried to dart to one side, then the other. It blocked me both times. I backed up. It followed. Oh, God; it was herding me toward the water. Step by step I went. There was a hollow thump when my feet hit the wooden planks of the boardwalk that ran along the lakeshore for miles. A couple more feet, and I'd have nowhere to go but into the deep, dark water.

The thing stopped. I stopped. It whined, crouched, leapt to its feet again. Gave a yowping bark. I nearly jumped out of my skin. What was it doing? It actually danced from foot to foot, like some kind of sticky, spidery-legged dog. It rushed past me to the very edge of the boardwalk, looked out over the water, and yowped again. It looked at me expectantly. I swear if it'd had a tail, it would have wagged it. It ran along the edge of the boardwalk away from me a few feet, then back. It made its weird yowping bark over the water.

There was someone floundering in the water! "Oh, my god; you tossed someone in!" I ran to the ledge and called out, "Hold on! I'll get help!" It was probably barely above freezing in there. Two Horseless Head Men dithered around the person. What could I do? I could swim okay, but if I jumped in, it might mean two people dead of hypothermia instead of one. The person was struggling to get their coat off. They went under. "Oh, crap." I looked around frantically for anything I could use to pull the person out. There was lots of debris lying around; there must be something I could use! Another yip from the monster. But it seemed to be leaving me alone. Frantically, I looked around for a stick, anything I could throw out for the person to grab. There! A life preserver, on a hook on the wall! I ran over and grabbed the white Styrofoam ring. I flung it, Frisbee-like, out over the water. The yellow nylon rope to which it was attached unfurled, twisting in the air. The life preserver landed in the water, but too far away. The person was going down again. I would have to pull the life preserver back by the rope and toss it again. No time! Beside me, the tar thing whined and whimpered, but it didn't try to attack me. "Good dog," I said. "Stay right there." I snapped the phone shut and shoved it into my front jeans pocket.

The person had managed to get her head above water again. She was gasping and coughing. She turned an anguished face to me, and my blood went as cold as if I had jumped into the lake. The dunking had swept her hair away from her face. It was my aunt Maryssa! She went under again, and the Horseless Head Men plunged after her. When they surfaced, I saw that each one had grabbed a shoulder of Auntie Mryss's sweater in its mouth. Her face was back above water. The Horseless Head Men seemed to be straining in the direction of the floating ring of the life preserver a few feet off, but they were only little. They couldn't hold her up and tow her at the same time. But Auntie started paddling her hands, so weakly. But it was enough. It probably only took a few seconds, but it seemed like hours before she finally grabbed on to the life preserver. I pulled on the rope, and she began moving toward me. The Horseless Head Men kept their grip on her lavender sweater. As she got closer, I could see how badly she was shivering. She looked exhausted. Her face was naturally pale, but right now it was gray, drained of all color. She was looking in my direction, but I couldn't tell if she was even seeing me. Then she closed her eyes, turned her head to the side, and laid it down on the life preserver. "Auntie, don't let go!" I shouted. "Hold on!" I didn't know whether she'd heard me, whether she was even still conscious, but she didn't let go her grip on the life preserver.

When she bumped gently against the dock, I dropped the rope and ran down the little flight of cement stairs that got you level with the water. I knelt on the bottom stair. The freezing water seeped into my jeans, but my blemish-covered legs barely felt it. I stretched my hand out. "Auntie Mryss," I said, "can you reach my hand?"

She rolled her head weakly up. Her hair, which she usually wore in a tight bun, had come undone. Sodden hair draped her face. "Sojourner?" she said. Her voice was hoarse and whispery. I could barely hear her.

"Yes, it's me! Give me your hand!" She reached a trembling arm toward me. I leaned forward as far as I dared. "Come on, Auntie. Just a little more." Her fingertips touched mine. Then I was holding her ice-cold hand, then her wrist. "Come on, Auntie," I crooned, "nearly there."

I pulled her in, got her upper half lying on the stairs. From the waist down, her legs were still in the water. She was too weak to clamber up the rest of the way. I had to grab her by the waistband and pull with all my strength. She groaned the whole time, and the Horseless Head Men flew around and wittered like worried old ladies. Finally I got all of her onto the bottom step. She was sobbing, her mouth open. "My Lord is my help and my savior," she said, over and over. "He answered my prayers. He sent you to fetch me out." I sat on the step above her, took her into my arms, and rocked her.

She was so cold! And trembling uncontrollably, from the core of her on out.

"Auntie, what you doing all the way down here?" She lived north of downtown, up past Dupont Street on the west side of the city.

The two Horseless Head Men stayed floating close above her. They made a noise, something like a pigeon cooing combined with a growling undertone of cat in heat. I rolled Auntie Mryss onto the ledge, took her into my arms. She was so wet she squelched.

"I came down here to see the miracle."

"The disaster, you mean."

"I mean the volcano. I lost my balance and fell in."

"So that thing didn't throw you in?" Hey; where was the creature, anyway?

"Nothing threw me in. And where's Spot?"

Uh-oh. Aunt Mryss was a little bit . . . eccentric. Spot was her imaginary guard dog. Dad growled at her if she talked about Spot, and Mum would ask her if she'd stopped taking her medication again, but I went along with it. Spot had become something Auntie and I shared; our private game. I'd thought she kinda knew Spot wasn't real, and she just liked giving her cousin a hard time. But now I wasn't so sure. I said, "We need to get you warm and dry, like right now." She sneezed. I shouldered my jacket off. "Put this on."

"But you're going to be cold."

"I'll be all right." A chilly fall breeze was blowing right

through the thin shirt I had on underneath. I was all over goose bumps.

"Where's Spot?" She took the jacket from me, but craned her neck, looked up to the boardwalk. "She was standing right beside you. I heard her bark."

My skin prickled. "That," I said, "was Spot? That thing freaking tried to kill me, Auntie!"

"You mind your language, pickney. And help me up." As I helped her stand on shaky legs, she said, "Spot wouldn't hurt you. After you and she know each other from since."

I helped her into my jacket. Immediately, water from her wet clothing started seeping through it. It was ruined. I sighed. First time I'd worn it, too. "Auntie, that monster chased me all the way from the Convention Centre to here." I wasn't going to tell her that I'd never really believed in Spot.

"She probably just came to bring you to me." She had another fit of shuddering.

"You need to get to a hospital." I pulled my cell out of my pocket and dialed Emergency.

"Emergency Services," said a voice on the phone.

"Hello, my aunt needs—"

"We're currently working beyond capacity with rescue operations throughout the city," said a tense recorded voice. There was screaming in the background. "Please leave a message stating your name, location, phone number, and the nature of your emergency—"

I put the phone away. "Okay, so that's not gonna work," I said. "All right, can you walk a little?" I asked her. "We have to find a taxi."

She nodded. "Y-yes. Not far, though."

I helped her up the stairs. Just three little steps, but by the time we got up them, she was panting and the little color that had come back into her face was gone again. She wasn't looking good, and the street was all the way at the other end of the parking lot. Maybe I could leave her here, go and get the cab, and have the driver come over here and pick her up? But I didn't want to leave her alone.

Three or four white guys on skateboards came rolling over. "She okay?" one of them asked as he came to a stop and stamped on one end of the board to flip the other end up into his hands. He saw the two Horseless Head Men. "Whoa."

One of the guys, a long drink of water wearing a parka and jammers, said, "Those things are everywhere, man. They creep me out."

"She fell into the lake," I told them. "She's freezing." Skateboards. Man, wouldn't that be a sweet way for the Raw Gyals to come onstage to the battle?

"Bring her over by us," the first guy said. He jerked his chin in the direction of the space beneath the overpass. "We got a fire."

"Um, I dunno . . ." I didn't know these guys.

Auntie Mryss decided for me. "Thank you, darlings," she said, her voice all quavery from the shuddering. One of them took her other arm, and together we half-carried, half-walked her in the direction of the fire. As we went, the guy asked my aunt, "So, how'd you get in the lake?" By the time we got to the spot under the highway overpass, Auntie was chatting away with the skateboard dudes like she'd known them forever. She'd asked them all whether their families were okay and had already told a beefy guy in a well-worn leather jacket that his hair would suit him better if he kept it out of his eyes. I hoped she wouldn't start asking them whether they knew Jesus. Though, come to think of it, that might actually be possible nowadays. Man, I was cold!

It was dark and damp under the bridge, and it smelled of

earth and wet cement and piss. There were blankets strung on lengths of rusty rebar as makeshift tents. There were empty junk food bags. Through a gap in one of the "tent" flaps, I could see overlapping garbage bags laid on the wet ground, and a stained, mildewed futon on top. There was a winter coat spread out as a blanket, and a rolled-up one for a pillow. Even Auntie Mryss was looking a bit doubtful now. The guys didn't have just one fire, but a big circle of five of them in metal garbage cans, off to the side of their camp. I said, "Wow."

Parka-and-jammers guy grinned. "Pretty cool, huh? You and this lady should go stand right in the middle. That's what we do when the cold begins to get to us."

"She's my aunt."

"No way!" He peered at me through the darkness. "But you're black or something, right?"

I sighed. "Points to you for being able to tell."

"So are you, like, adopted?"

"No, I am," said Auntie Mryss firmly. She was messing with him.

"Oh," said the guy, clearly confused. "Okay."

Mryss winked at me. I smiled back. I could just hear Dad if he had caught her in a lie like that; "What a way you too liard, Maryssa!" He would probably have thought it was funny, though. Acting up like that was okay by him, so long as it wasn't his children doing it.

I started to take Auntie into the circle. One of the guys leapt ahead of us. He was carrying a bright blue plastic milk crate. He put it down inside the circle. "So she can sit," he said, brushing it off with his hand. "Want me to get you one, too?"

"No, I gotta go find a cab, get her back home."

He nodded. "Sweet." He ducked shyly away. The Horseless Head Men were frolicking into and out of the flames, just like kids playing in the sprinkler jets in summer. They were fireproof, then. Handy.

I led Auntie into the circle of warmth. The heat felt like we were snuggling down under a blanket on a cold night. The flickering leaves of flame gave everything and everyone a glow. You could almost forget you were under a stinky old bridge in a city that had gone to hell in a handcart over the past day. I sat my aunt down on the milk crate. Her hands were still like ice, but her lips seemed to be less bluish. "What nice young men," she said.

"I guess." I rubbed her shoulders briskly, squeezed the water out of her hair. "We have to get you out of those wet clothes. I want to go hail a cab, but I don't want to leave you alone with those guys."

She patted my hand. "I'll be fine." She jerked her chin in the direction of the Horseless Head Men. "My little friends will look after me."

I tried wave to down three cabs before one of them would stop, and I waved down another two before one would agree to stay put while I fetched my aunt. When I got back to where the skateboard guys were camped, they were all sitting on their boards in front of Mryss. Everyone was laughing and talking. Auntie Mryss was cradling a cup of something warm and steamy in both her hands. Her hair was dry and she'd put it back up into her usual bun. The two Horseless Head Men were nestled in her lap. She saw me. "Sojourner, my darling, come over here, nuh? Alan was just telling us about going fishing up north last summer."

"Auntie, you changed your clothes?" I'd never seen her in jeans before. And under my jacket, she was wearing a different color sweater than she had been.

"I couldn't stay soaked the way I was. I would have caught my death."

"I'm so sorry! I couldn't get a taxi sooner."

"Don't fret, child. One of these gentlemen lent me a sweater and a pair of slacks."

"Auntie, they're called jeans." And they were probably nasty and smelly, what with guy sweat and these guys camping out in the dirt under a bridge. "Listen, we have to hurry. I don't think the cab will wait long."

Maryssa smiled at me. "You ever notice how people say, 'The cab won't wait'? As though it's the car that's alive, not the driver?"

"Yeah!" said one of the guys. He frowned. "Though I think I saw a living cab today. God, that was freaky."

Auntie handed her cup to him. She stood, tumbling the Horseless Head Men out of her lap. They made surprised little squeaks and bounced right back into the air as they hit the ground.

"Those things really weird me out," said one of the guys.

Auntie put an arm around me. She told them, "Sojourner is my favorite niece, and she is looking after me real well."

"I'm your only niece. Or second cousin, or something."

She kissed my cheek. "Sweeter than honey from the bee is the love of a thoughtful child."

Yikes. She was about to bust out with the holy-rolling. Time to get her out of there. "Uh, bye," I said to the skateboard dudes. "And . . . thanks."

"Don't mention it," said the chunky one with the blue hair.

"Cab's this way, Auntie."

When we reached the cab, I opened the car door, helped her in, and got in beside her. Good thing she was dry now. The driver was looking nervous enough already. I hadn't been looking forward to convincing him to let a soaking wet person inside the car. The Horseless Head Men got in with us.

"Ladies," said the cabdriver, "please, these animals are not coming into my car."

"That's all right, dear," replied Auntie Mryss. "They will follow along behind."

Gently, she shooed the Horseless Head Men out. They hovered near her window. I told the cabdriver the address.

"Yes, Miss."

He pulled out, and drove around a woman with a shopping cart full of fur coats. Or maybe they weren't fur coats. Was the furry pile heaving a little in its middle? Before I could get a good look, the driver had pulled too far away. I shuddered. The driver headed toward the highway. The Horseless Head Men came along with us, hovering at the level of Auntie's window and moving smoothly sideways, in tandem. They would be a hoot on a dance team.

CHAPTER TWELVE

Traffic was backed up on Dufferin Street, where Auntie lived. Our car inched forward. I watched the charge on the meter add up. Auntie had left her handbag in Lake Ontario, so I'd told her that I would pay the fare. At this rate, paying for the cab would use up most of the money that Glory had lent me.

The driver said, "Pay no attention to the meter, Miss. There is no charge today. I only put it on out of habit." He turned the meter off.

"But it's such a long trip!" Auntie said. "We should give you at least some of it."

He shook his head. "Thank you, no, Madam. Maybe the world is finally ending and maybe it isn't. But there are people on the road today who have no way of getting home. This is something I can do."

Auntie beamed. "Thank you, driver. God bless you."

But something was bothering me. I asked him, "How did you know I was thinking about the fare?"

In the rearview mirror, I could see the quiet smile on his face. "Lucky guess, miss."

I wondered.

Finally, the cause of the traffic jam was in front of us, in the middle of the road. People had been slowing to look. But we couldn't tell what was going on; it was hidden by a knot of people, in cars and on foot. There were more oglers standing on the sidewalk, both sides, even though they probably couldn't see a rass. But then the crowd made an "Ohh" sound and moved backward.

"*Hai Ram!*" exclaimed our driver, stomping on the brake.

"Holy shit!" I said.

Auntie Mryss said, "Lord Jesus."

It was a fight between a big black tumbleweed and a— "Is that an archaeopteryx?" I asked. Our biology teacher had told us that the first winged dinosaurs had been pigeon-sized. The one flopping all over the road was humongous; about the size of a bus.

It was still losing, though. The tumbleweed was only maybe six feet across, and it didn't even have limbs, but it had the dino bird down on the ground, pinned by the neck and by one wing. The bird batted its free wing against the ground and tossed its head on its snaky neck. Aunt Mryss growled, "Always getting into mischief."

"Madam," said the driver, "is there a side street to get to where you are going?"

The dino bird tried to attack the tumbleweed with its sharp beak, but the angle was wrong. Instead, the tumbleweed started worrying at the body of the dino bird. The tumbleweed had serious teeth. And angry yellow eyes. Then it hawked up some black gunk that stuck to the bird's feathers and started to spread. "Hey," I said, "that kinda looks like—"

Aunt Mryss pressed the button to open the car window. She put her head through the window and yelled, "Spot!"

I said, "Oh, my god. One of those things is Spot, too? How many Spots do you have?"

"Just the one. A rolling calf can take different forms, you know." She called out, "Spot, you stop that right now! Leave that poor thing alone!"

People in the crowd gaped at her. The tumbleweed stopped tearing at the bird and turned its yellow eyes our way. So now I knew which of the two of them was Spot. I resisted the urge to hide below the level of the window.

The taxi driver turned around in his seat to goggle at us. "What is she doing?" he asked me. "She is knowing that horrid creature?"

"I'm sorry, this is all new to me, too. Who knew Spot was real?"

Auntie Mryss said, "So what you thought Spot was all these years? My imaginary friend?"

"Uh . . ."

Aunt Mryss called out the window, "Bad girl! You go home right this minute!"

"What is that thing, Auntie?"

"Rolling calf," she replied.

When we were little, Dad used to tell me and Rich scary stories about the rolling calf. About how it would hunt you down if it found you outside late at night, up to no good. The rolling calf's fur—did you call a cow's hair "fur"? Man, all this stuff was making me learn things I didn't know I'd ever need to know. Anyway, its hair or whatever was black and threw off sparks. Just like it had when it had chased me, it was wearing links of heavy chain around it, like some kind of kinky harness. Looked like Spot and the dino bird had been fighting over a dead cat lying in the street. I didn't want to know what they wanted it for. Real cows don't eat meat. Wouldn't that be, like, cannibalism, or something? If they ate beef, anyway?

Auntie shouted, "Go home, I said!"

The rolling calf whined and dithered for a second. Then it left the dino bird and rolled off in the direction of Maryssa's place, tumbling round and sometimes bouncing up into the air, just like a real tumbleweed. Its chains dragged behind it, making an almost clanking noise. Suddenly I wasn't so eager to go to my aunt's place anymore. "Auntie, are you sure that you want it to go to your house?"

"Don't be silly, it's her home, too. Besides, she's harmless. Mostly."

The taxi driver said, "My wife, she has a little wooden person following her. Since this volcano, you know? All kinds of bad things came out of that volcano. I would like to chop the little wooden person up to bits. It watches me. But my wife, she says leave the little wooden person alone."

Maryssa gave him one of her looks. "Then you should leave it alone. Please to take me home now, driver. The traffic is clear. I need to feed Spot. Poor thing, she must be hungry."

She was going home to feed a monster that could take down a giant winged lizard-bird. Oh, goodie.

The driver turned to face front in his seat again. As he was beginning to drive off, the dragon-bird moved weakly.

"Whoa." I tapped Auntie Mryss on the shoulder and pointed. "It's not dead!"

Auntie Mryss saw what I meant. "Pull over, driver."

The driver grumbled a little about people who didn't know whether they were coming or going, but he pulled over to the curb. The bird tried to stand, wobbled back down into a crouch. Its neck was bleeding, red soaking its white plumage. A Hummer careened around it, honking its horn. I swear it missed the bird by inches. The Hummer was about half the bird's size.

Auntie said, "Lord have mercy. And all because of Spot. You go and see to it, Sojourner."

"Me? No way! Look at the size of that thing! Besides, I have to go with you, to make sure you're okay. You could have hypothermia."

"I'll be okay. My little friends will look after me."

The Horseless Head Men grinned at me through the window. Not like they'd ever stopped grinning. "Auntie, that thing could eat me whole and never even notice."

"Don't be foolish. It's half-dead. It couldn't hurt a flea right now. If you leave it there, a car's going to hit it, and then how you're going to feel?"

Sure enough, one of those chopped-in-half-looking smart cars ran right into the bird's side. The bird was so huge, it was almost like me being run over by a squirrel, but three more cars banged into the smart car, one behind the other, and the bird screamed. Traffic was piling up, people were putting their heads out their windows and swearing, horns were blowing, brakes screeching.

"I don't know what to do," I told Auntie.

She smiled. "That's the beginning of wisdom. Knowing that you don't know anything."

"It is?"

"Just go. Be careful, and just do your best. God will understand."

If my mom knew that crazy Aunt Maryssa was sending me out to face down an injured wild creature many times my size with only her faith in God to protect me, she would have gone postal. Thing was, it wasn't just Aunt Mryss. I sort of did want to help the bird. "Okay," I said, "I'll give it a go. I'll meet you at your place afterward." If I didn't turn into lunch for the bird. I left the taxi, dodged two cars and a UPS truck, and went toward the bird.

Two of the drivers in the fender bender had gotten out of their cars; a white guy wearing a Blue Jays bomber jacket, and a white woman about my mom's age. The third driver cowered behind his wheel, staring openmouthed at the bird. The bird was snapping at the smart car. Its breathing was shallow and fast.

Something with lungs that big shouldn't have to pant. I said to the two drivers, "Can you guys back up? I think you're hurting it." But the bird solved that problem by dragging itself a little way away so that the car wasn't touching it anymore. That seemed to have used up all its energy. It put its head down and made little moaning sounds.

The woman looked stern. "Is this your pet, young lady? See what you've gone and done by letting it roam about?"

The guy in the bomber jacket looked up at the bird. "It's not like she could put a leash on it," he said. He sounded too calm, as though he was thinking really hard about staying calm.

"It's not mine. My aunt just sent me to try to help it."

"And what does she think a teenager's going to do? That animal is injured! Someone should fetch trained professionals."

I sighed. "You guys have cars. Why don't one of you go get some help for it?"

"Me?" said the woman. "But I don't . . . but I can't . . ."

Bomber jacket guy said, still in this weirdly reasonable way, "It's getting blood on the roof of my car."

There was a screech of tires. The third driver had thrown his car into reverse, then into forward again. He took the car up onto the sidewalk to get around the bird and drove away.

Bomber jacket guy was still staring up at the bird. "I'm out looking for my kid sister. Nobody's seen or heard from her since the volcano. So, uh, good luck with that."

"I hope you find your sister," I told him. "My big brother's missing."

"That sucks. I'm really sorry." He got back into his car and pulled away, driving slowly so he could check down alleyways.

A fat drop of big bird blood fell onto the woman's sturdy black shoes. She looked down, yelped, pulled her foot away. "Okay," she said to me, "I'll go for help. Um, would you like to come along?"

She was offering me a graceful way out of this situation. "Thanks. But I think someone should stay with it."

"But you . . . Okay. If you're sure?"

I looked up at the bird. I'd bet the top of its head was a good twelve feet off the ground, and it wasn't even standing. "No way am I sure."

"Well, good, then. Fine." She hadn't heard a word I'd said. She was already backing away toward her car. "I'll just . . . I'll be right back. With help. I really will."

Sure she would. "Don't let the door slap your ass on the way out!" I yelled as she left in a screech of tires. I'd always wanted to say that. The woman's quick exit was spoiled a little by her having to stop and inch her car through the growing crowd.

Slowly, I approached the bird. It turned one despairing eye on me. The eyeball was the size of a basketball.

"It's okay, boy," I said. "Or girl. I'm not going to hurt you." I took one more step. The bird raised its head and hissed. I leapt back, ready to turn tail and run. But hissing was all it could do. Its head sank to the ground again. It was in a bad way. It was still losing blood, and maybe it had other injuries as well. "Christ. I hope Auntie Mryss tears Spot a new one for doing this." Though it was hard to imagine the thing I'd seen putting up with any back talk from one small, old woman. I just couldn't get it out of my mind that Spot had been real all along. And Sasquatches. What else was real, then? Well, duh, Scotch; you name it. Sasquatches, demonic Tinker Bells, purple hippos wearing party hats; they were all real now.

The bird shuddered out a big breath. It was a few long seconds before it breathed again. It was going to die while I stood here, doing nothing. Slowly, I went closer to its head. "Shh, boy. Or girl. Or whatever. It's okay." It really wasn't, though.

The bird's eye rolled when it saw me. It struck out weakly with its beak at me. But even that had plenty of power, coming from a creature its size. I had to do a fancy leap backward to avoid its big head with its cruel eagle's beak. But the tightness of my jeans around my tainted legs slowed me down. The bird's beak connected with my leg. I screamed and fell onto the pavement. I rolled out of the bird's reach. "Ow! I'm trying to help you, you stupid thing!" Dimly I heard the crowd making "Oo" and "Ahh" noises. Not a one of those so-and-sos would help me, though.

The bird cried out, laid its head down. Didn't look like it had any more fight left. But just in case, I got a few more feet out of its reach. And finally, I had to look at my leg. There was a long slash right through my jeans, on the outside of my leg from just below my knee to just above my ankle. The top of my leather boots had stopped the bird's beak from going any lower. The gash in my leg was deep enough to lay a pencil in. I could see the white fat underlayer of my skin, exposed. And then blood began welling up out of the wound. Now that the shock had worn off a little, I could feel the pain of the injury. It hurt so bad. Like my leg had been stung by a thousand bees. A deep, burning pain. Relentless. I sat and rocked, doing this soft, constant whimper I had almost no control over. I couldn't help it, I started to cry, with fear, with pain. "Can somebody help me?" I shouted to the crowd. A couple of people actually started toward me, but the bird lifted its head. It screamed a challenge at them and struck out. No one could get close.

Someone threw a rock at the bird. It missed by a mile. "Stop it!" I yelled. "You're going to hit me, too! What is it with people and throwing stones?"

"Miss!" yelled someone from the crowd. A woman, maybe in her thirties, looked Latina, short hair, broad shoulders, wearing a light blue shirt with the red crest of the Toronto Transit Commission on the pocket. "You need to get away from it so we can get close to you!" A few more people shouted in agreement, urged me to get out of there.

"I can't use my leg!" I sobbed.

The woman yelled again, "Can you make it over here?"

Oh, God. Oh, God. I hurt so much, I just wanted to curl up into a ball and whimper until someone made the pain go away. "I'll try!"

"Quickly!"

I managed to push myself into a standing position on my good leg. Every movement shot pain through the sliced-up one. I was shaking. And my nose was all snotty. They would have to cut my jeans off me to treat my leg, and then they would see the taint crusting my body like old, chewed-up gum.

I screwed my eyes up tight and took a deep breath. I started screaming in anticipation of the searing pain I would feel when I put my weight on my slashed leg. I stared down at the leg. My jeans had a spreading purple stain where the blue of the denim mixed with my red blood. And something else was leaking from the wound; an oily, black liquid. Startled, I put my bad foot down without thinking about it.

I stopped midscream. It hadn't hurt. In fact, the gash wasn't even there anymore. To be sure, I pulled open the rip in my jeans.

"Miss? Are you okay?"

I shouted, "Yeah! Just give me a minute!"

My jeans were still soaked with blood, but my flesh was whole again. Even the awful black blemish had sealed right up, as though there'd never been a long gouge through my calf. My leg was a teeny bit tender, that was all.

"Miss, get out of the way! We have a man here with a hunting rifle!"

"No!" I scrambled to my feet. "No, it's okay! I'm okay! See?" I took a few strong steps to show them. The woman looked confused. Beside her, a man lowered his rifle. Before today, I'd never seen a real rifle before, not even at a distance. My mom always harped on about how it was better that she and Dad were raising us here instead of in the U.S., where "everybody and their dog" had a gun.

Weakly, the bird tried to strike me again. It missed. Its head flopped to the ground. It'd lost a ton of blood, and who knew what internal injuries it had? The woman shouted, "We still need to shoot it, Miss! It's a danger to everyone!" The man raised his rifle again.

"No, no; don't! It's dying, can't you see that?" How could I keep him from shooting it? Maybe if I were on it, he wouldn't shoot because he'd be afraid to hit me. I ran right up to the bird and started climbing. The skin on my back was crawling at the thought that it was now exposed to the guy with the gun. I yelled, "Don't shoot! Just give me a freaking minute, okay?" The bird's feathers were more like young tree branches; they made good handholds. They also smelled like rancid fish oil. And it had fleas. Fighting not to gag, not to freak at the sensation of fleas running over my hands, I climbed onto the bird's back, up near its neck. That added the smell of raw blood to the rest of the nastiness. I avoided the tarry patches where Spot had mired the bird's feathers. I straddled it, near its neck. It didn't react at all. "That's right, baby," I crooned to the bird, "don't kill me." Not that it could, in its present state. I didn't even know if it was still alive.

From my perch, I looked out over the crowd. Some of them had gotten bored already and were wandering away. I thought I saw a Sasquatch among them. It was wearing jeans and a loose hoodie with the hood pulled up over its head. A few people were still there, including the woman who'd tried to help me and the man with the gun. The two of them were talking to each other. Then the woman nodded, and she and the man made their way cautiously over to the side of the bird.

The man looked angry. "What're you playing at?" he said. "You told this lady you were injured."

"I didn't tell her anything! She could see it for herself!"

The woman said, "You could have faked that."

The man said, "Yeah. I know you kids today. Do anything to get attention."

I couldn't see how this could end well. So I didn't reply. Instead, I thought hard. I needed a vet; one that knew how to treat the granddaddy of all archaeopteryxes. Archaeopteryxi?

Wait. I did know someone who could take care of huge birds that both were and weren't birds. How to get her here, though? What had she said to her house? The soundshapes and rhythms of the old lady's words danced in my mind, like toes tapping out a story to music. I had it. I murmured, "Dacha maya, idti syuda." I was pretty sure it went something like that.

Now the man looked really mad. "What the hell? Are you making fun of me?"

I wasn't. I was just using my superpower. "Dacha maya, idti syuda."

The woman shook her head. "She's saying words. Honey,

what language is that? Do you know where you are?" To the man, she said, "I think she might be delusional."

"Dacha maya, idti syuda." Come on, come on.

"Well, I say we drag her down off that thing, kill it, and march her right over to the loony bin."

"Dacha maya, idti syuda." Maybe I was saying it wrong? I wasn't. I knew I wasn't, like I knew where each part of my body was in space when I did a somersault.

"I don't know," said the woman. "We don't want to agitate her. Or that thing she's riding."

"Lady, she looks like she's already been plenty agitated. Shaken and stirred, I'd say." He looked up at me. "Miss, you come down here right now, you hear me?"

The woman said, "You think she's going to come down while you're brandishing a gun at her? She's schizophrenic, not stupid."

Oh, so now I was schizo? "Dacha maya, idti syuda."

"Do you even have a permit for that weapon?"

"Dacha maya, idti syuda." Crap. It wasn't working. I felt like such an idiot. "Dacha maya, idti syuda!" Maybe the old woman had been lying about being able to find me anywhere.

The man said, "Oh, so when it's convenient for you, you're all like, 'Please, mister, please shoot wild, scary animals for me.' But now—"

A shadow fell on us. A big one. There was shouting from the crowd, and a lot of pushing and shoving to get out of the way. The man looked up and gaped. He fired a shot. The bullet buried itself in one of the wooden beams at the corner of the flying house. The old witch's house had arrived. "Finally," I muttered. "Took you long enough."

With one long, chicken-skinned claw, the house flicked the rifle out of the man's hands. It ran to where the rifle landed and stomped on it a few times. It had learned quickly about rifles.

"Good house," said the Toronto Transit Commission woman approvingly. "He was going to hurt someone with that thing."

The giant bird chose that moment to show signs of life. It raised its head and began to struggle to its feet.

The now rifle-less man said, "You're all crazy. This is crazy. I'm outta here." He took off at a run. Me, I slid down off the bird's back to where the woman was standing.

"Lady," I said, "we gotta run." I grabbed her hand and tugged her out of the way just as the bird took a swipe at where she'd been a split second before. I took her behind the legs of the witch's house.

"Is this safe?" she asked, looking up at the underside of the house.

"So long as it doesn't sit down."

"I was more afraid of it *shitting* down."

"Oh, crap."

"Precisely. How about behind that car over there?" She pointed to a yellow Prius that was on the sidewalk, kissing a telephone pole. So we went over there to watch what would happen next. "This is so exciting!" she said. "Much better than Sunday afternoon classes at my dojo."

The bird, which had been wobbly on its feet anyway, plopped back down in a puddle of its own congealing blood. The house put itself right in front of the bird. The bird cocked its head sideways at the house. The house's eye shutters opened and closed.

The house's front door flew open so hard that it cracked against the outside wall. "Dyevuchka," came a voice from inside, "where are you? What are you doing, ordering my house around as though it's yours? Come and take your punishment, brazen child. You know you can't hide."

True. I couldn't. I might be in a witch's soup pot tonight, and all for what? A big, half-dead dinosaur bird that'd just as soon kill me as look at me. "I'm coming!" I stepped out from behind the car and began making my way back over there. If this didn't work, I was toast. "Just take a look outside first, will you?"

"I will not. Come along, now. Izbouchka, let her in."

Izbouchka did nothing of the sort. She had a good look at the injured bird. Where an ordinary bird would have cocked its head to look at something that had made it curious, Izbouchka had to cock her whole body to stare at the giant bird. I heard stuff tumbling inside, things breaking as the witch's house tilted at an angle, with her inside. "Izbouchka!" she yelled, then a string of words that didn't sound polite at all.

"I'm sorry!" I shouted. "Just come out, please? Just for a second?"

"Oh, I'm going to peel your skin off to make myself a new pair of boots. I'm going to string your teeth together for a necklace. I'm going to roast you like a suckling pig and feed your bones to Izbouchka."

Izbouchka righted herself.

The old lady stuck her head out of a window that hadn't been there a second before. She was wearing curlers in her hair. I dared not laugh. Instead, I pointed at the bird. "Um, this—whatever it is—got into a fight with my aunt's pet rolling calf."

She looked. "Oh, my," she said.

"I know, right? It looks like it's lost a lot of blood, and I can't take care of it. My parents'd freak. Besides, I think it's more likely to eat me than be grateful. Anyway, I, um, I just thought that you'd know how to handle a big flying creature that's pointy at most of its ends, and I wanted to ask your advice, you know? I'm really sorry to inconvenience you."

She gave me a stern look. "We'll see."

What'd that mean? But I couldn't ask her. She'd pulled her

head back inside Izbouchka, and the window had disappeared. A second later, a door appeared. Izbouchka crouched down, and a set of stairs from the porch to the ground appeared. The door opened, and the old lady marched out. She'd tied a scarf around her curlers. She came down the stairs and went over to the bird. It just crouched there, tar soaked into and dripping from its feathers, panting for breath and trying to blink more tar out of its reddened eyes. It looked like it'd been caught in the biggest oil spill ever. Plus there was all that blood.

The witch shook her head. "He's done for," she said. "His injuries are too serious. And there's no way to get all that stuff off without taking his feathers and skin along with it." She made a tutting noise. "Pity the feathers are ruined. They would have made me a wonderful cloak."

"Gross. You mean he's going to die?"

"Yes."

Izbouchka stood. The strangest noise came from inside her; kind of a *whump!*

The old lady's eyes went wide. "Dacha, no! Stop that this instant!"

But she didn't. The house tilted her body until her roof was pointing at the bird. Inside the house, I heard the crash and bang of things being tossed around and breaking. "Izbouchka!"

A chimney slid out of Izbouchka's roof. "Run!" said the old lady. She hustled me over to the side of the road. She could move pretty quickly for an old lady.

Izbouchka coughed, an almost ladylike sound. "I'm sorry," the old lady said to me.

"For what?" I turned to look at what was happening.

Flame came spurting out of Izbouchka's chimney; a roaring torch of it a good six feet long. People who were still watching shouted in surprise.

Izbouchka aimed her flame at the bird. The bird was covered in tar; it caught fire right away. I yelped. The crowd backed farther away. "Stop her!" I yelled. "She's going to kill it!"

The witch shook her head. "I can't stop her."

The tarred bird was screaming now, trying to stand. It threw its head back and extended its wings. Flame licked all the way along them, outlining them in orange light. It was glorious to see, and it made me feel sick to my stomach. "She's hurting it," I moaned. Tears were running down my face.

The burning bird collapsed in on itself. For a second, it glowed from within and I could see its bones. Then the flames disappeared and the lump left in the road was just a big piece of coal. "What did you do?" I screeched at Izbouchka. I started to rush toward the house, but the witch held me back.

The charred corpse of the giant bird flared into flame again, so bright. No, not flame. A bird-shaped body was rising out of the ashes. Its plumage was red and orange, shiny new and glowing in the dark. It stretched its wings out and cawed so loudly that it hurt my ears. People in the crowd covered their ears, too. Over by the pretzled Prius, the bus driver watched, her face alight with wonder.

"Is that the same bird?" I asked the old lady.

She gave a rueful smile. "No one has ever known."

"My bio teacher never told us that the Archaeopteryx could do that."

"The arka what?" asked the old woman.

Izbouchka righted herself again. More sounds of china and glass breaking. "I so hate it when she does that," said the witch. "How would you like to be my next Vassilisa? Just a little light cleaning work."

I put my hands on my hips and glared at her. "Tell me you did not just offer me a job as your maid!"

She shrugged. "Your choice. It would have been a way for you to make up for your offense. But as you wish." The threat in her voice made me shiver.

The giant bird turned its eagle gaze on Izbouchka. It hissed. Then it extended its neck, cocked its head sideways, and looked Izbouchka up and down. It made a rumbly inquiring sound in its throat. Izbouchka made her own question sound back. I guess that was the answer the other bird wanted, because it leaned over and nuzzled Izbouchka's awning with its beak. Izbouchka's ceiling tiles ruffled up, making a sound almost like a girlish giggle.

"Well!" said the witch. "Who would have thought?"

Izbouchka's chimney was nuzzling the bird back. The bird tried to climb on top of her. I wasn't sure I was old enough to be watching this, no matter how much porn I'd scoped on gottabejelly.com. The witch yelled something at Izbouchka in Russian. Izbouchka slid out from under the bird and slammed open her front door. The witch said to me, "Maybe luck is with you this time. Perhaps you won't have to pay the price for presuming to summon me." Before I could ask her what she meant, she swooped up her stairs and into Izbouchka again. The door slammed shut and disappeared. The stairs rolled themselves back up.

Izbouchka took a running start, then leapt into the air. The giant bird squawked. That was *"Come back, hot thing!"* if I'd ever heard it, and I had. A little unsteady on its new feet, it stood. It leapt into the air, too, and flew after Izbouchka. They headed south, in the direction of Animikika. I guess a little molten lava wasn't the kind of thing those two needed to worry about. Pretty soon, they disappeared into the volcano smog.

CHAPTER THIRTEEN

I rode another bicycle I'd found to Aunt Maryssa's place. People had just abandoned their rides all over the place. The bike was a little short for my long legs, but its gears were sweet smooth. Even though Auntie had my jacket, riding kept me warm. But it didn't do anything to help the chafing. At least the blemish didn't seem to have spread much farther. I had a couple of near accidents, because as I rode, I kept peeking down at the leg the fire bird had gouged. I could see the smooth, rubbery skin of the blemish where there should have been an open wound. It didn't even feel tender anymore. It didn't feel anything. What was that black gunk that had come out of the cut just before it had healed over? It'd had the same consistency as blood. I touched my forehead. The cut I'd gotten from the piece of flying eggshell was gone. Man, I wished that I had Ben and Gloria to talk to right now! But Gloria was probably never going to talk to me again. I wished I had Tafari to hold me and argue with me until I did something sensible about the weird shit that was happening to my body.

If only I knew what that sensible thing was. I wished I had Rich to tease me and make fun of me and laugh at Mum and Dad behind their backs with me. Hell, I even wished I had Mum and Dad.

My life had been so simple. Yesterday, all I'd wanted was to win that street dance battle and make enough cash to put down on an apartment with my big bro. Today, I was dodging boggarts and abominable snowmen in the streets, my missing brother was sending me creepy phone messages, the countries of the world were in chaos, and with every passing hour I turned into more of a tar baby; a freak on the outside as well as on the inside.

At least I had Aunt Mryss. She was a one-woman Chaos all by herself, but that only meant she was dealing with all this strangeness as though it were a normal day for her. Maybe it was.

That humongous bird; was it a different one from the one Izbouchka had torched? Or had she just helped the injured one to somehow heal itself?

I stopped the bike at Aunt Maryssa's bungalow on the corner of Dufferin and that little side street with the butcher shop. She came out onto her front porch to let me in. She was dressed warmly, and her color was back. Boy, was I glad to see that.

I didn't have any way to chain the bike up. "Can I bring it inside?" I shouted to her.

She replied, "A bird in the hand is better than two in the bush." I guessed that meant yes. She always talked that way, like a combination between church and a wizard's prophecy. I went to open the gate. Her hedge rustled, and the two Horseless Head Men popped out of it. I jumped. "Don't fear them," Maryssa called out, "for the lion shall lie down with the lamb."

All that talk about lambs. She was making me hungry. I opened the gate and wheeled my bike past the Horseless Head Men. One of them burbled at me as I passed. "Nice day," I said to it.

When I reached the foot of the short set of stairs up to the porch, Maryssa said, "Bring the bicycle come. Put it inside. But brush off the wheels-them first. Nah want no mud on my nice carpet."

I knelt by the bike and started brushing the wheels off. "You'll never believe what happened to that big weird bird!" I told her.

"Poor thing. Don't tell me it dead?" With her strong accent, she sounded so much like my dad that I started to tear up. I'd heard white people ask her where in Ireland she was from, or Spain. Because she was white it never occurred to most of them that what they were hearing was Jamaican.

"No, it didn't die. Well, it did and it didn't." I stood up. "The thing is, I'm not sure. But it was alive again at the end, and I think it's okay."

She nodded. She seemed satisfied with that. "You hungry?"

"Like a horse."

"Come and eat, then." She put her two pinkie fingers to her lips and whistled. The Horseless Head Men were there instantly, squabbling with each other. "Behave yourselves," she said. "Plenty of room for the two of you." To my surprise, they settled down and shuffled into place on her left shoulder. Not that they actually sat on it. They bobbed in the air just above it.

"They have to come inside with us, Auntie?"

"Feeding time."

Horseless Head Men ate? This I had to see.

Auntie Mryss waved me on in ahead of her. Behind me, I heard a sharp knock. Didn't need to turn around to know what it was; Maryssa, rapping on the doorjamb. "Out, Spot!" she said. Out of habit, I said it along with her. Not as enthusiastically as I used to, though. Now that I knew what Spot was, I wasn't so keen to have it come out of anywhere. Well, it had seemed to listen to Auntie Mryss. I was going to have to put my trust in that. I leaned the bike up against one wall of the hallway and waited for her to lock the door. She turned toward me, smiled, and opened her arms. I went into them, closed my eyes, and sighed with happy. Someone I knew. Who loved me. Someone solid and familiar, and just a little mad. That was the thing about Mryss; everybody else I knew tried to keep their madness under wraps, to pretend they were normal. Even me. Mryss had never bothered to try. "Auntie Maryssa," I said, "I'm so glad you're okay."

"I thought I was unlucky because I had no shoes. But then I met a man with no feet."

"You betcha," I responded. I had no clue what she was on about. And what was making that quiet humming sound? I opened my eyes to find myself nose to snouts with the two Horseless Head Men, who were peering curiously at me. They were the ones humming. "Uh." I stepped out of Maryssa's arms, away from them. "What smells so good?"

"For I have prepared a table in the presence of mine enemy," replied Maryssa, "and killed the fatted calf." She was walking down the hallway, in the direction of the kitchen. "I know you. You always hungry. Eat more than your brother, even."

I scurried after the sound of her voice. I wanted to put off the moment when I told her how badly I'd been messing up. I asked her, "You going to tell me more about Spot?"

The kitchen was the same old kitchen. Dunno why I'd half-expected it to have changed. Same white walls. Same small Formica table with the brown-on-beige flowers and that silver plastic fake aluminum rim running along the bottom of the tabletop. Same faint smell of the bleach she cleaned everything with. But everything here was the same, as though all the good hadn't gone out of my world. I sniffed.

"What you weeping for, girl?" asked Maryssa. She was poking about in one of the cupboards above the sink (same cream-colored, ice-cream-thick enamel paint, same brass handles). She took out a plate and set it on the counter. As she moved around the kitchen, the two Horseless Head Men stayed with her, floating a quarter inch in the air above her shoulder. They were beginning to grow on me.

I pulled a chair out from the table and sat down (the seats matched the ugly pattern on the table, only in vinyl, half of them torn down the middle). I sat down. "Mum and Dad are going to kill me. Rich is missing, and it's my fault. One of my best friends isn't talking to me." My eyes were welling up for real now.

Maryssa turned and gave me a measuring look, but she didn't say anything. She spooned rice onto my plate from one of the two pots on the stove and ackee and saltfish from the other. She plonked the plate down in front of me. "Some have meat, but cannot eat," she said.

Was that supposed to mean something? Everything Maryssa said seemed to have another meaning woven into it, like the ribbons Mum used to plait into my hair. The salty smell of the plate of ackee and saltfish in front of me made my mouth water. "My favorite!"

She went over to the fridge and opened it. "Your favorite food is any food."

I picked up the fork she'd put down beside the plate and started shoveling the meal into me. Creamy yellow lumps of ackee, bits of salt cod, tiny green leaves of French thyme, and of course, plenty of pepper. It didn't taste quite right, though. It needed something else. Maybe I could sneak some plastic wrap when she wasn't looking.

Maryssa was slicing into an avocado she'd taken from the fridge; a Jamaican alligator pear, as big as a cantaloupe, with smooth, bright yellow-green skin. Not those tiny, bumpy-skinned avocados from the regular grocery store that barely lasted two bites. She put two huge wedges of it on the side of the plate. I stuffed one of them into my mouth right away, even though I was still working on a mouthful of ackee and saltfish. Through a mouthful of food, I said, "So, like I was telling you—"

"Manners," she said, and clucked. "Don't talk at me with your mouth full like that."

"But Rich—"

"Is a grown man. He can look after himself."

"Oh. I guess so. I kind of forgot." So I continued about the serious business of chewing. God, the taste. I finally got the whole mouthful down, and said, "Ackee is kind of like if scrambled eggs were a vegetable, you know?"

She snorted. She sat down at the table, across from me. One of the Horseless Head Men floated over to inspect my meal.

"Shoo. Auntie Mryss, didn't you say you were going to feed those things?"

"They been feeding right here sitting on me the whole time."

Okay, so they weren't growing on me after all. "You mean like . . . vampires or something?" Did the nasty little things have fangs?

She laughed. "In a kind of a way, I am the blood and the life," she replied, "but these don't want neither from me."

"Well, thank goodness for that."

"Though if they wanted it," she said, her face serious, "I would give it."

"Auntie Mryss, don't. You're creeping me out."

She only smiled and took one of the Horseless Head Men off her shoulder. It sat purring in her palm while she stroked its head. The other went and floated in the sunny window, purring too, like some kind of levitating cat. Hard to believe the two of them had been strong enough to keep her from drowning.

I kept eating. I wanted to hear about Spot. Plus I was hungry.

Plus it was good food, even if a little bit funny-tasting. "I wonder what's happening with Mum and Dad," I said to Maryssa. "They must be worried sick." Maybe if I eased into it. What was happening to me. Rich's agonized voice on the phone.

"Mm-hmm," she said, looking grim. Uh-oh. Bad topic. It really pissed her off that Dad didn't visit her more often. I came a lot, though. It kinda pissed me off that I wasn't enough for her.

"You're managing okay?" I asked her. "I mean, after being in the lake and everything?"

"Poco-poco, you know? Poco-poco."

She said that a lot. I'd asked my dad what it meant. "So-so" in Spanish, he said. I had a thought. Didn't know why it hadn't occurred to me before this. "Hey, Maryssa?"

She glared at me.

"I mean, Aunt Mryss? How come you say that? You know, 'poco-poco.' How come you say it in Spanish?"

She kissed her teeth, rolled her eyes. "Pickney-gyal, you nah know that Jamaica was Spanish one time? So what all that book learning you do in school good for?" But I knew what it meant when the corners of her eyes crinkled up like that. She was pleased that I'd asked her.

"Spanish? When?"

She shrugged. "Centuries. But never mind that. What is this thing you keep trying to tell me?"

Oh, bite me. I'd started it. I had to finish it.

"Auntie, I go places in my dreams. Last night I think I did so for real." What would she say? It was so hard talking to adults about real shit, important shit.

"Finish your food. You been finding yourself on sojourn in a strange land."

Sojourner. Visitor.

She looked out the window. "Heaven forgive," she said, "but I wish it could be me." She sounded so wistful about it. Then she smiled down at the Horseless Head Man in her hand. "But lo, mine own have come to me."

"You don't want to go where I went, Auntie." I took a deep breath, put down my fork, pushed the sleeve of my left arm up, and exposed the black, tarry patch. I showed it to her. "And on top of that, look what else is happening to me."

Her eyes went wide and she leaned forward to see better. "Holy shit. What the rass that is?"

Another time, I would have laughed. Aunt Mryss was always saying things you didn't expect to come out of her sanctified mouth. Instead, I rolled up my left pant leg, showed her my leg. "Remember those spots I was getting? Well, they're spreading. And then I got Rich to touch that weird light that came out of the ground, and bang! I was dreaming, only awake. And then Rich was gone." I was blabbering, the words coming faster and faster, the tears starting again. "And when me and Punum woke up, the whole world had changed and all this horrible stuff was happening, and this black stuff is spreading everywhere on me, and people are dying, and Auntie Mryss, suppose it was all my fault? Suppose I made all of this happen by getting Rich to touch that thing? And what am I going to do when I'm one big blemish from head to toe? If the whole world hasn't blown up by then, or, I dunno, if a big space monster hasn't gobbled down the whole planet like a muffin?"

"First of all," she said, "don't worry 'bout Rich. He called me just now, before you reach here."

My heart did a somersault. "For real? Where is he? Is he okay? Did he report to his parole officer?"

She frowned. "Though, come to think of it, he sounded strange."

My heart crashed back down into my chest. "Strange how?"

"I don't exactly know. Like his mind was on something else." Lightly, she tossed the Horseless Head Man into the air. It chirped happily, took itself on a sail about the room. Auntie pointed a finger at me. "Second thing. You call your parents yet?"

"Yeah. But we got cut off. My phone ran out of minutes."

She nodded. "Awoh. You going to call them when you finish eating."

"Yes, Auntie." Mom would come and get me in the car. If the car still existed. If the highway still ran in the same direction. I found I was looking forward to sleeping in my own bed, in my own house.

"Third thing," said Mryss.

"Yes?"

"So you're changing. You mean to tell me you don't already change every day?"

"I don't understand."

"Everybody change every day. Change is hard." She put an *h* in front of each "every," and took it away from the front of "hard." "You grow bigger, you grow taller, you get fat, you get maawga, you grow titties, the boys-them start to smell good, maybe even the girls, ee? You young people. In my day, we wouldn't talk that out loud."

I could feel myself blushing. "But not like this! I'm not supposed to change like this!"

Just then, the house rocked with the force of something outside hitting it. I cried out, "What the hell was that?"

Auntie Mryss was already up out of her chair, the Horseless Head Men zipping around her. She rushed to the kitchen window, threw it open, and yelled, "Spot! Stop that! Stop it, now!" She turned to me. "Sorry, darling. But now she turn flesh, like she can't behave herself any at all. She want to go out, she want to come in." She shook her head, smiled. "She want to see all there is to see, frighten all them that could frighten."

Well, that frightening thing was working on me, anyway. I stood up. "She just about killed that huge bird!"

"Yes, well, me and she had a little talk about that. She going to behave from now on."

Right. "All the same, I think I'd better go now. Thanks for the meal, Auntie."

She stood up, too. "Well, come and meet her, then, nuh? Now that you don't have to pretend you can see her?" Her eyes twinkled. Damn. All these years, she'd known I was humoring her.

"Spot," said Maryssa, "time for din-dins, sweetie."

More banging. Something large in the backyard was throwing itself repeatedly against the kitchen door.

Auntie called out, "In through the cat flap, Spot! Like I showed you!" Auntie's old cat, Plato, had died last year.

Something wedged a big nose in through the cat flap. That was all that could fit. The nose snuffled around eagerly. It was a damp, sticky nose, matte black. I could hear the rolling calf's yowping bark, the rattle of chains. The Horseless Head Men were hovering on either side of the nose, taunting it by tapping on it; first the left side, then the right. I said, "I wish they wouldn't do that." The nose twitched in curiosity. The rolling calf shoved at the door, which rattled on its hinges. Maryssa put a bowl down near the door. It was her cake bowl; the big aluminum one in which she stirred the batter for the rum-soaked, fruity black cake she made every Christmas. The thing on the other side began to scrabble, to whimper. I think I was whimpering, too.

"Stop that," Maryssa ordered the rolling calf. "Just come in." She winked at me. "She trying to get me to open the door for her, so she don't have to small herself up. Think I don't have the brains God give a guinea hen."

There came another scrabble, a final whimper. Then the nose heaved itself through the cat flap, and along with it, the rest of its body. At first I thought Spot was just oozing her melted tar self through, but as she came, she kind of shrunk. By the time she had poured herself into the kitchen, she was a three-legged black kitten, barely big enough to fit into my two hands. She looked at Maryssa, at me. Her eyes were red. She had a delicate chain around her neck. "Mew," she said, in a tiny kitten voice. Her small mouth was black and wet inside.

Maryssa chuckled. "'Mew' yourself, Madam Spot. You nah fool nobody. Koo your food there." She pointed to the bowl, which was a good two times bigger around than the kitten, and full to the brim.

The kitten's ears perked. She trotted over to the bowl. She had to go past me. I sat down and lifted both my feet up, so there was no chance of her touching me. Her missing front leg didn't slow her down much. She began to lap up the dark brown syrup inside the bowl. When she lapped, she sounded like a much larger animal lapping. Say, like a three-legged monster that came up to my waist. The bowl was half-empty in two-twos.

"What's she eating?"

"Rolling calf food; molasses."

"It smells really good." It did. My mouth was actually watering. It didn't smell exactly like molasses. More like molasses manufactured in heaven. "Can I have some?"

"After you call your parents."

The kitten was done with her meal. Quick as thought, she leapt up into my lap. I yelped and stood up to toss her off. One of the Horseless Head Men swooped down and caught her up by the scruff of her neck.

"Sojourner!" said Auntie. "Mind your manners!" She took

the kitten from the Horseless Head Man. "I told you, Spot not going to hurt you. See?"

She held her hands out. The kitten had tucked herself into one of her palms and was diligently licking itself clean. She was purring.

"Take her."

My heart was pounding, but I reached out and tried not to flinch as Auntie Mryss put the kitten into my hands. Her fur was, well, furry. And soft. A little damp; one or two fine hairs stuck against my hand for an instant, but that could have been because she had been cleaning herself. I could feel her tiny body vibrating with the rhythm of her contented purring. I put her in my lap. I stroked her with a fingertip at first. Then with my whole hand. She looked up at me, half-closed her eyes. She was zoning out on food and stroking. "Aw," I said, "she's cute."

"Didn't I tell you so?"

"It's so weird that I can see her now."

Auntie gave the kitten a bemused look. "I tell you true, Sojourner; I never used to be able to see her either." She raised her eyes to mine. "A lie is a sin, so I must tell the truth; all this time, I knew full well I was only making believe that I had a dog."

I laughed.

"And I never pictured her as a rolling calf."

Uh-oh. "As what, then?"

"A dog. A big brown and white dog. I was so surprised this morning when I called for Spot and this is what came in through the cat door. And when I let her back out into the yard and she grew to her full size . . . Lawdamassy! I nearly dropped my drawers, I was so surprised."

"Uh, Auntie, then how do you know this is Spot?"

She frowned. "Come to think of it, I don't, you know."

I'd been rubbing under Spot's chin. I pulled my hand away. She narrowed her eyes at me and coughed. A black gobbet flew from her maw and landed on my wrist. Immediately, it began to spread. "Jesus Christ!" This time I did dump her from my lap. She landed on the floor with a light thud. I ran to the sink, turned on the water, tried to scrub the new blemish off. It wouldn't budge. It was spreading up my forearm. "Look!" I screamed at Auntie Mryss, showing her my arm. "Look at what she did to me!"

Mryss's jaw dropped. "Lord Jesus. Stay right there," she said. "I going to call for help." She dashed out of the kitchen, probably to the land line in the living room. The Horseless Head Men followed her, wittering.

I stared at my arm in horror. The spread of the blemish had slowed a little, but I could still see it creeping along my skin, feel the itch as it spread. I felt the moment when it reached and merged with the one on my elbow.

There was a hissing sound at my feet. I looked down. The kitten was no longer a cute, three-legged ball of fluff. It was now the size of a raccoon. One ear was missing. The rolling calf bristled. It absorbed its tail. "Auntie!"

The links of its delicate collar swelled back into heavy-duty chain. Its body filled out, became spherical, its surface undulating and puffing out until all that was left of its face were red eyes, a damp snout, and that black, gummy mouth, working and growling, sinking back into the body of the skittering thing and reappearing to face me, no matter how I dodged about the kitchen. "Auntie!"

With a clink of its chains, the rolling calf advanced upon me. I backed away. It kept coming. My back hit the kitchen door. The rolling calf kept coming. I reached behind me, turned the knob, opened the door, and edged outside. Spot, if it was Spot, slammed into the door as I closed it. I heard the door crack. I shrieked. I turned tail and ran for my life, right onto Mryss's backyard lawn. In the dark and in my panic, I couldn't make out where I was going. My foot sank ankle-deep into something soft that I prayed was a pile of leaves. A few steps later, my other foot crashed into something else that felt like an open paint can. My toes jammed painfully hard into it, and the metal mouth of it cracked against my ankle. "Ow! Damn it!"

Another crash came from Auntie's back door, and then the whirring thump of the rolling calf in its spinning stride. Something plopped onto the ground near me. Spot was flinging more of its gooey stuff at me. I shook my foot free of whatever I'd stepped in and ran a few paces more, straight into the chain-link fence between Mryss's yard and the neighbor's. I'd never been good at climbing those. I practically sailed over this one, never mind what might have been leafy grape vines entwining it. I jumped down into the other yard. A dog started barking. "Oh, bite me," I muttered. Perhaps not the best thing to say under the circumstances. Next thing I knew, I was being rushed by a big white poodle, fully groomed and shaved with its fur in those goofy pompons. Full-sized dog, though. With full-sized teeth. It leapt at me. There was nothing I could do. Then a shadow blacker than nighttime leapt between me and the dog. With a yelp, the dog tumbled sideways. And was swallowed up by blackness darker than the night. The rolling calf faced me down.

"Sojourner! Where you?" It was Auntie Mryss.

"Auntie, stay away! Run to the neighbors and hide there!" Crap. Suppose the rolling calf understood me and went after Auntie Mryss? "Go away," I said to it. "I hate you!"

It growled. It gathered itself and leapt at me. I screamed and threw my hands up in front of my face. So it was my bare hands that took the first impact.

It was like gum. Wet, spit-sticky, nasty gum that had been chewed for so long it was stringy, stretching on and on forever and never breaking. It hit my hands with a warm splat. My hands were too small to hold back the hurtling mass of it. The rest landed on my face and neck. I tried to inhale for a scream, but the gunk was stretched like a membrane between my lips and across my nostrils, and I got no air. I clawed at it with hands so covered in gunk that they were useless mittens. I couldn't even open my eyes. I couldn't see or hear, but I could feel. Quick as thought, more of the tarry stuff slipped under my collar and spread down my torso, while the gunk on my hands spread up my arms to meet it. I fell to my knees. Green stars crawled across the universe of blackness behind my eyelids. My ears were ringing. I was suffocating. I clawed and clawed at my face, but couldn't get the stuff off.

And then my mouth was clear. I sucked in air, coughed as I took in too big a breath. My eyelids could open, although they stuck a little on the first blink, pulling hair-thin taffy strands of the black stuff across my eyes. I blinked them clear, struggled to my feet. The lights were coming on in the house of the yard I was in. They apparently had electricity. "Magellan?" called a man's voice. "Where are you? Come here, boy!"

The rolling calf was still in front of me. It seemed a little smaller. I backed up. It followed, but it didn't attack.

"Magellan?"

"Shoo!" I said to the rolling calf. "Nasty, ugly thing." It whimpered.

The back door of the house opened a crack. A man's head appeared around it. "Magellan?"

If Magellan was his poodle, he wasn't ever going to see it again. And if he came outside, that might be the end of him, too. Oh, God. "All right, fine," I said to the rolling calf, "is catch you want to play? Come then, nuh?" I was already running around the side of the house, heading for the front. Behind me, I could hear the splotch and whir of the rolling calf in pursuit. I sped down the front driveway of the house. I leapt over an overturned recycling bin that had spilled crushed plastic bottles and cereal boxes into the road. Then I was out onto Dufferin Street, pelting down it as quickly as I could with my blemish-coated legs straining against the seams of my jeans and shortening my stride.

In the dance movies, people can dance their way out of any trouble. If some bad guy's coming at you, just take him out with a flying roundhouse kick, right? After all, aren't you a capoeirista along with being able to get buck with the best of them and pick up the tango after watching someone do it for, like, five seconds? Oh, yeah, and let's just pretend that standing on one foot while you fling one leg up in the air and swing it in a circle doesn't leave you unbalanced with your crotch open to attack from someone who has the sense to just throw a quick jab at you and get out of the way. If this was a dance movie, I'd have done a flying leap and tumbled over that crumpled motorbike, instead of bashing my shins into it, tripping over it, and scrambling up into a run again. I'd have done a quadruple somersault right over the discarded condoms and broken glass in that alleyway, instead of scurrying through the dreck like a frightened mouse.

But this wasn't a dance movie. I was tiring, and Spot was gaining on me. I dove under an SUV, sliding on my elbows and thighs on the asphalt to get under it as quickly as I could. Those were going to hurt. At the moment, I wasn't paying them any mind. I concentrated on not gasping too loudly for breath. Yeah, so this wasn't a dance movie. But you know what? Being in great fucking shape and flexible with it doesn't hurt, either. So long as you don't try the dumb, flashy moves when you should be throwing down a head butt and a swift kick to the nuts and then running like hell. Spot whirled right past me and kept going till I couldn't see her anymore. But because this wasn't a dance movie, I didn't leap right out from under that SUV the second the bad guy was gone and get on with my life. I stayed under there with tears rolling down my face.

At least, I knew I was crying, but I couldn't feel the tears tracking down my skin. I lifted my arm to put my hand to my face. My palm was covered with gunk from Spot. The dust from the road was sticking to it. The gunk was covering both my hands, all the way up my wrists and probably farther. I didn't want to roll my sleeves up to check. Sobbing, I scraped the dirt off one palm as best I could with my other hand. I couldn't feel where the blemish ended and my skin began. I put my hand to my face to feel the tears. It was like I was wearing vinyl gloves; you know, those thin ones that doctors use? And my face. Oh, God, my face. It was completely covered. I tried to feel my hair. My beautiful hair! It had become lumpy strings of rubber, so heavy that my hair hung down for the first time ever in my life.

The gunk covered my neck. It had slid down underneath the collar of my blouse. I checked out the skin on my chest and my front. I couldn't tell for sure with my muffled hands, but it looked as though I was entirely covered. I tried plucking the stuff off me, but my skin just lifted with it. I would hurt myself if I kept it up, so I stopped. And the worst of it? I was beginning to think that the stuff that Spot had glopped all over me was the same as the blemishes that had been blossoming on my skin for a couple of months now. Horror filled me, rose up my gullet, as strong in the back of my mouth as the taste of rot. "Oh, no," I moaned. I started pulling on the skin on my arms, my neck, my chest. I couldn't help it. All I could think was getitoffgetitoff. I raked my fingers down the side of my face. "No, no. Oh, God, please." There wasn't enough room to move under the SUV. I rolled out from under there. I stood up. About halfway down the block was a bank with a big mirrored window. I headed over there, using parked cars for cover when I could. A little boy walking hand in hand with his mother saw me. He made a face. "Euw. Mum, look!"

"Not right now, Sam." Sam's mum was red-eyed and red-nosed, her voice tired. She was struggling one-handed with about six plastic shopping bags. I could see a few liter bottles of water sticking out of one, and a jumbo package of toilet paper out of another. She had yellow roses growing from her shoulders.

"But, Mum!" He pointed at me. "Is that the Incredible Hulk?

His mum started a fit of sneezing. She put the bags down, rummaged around in them, tore into something inside, and pulled out a handful of tissues. She blew into them before she glanced my way. She looked me up and down, shrugged. "Cry me a river," she said to me. She gestured at the roses. "I'm allergic."

She sneezed again, picked her bags up, took Sam's hand, and trudged on. Sam kept staring back at me, even when he practically had to turn his head all the way around to do so. Actually, he might really have turned it all the way around.

I approached the bank window slowly, from the side. Closed my eyes. Went and stood in front of the window. Opened my eyes.

Oh. My. God.

I was gross. I looked like a lumpy asphalt snowman that had outgrown its clothes. My cute pink blouse had smears of Spot on it, and was grimy from all the sweating and rolling around in the dirt that I'd been doing. It was ruined. I'd paid a week's salary for that blouse! My jeans were torn out at the knees. Lumpy black Spot skin showed through the holes. The jeans had become so tight that they were cutting into my tummy. My head was just this big, round ball with reddened eyes in it. Spot gunk had filled in the curves of my nose so that only my nostril holes showed. I couldn't even see my mouth unless I opened it, and then it was just a slit with teeth and a tongue behind it. My hair was all lumpy black strands. My head looked like a badly made Koosh ball. My hands were thick-fingered, slightly sticky mittens. As I turned them over to look at my palms, a piece of broken glass that had stuck to one palm came loose and fell off. My palms were powdery with dust that was clinging to them. My feet, squished into boots that were now a good two sizes too small, felt like someone had put them in a vise and was tightening it.

Every kid who'd ever read a comic knew how this was supposed to go; if you got covered in the black skin, you would be evil and have scary teeth, but you'd have bitchin' powers, like super strength. And you would be even hotter and sexier than before. You weren't supposed to end up looking like a five-eight pile of walking rubber doo-doo.

When I cried, the tears were black.

An old lady came around the corner of the bank. She screamed when she saw me. Her hair was turquoise and glowing, upswept into a cage that rose about a foot above her head. Pink and green butterflies fluttered around inside.

"I'm sorry," I said, taking a step closer to her. "I just need to get all this crap off me." The giant bird had had to have this stuff burned off. What was I going to do? "Somebody needs to find Spot," I told her. "Like, the animal control people, or something."

The old lady backed away as I came closer. "Please don't hurt me," she said.

She was whispering, but I could hear her just fine. I could see her clearly, too. "Lady, I'm not going to hurt you. I'm just a teenager, okay? I mean, a girl. A girl teenager. And I need help. Something attacked me and—"

Something hard thumped onto my chest and fell off. Had Spot come back? "You leave her alone!" cried a girl's voice. She was black, about my age, wearing jeans and a T-shirt. Her feet weren't touching the ground. She had come up beside the old lady, and her arm was cocked back to throw another rock. She'd thrown a rock at me!

"Hey! Stop that! You could have hurt me!"

"I said, get away!" She threw another rock. It went wide. The recoil pushed her backward a little. "Don't have the hang of this yet," she muttered to herself as she floated back to the old woman's side. It was a weird float. She was striding, as though she were walking on the air. A guy ran up to join the girl. His ears were little white wings.

"Clarissa, be careful!" He stopped and gaped at me. "God. What is that thing?"

"It jumped out from under that car at me!" the old lady told him.

My blood was pounding so loudly in my ears that I couldn't hear anything else. I grabbed the old woman by the collar. She gave a little scream. "Don't tell lies about me! I didn't do anything like that! I'm not like that!"

The girl yelled, "Go on! Scram!" She threw another rock. It didn't hit me. The one her friend picked up and pelted me with did, though. Hard, on the shoulder. So I got out of there.

CHAPTER FOURTEEN

Once more, I wandered the city on foot for hours. But this time I kept to alleyways and hidden places. For a while I'd seriously freaked out. I'd tried clawing the black rind off me. I only ended up gouging my own skin. There were lines of blood on my face, even though the gouges underneath had healed. I began to avoid any kind of reflective surface. I couldn't stand looking at myself. Suppose this change was permanent? What kind of life would I have? No boy would look twice at me. I wouldn't be able to take part in the battle next week. I mean, imagine this body in that short skirt? The audience would either guffaw or puke. I probably couldn't work at the fast-food joint anymore; George, my manager, would never let these hands near the burger patties. And what if this stuff dripped when it got hot, like asphalt in the summer? I was a freak. At school, people would whisper behind my back. I was going to live with my parents forever.

Sometimes I would spy something that looked like Spot, and I'd have to hide. And everywhere I went, people pointed, or screamed, or made disgusted sounds and faces, or backed away, or tried to hurt me. People freaking hurled rocks at me! Though I didn't feel any pain when they bounced off my new skin. If I'd been like this when the girls at LeBrun had stoned me, I probably wouldn't even have noticed. And my hair was more gummed-up now with something worse than the sticky wads of chewed Dubble Bubble that those bitches had jammed all up in my hair. At the time, Mom had said they'd done it because they envied my natural ringlets. She'd had to cut my hair short, and I'd been devastated, but it grew back in, and it was still all curly. Plus by then I was in a new, better school. But where was I now? In Shitsville. Looking like actual shit, with people throwing rocks at me. All over again.

A lady walking in the opposite direction on the sidewalk caught my eye. Asian lady, I couldn't tell how old. They were kinda like us that way; not so much with the wrinkles until they were really ancient. Mrs. Hoshiama who taught Writing Craft at school was nearly forty, but you wouldn't know she was any older than twenty-five. Anyway, this lady didn't lose her shit when she saw me. She just nodded. She was wearing one of those long suede coats with a fur-lined hoodie, and a kicking pair of pointy-toed boots. They would have looked better in black instead of beige. Or in purple; that would have been way cool. She had a little green frog thing sitting on her shoulder, only it had arms and legs like a person, and its head looked like a bowl. It seemed to be whispering into her ear; how neat was that! I almost stopped blubbering, it was so amazing. As the lady drew level with me, she goggled, then tried to look casual, as though I was something she saw every day. She'd noticed that I was crying; I could see it on her face. For a second, she slowed, looking concerned, but she kept on going. It's not cool in Toronto to talk to strangers just 'cause. If I'd just been hit by a car, maybe. Not for a piddly little thing like me sobbing my heart out. The frog thing turned its head to watch me as they went past. I waved at it. It waved back. The friendly gesture made me feel a little bit better, so I used the sleeve of my blouse to dab the tears from my eyes. They made a black stain. So much for feeling better.

God, I missed my mom and dad, and who would ever have believed I could do that? And I missed Richard. I missed the way he would wake me up at ungodly hours of the night, eager to try out his new rhymes on me, no matter how much I cussed him. I missed him teasing me about my eye makeup, calling it "raccoon eyes." I missed him sniggering when he caught me with the most recent HP novel, or reading manga. I missed him saying, "What're you doing with that shit? You don't even know you're black, do you?" If I could have brought him back right that minute, I would never ever cuss him out again if he woke me up at three in the morning with some lame rhyme about the suffering of the black man. I would listen with my eyes wide open like I was really awake, and I would tell him it was the best thing he'd ever done.

I was thirsty. All the public water fountains had been turned off now that summer was over. Though I did find one that spat out mini batteries when you turned the handle. I had a few bucks left in my pocket, but even if I could have found any store that would let me in long enough to buy a bottled water, the few that were open had lines out the door from panicked people stocking up on food, water, batteries, pads. And, boy, was I hungry. My last meal had been back at Auntie Mryss's. A roll of Saran wrap would really have gone down well right about now.

Right. Then there was that; weird appetite, black tears, black blood. Obviously, I had changed on the inside as well as on the outside. Was it making me sick? Was it contagious? Would it get worse? 'Cause, see, there was something worrying me even more about the stuff covering me. It sweated. I'd inspected it when I'd found a streetlight that was working, that hadn't taken it into its head to turn into a tower of dead rabbits with lightbulbs jammed into their mouths, or a giant yellow highlighter. Under the light, I'd been able to see that my new covering had pores, and tiny hairs that looked a whole lot like the hairs I had on my real forearms. I'd once compared forearms with a guy I'd gone with a couple of times. Jimmy Papadopoulos. He was Greek, his skin a little darker than mine without a summer tan, which bugged me. He had the normal guy hairs covering his forearms; easy to see from a few steps away. Maybe even easier, given his heritage. He'd never really looked at a grown girl's skin up close, though. He was surprised to learn that we had body hair, too, though it was usually much finer than on guys. Sweet guy. We never dated, only knocked boots once or twice, but he didn't start treating me weird afterward.

You know, my folks weren't bad people, at least not all the time. They sometimes did kind of neat stuff, when they weren't turning themselves inside out trying to keep me "in line." Like the stories they used to tell me as a kid. I guess that was cool. For years I'd convinced myself that Brer Anansi was a girl, because Dad sometimes said, "Brer 'Nansi." I thought he was saying the girl's name Nancy. Turned out it was a short form of "Anansi," like "Brer" was a short form for "brother." But even after I found that out, I still liked to think of Brer 'Nansi as a girl, because I was a girl. Brer 'Nansi was the star of all the stories about him, even when he screwed up and the other animals were getting back at him for it. He was larger than life; he was a hero. I wanted to be like that. But as it turned out, I wasn't the hero of this story.

I was the tar baby.

I ended up in High Park. I was thinking maybe I could find

a tree or something to sleep in. Maybe I could make a nest, like a gorilla. Could Spot climb trees? By now, I was so exhausted that I almost didn't care. Maybe I could get a job as a gorilla. Maybe the Toronto Zoo would take me. They could put me in a cage, feed me bananas and gorilla kibble, and leave me there for people to stare at.

My phone rang. My phone shouldn't have been able to ring.

With thick, rubber-coated fingers, I fought to get the phone out of the pocket of my jeans, which were now so tight on me that I could barely slip a couple of fingers into my pocket. "Please keep ringing," I begged. I managed to get the phone out, then I fumbled it and it fell. "Damn it!"

It landed on the soft High Park earth. It was still ringing. I snatched it up, and an instant lasted an eternity as I tried to flip it open with my sausage fingers. I did it. Held the phone to my ear. "Hello?"

Still that eerie noise of millions of people wailing, but way in the background this time. "Scotch?"

"Richard? Are you okay? Where are you?"

"I think I'm in the phones." His voice was weird, kind of like he was using an Auto-Tune, only scary, not goofy-sounding.

I leaned against a maple tree. "Did you say, 'in the phones'? This connection's really bad. I'm having a hard time understanding you."

"Hold on. Let me try someth— There. Is that better?" His voice had changed to normal.

"Yes."

"Sweet! I'm beginning to figure this thing out. I made myself a voice by cutting together bits and pieces of other people's voices, you know? Just took me a while to get the samples short enough and pick the notes that matched my own voice. Sis, this stuff is so cool! What's happening out there in the world? The conversations going across the phone lines are incredible, not to mention the stuff on TV."

"Where did you say you were?"

"Okay, I know it sounds wack, but I think I really am in the phones."

The skin on my itchy Koosh ball scalp prickled. "Your voice is in the phones, you mean?"

"Well, yeah. Only it's more than that. It's gotta be my brain, too, right? Or else I wouldn't be talking to you, or extending my reach like this, working out how to bypass the locks so I can activate a phone that doesn't have any minutes on it. I can get GPS on this thing! Hell, I think I *am* the GPS!"

"And I'm the Creature from the Black Lagoon. Are you sure you're not in a hospital room somewhere, stoned on morphine and hallucinating?"

"I don't think so. I made your phone work, didn't I? And while I have you on the line, lemme tell you; I'm so gonna get back at you for ratting me out to Mom and Dad."

"I'm sorry!"

"That doesn't cut it, Scotch." His voice had started breaking up into lots of little voices again. "HOW COULD YOU DO THAT TO ME?"

It was the angry wail of a million trapped people. It gonged through me like Judgment Day. I fell on my knees. "I'm sorry," I whispered.

There was a long silence.

"Rich?"

"Yeah, well, three months in jail is nothing compared to what's happening to me now." His voice was back to sounding normal.

"I'm sorry."

"What're you sorry for now? It's not your fault I ended up in here."

"But I made you touch that bubble!"

He snorted. "As if you could make me do anything. Listen, Sis; I apologize."

"Huh?"

"I knew you were in trouble at LeBrun High, but I didn't know how bad it was."

"But I told you what it was like! I told you and told you! And you just laughed at me!"

"I thought you were just being a girl. You know, all whiny and shit. Who knew girls could be that evil to other girls?"

"Well, now you know."

"I guess I deserved you telling Mom and Dad on me."

"I thought you did, but I was wrong. I was just a big ball of mad at everybody, and scared."

"Yeah, welcome to being a teenager."

I chuckled at that. He laughed with me, and for a second, we were just brother and sister again. Then he said, "The thing is, I don't think I'm ever going to get out of here. Hey; what are you doing in High Park?"

"Hang on; can you see me?" God, I hoped he couldn't see me like this.

"Working on it. Surveillance cameras use a different bandwidth."

"Rich, where's your body?"

"I think it's gone. When that weird white gel sucked me in, I felt it kinda . . . dissolve."

"Oh, shit." I didn't think I had any more tears. "Are you dead?"

"I thought I was at first. God, I've never been so scared in my life. Felt like someone had stretched me out so thin I could cover the whole planet. And then there were all these voices. It sounded like one big wail."

"Yeah, I heard it."

"Anyway, that's not why I called. I called to yell at you. And to apologize. And to tell you this; you need to get home, Scotch. Mom and Dad are going nuts looking for you."

"But I—"

"Don't tell about me, okay? Not yet. I'm putting you through to them now."

"Rich! Wait!"

But there was the sound of a phone ringing on the other end, and a click.

"Hello? Sojourner, is that you?"

"Hey, Dad." It was so good to hear his voice. I hadn't expected to feel that way.

"Where are you, child? You frightened me and your mother half to death when the phone cut off like that."

"Sorry. I ran out of minutes."

"You all right? You hurt? Tell us where you are, and we'll come and get you. Your mother drove through hell and back to get us home to you children. And where's Rich? He called us, but he wouldn't stay on the line."

"He's . . . he's all right."

"Oh, thank God. Thank God."

My father was weeping. For Rich. I said, "He's got, uh, somewhere to stay, but he can't make it home right now."

How was he going to react when I told him what had actually happened to Rich? "Dad, I'm in High Park."

"What you doing all the way down there, right in the middle of the Chaos? Hold on. Tell your mother how to find you."

Mom came on the line. "Sojourner?"

"Mom, please come get me quickly, okay? I'm so scared and lonely out here. Only, Mom? I look kinda different."

"Baby girl, I don't care whether you've grown three more arms or you're suddenly eight feet tall. Tell me where you are, and your daddy and I will move heaven and earth to be there."

Through my sobs, I managed to tell her how to find me. "I'll come out to the street, okay?"

"Okay. Hold tight, sweetheart. We're coming. The car has cheetah legs instead of wheels now, but it runs like the wind."

I sighed in relief and slipped my phone back into my pocket. I started heading for the edge of the park. It was going to be okay. My folks were coming for me, and they'd take me home and feed me and I could sleep in my own bed. They'd figure out some way to help Rich. The rest of the world might be going to hell in a handcart, but I would have my life back.

With a wet, chewy growl, Spot leapt at me and bowled me over. We rolled end over end until I was dizzy. We finally crashed to a halt against tree. Spot snapped at me. I held her back with my hands. I tried to pull away, but my hands stuck to her. I planted my feet against her and pushed. My hands came free with a sucking pop. Spot didn't stick to my shoes. But she lunged and sank her teeth into my forearm. I screamed. The pain of the bite was bad. So was the sting of Spot's venom oozing into my veins, replacing the blood . . .

I yanked my arm away from her as hard as I could. The flesh tore. The red blood stood out starkly against my black rind. But there was already a ribbon of black curling through the red. I slapped my other hand around the cut and ran. I could see the highway. I was so close! If I could just reach the edge of the park . . . If my folks could just be there to rescue me . . . But my feet had swollen a lot with the new skin and all the walking. Every step stubbed my toes against the toe box of my boots so hard, I thought a few of them had broken. Pretty soon I slowed to a hobble. Spot leapt onto my back and pushed me to the ground. She sank her fangs into my shoulder. I rolled over, trying to shake her off, but it was no use. I ended up on my front with Spot still stuck to me. There was that creeping sensation in my veins again, of Spot's venom spreading from where she'd bitten my back. I was too weak to fight anymore. My head thumped down onto the ground. The lights from the highway swam in front of my eyes.

There was a whooshing sound. From above me, a voice said something like, "Oo blue duck!" I heard a thwack and a yipping yelp, the kind a dog makes when you step on its foot. The dead weight of Spot was gone. A pair of feet thumped down close to my head. I saw black boots, and the hem of a black skirt that came down to the wearer's ankles. "Look at that," she said. "You should have come to be my new Vassilisa. It would have been weeks before I would have tried to harm you." She cackled. "Now you're just easy pickings for any old villain that comes along."

"How did you recognize me?" I whispered.

"Dyevuchka, I would know you anywhere, in any disguise. You carry your taint around with you." She giggled; a hideous noise. "Taints are like opinions; everyone has one. See, that's funny because it's a pun."

I didn't care. I was half-conscious. The poison was spreading. I couldn't do a thing as she picked me up and heaved me over the side of her eggshell chariot to land hard inside it in a tangle of arms and legs. She looked older than God, but she was really strong. She joined me inside the eggshell. I felt the eggshell leap into the air and heard the swooshing sound of the giant pestle the witch used as an oar. Then I passed out.

The bump of our landing woke me up. I opened my eyes. I was lying piled in a heap on the bottom of the gently curved, yellowish-white eggshell. It had holes drilled in the bottom. Probably that was how the old lady kept it from flooding in rainstorms.

My neck was cricked at an uncomfortable angle, and I was

lying on one arm, which had gone numb and tingly. I shifted into a more comfortable position. I could see the crowns of trees, and behind them, the sky. It was brightening to daylight. I felt strange. Just, I dunno, different. Not as weak as last night, when Spot had injected venom into me.

A wrinkled face moved in to block the view. "We're here," said the old woman. She was wearing a scarf over tangles of gray hair. She'd knotted the scarf under her chin.

I sat bolt upright. "Mom! My folks!"

"Never mind that. Get out." She climbed out herself over the side of the eggshell and stood waiting for me. "And no tricks, mind."

I reached a hand up to grab the rim of the eggshell. A matte black, lumpy hand, like a glove filled with rocks. "Oh." In the back of my mind I'd been hoping that I'd wake up and find everything back to normal again. Me back to normal again. Stupid Scotch; I'd woken up inside a giant flying eggshell piloted by an old white witch; how normal could that be? Old bat probably wanted to roast me alive and serve me for dinner. The fear came rushing back. Seemed like the past few days had been nothing but.

"Come on, then," she said irritably.

I stood. I was a little wobbly. I looked around. Maybe I could run and hide somewhere, and call my folks again.

We were in a clearing, with trees all around. The trees didn't look quite right. Was that a mulberry? Except the fruit on it looked like tomatoes; purple and yellow striped tomatoes. And over there; coconut trees? In Toronto? There were bushes growing all around the edge of the clearing, with ivy winding over and around them to make the clearing difficult to get to. If ivy leaves were long, pink tongues, that is.

I clambered over the side of the eggshell. As my feet came

down onto the ground, the witch grabbed me by the scruff of my neck. Did I mention that she was strong? "Just to make sure you don't try to go anywhere," she said. There was a smile in her voice. I tried not to think about what that might mean. I didn't succeed.

There was a tramping sound from outside the clearing. Izbouchka came into view, stepping on and crushing bushes that were in her way.

"Hello, darling," said the old lady. "Rocky keeping the egg warm for you?"

Izbouchka made a soft whistling sound through her chimney. She folded her legs and settled down on top of them, almost exactly like a higgler woman gathering her skirt around her to settle in for a day of selling her wares at the market. As soon as she was still, a pigeon flew in through the soft, sparkling morning sunlight and landed on her porch railing. Then another and another, with sparrows flitting in among them. They all jostled for place on the railing. When there was no more space, the newcomers took up perches along the edge of Izbouchka's bumpy roof of human skulls. There must have been hundreds of birds. Looked like she was wearing a big ol' Sunday-go-to-meeting hat trimmed with birds. Except, you know, a hat from hell, because of the skulls. The pigeons cooed, the sparrows chirped, and Izbouchka made this kind of purring noise back at them. For them, she opened her stealth window eyes and batted the lids every so often with a rattling of her shutters that sounded like a light, happy laugh. The kind of laugh of sitting under a spreading tree with your friends on Toronto Island on a bright summer afternoon, and you've all just had ice cream and you're thinking maybe you'll go ride the swan boats on Centre Island, and you and Glory are teasing Ben about his tight white T-shirt and he's blushing 'cause he's not mad, 'cause he understands that it's your way of telling him he's looking really cute and buff this summer and he'll probably have to beat the boys away with a stick, not like last summer, when he was always fretting about his zits and his hair, and he wore thick, baggy sweatshirts all season. And this year he still has zits, but something's changed about him and the zits just stop mattering so much. Like that, you know? Just a chick and her pals, hanging out and shooting the breeze. The witch sighed. "You wouldn't think they were so charming if you were the one spending hours sweeping dung off the porch."

Izbouchka made a sharp noise.

"Oh, you're right about that," the witch replied. "The manure is good for the radishes. Just don't let this lot into the kasha bin, like you did with your other friends." She turned to me, shaking her head. "That buckwheat was supposed to last us all winter. There was so little, I had to add the ground-up bones of a Vassilisa to the porridge to thicken it." She made a face. "Chalky. All winter, the porridge was chalky."

She twirled her pestle, looking thoughtful. She said, "Though, that winter, both the eggs Izbouchka laid had good, thick shells. Neither of them broke." She nodded slowly to herself. Then she seemed to make up her mind about something. She said, "Well, child; time to go in."

I tried to pull away, but it was like being moored with heavy chain to a big cement block. So I stayed there beside her while she said something I didn't understand to her house, and it stood up and gently shook the little birds off. They flew away. "You might have kept one or two," she scolded Izbouchka. "That fat one with the black wing tips would have been just right with some onion and sage stuffing."

Izbouchka made a yowly cat noise of protest at that. But she obediently turned all the way around until her other side was facing us. There was the door; at the back of the house, not the front. There was a human-looking skull embedded in the door where a normal door would have a bolt. The witch said something else in her language. The skull's mouth opened with a metallic thunk, like the sound you hear when a bolt slides open in a big, old lock. The door swung open. It was black inside the house. The witch pushed me on ahead of her toward the door. "Come along," she said, "good little Vassilisa."

Oh, crap. I was going to be a Vassilisa after all. I was going to be her black maid who swept up the pigeon shit and cleaned her toilet and dusted. 'Cause who else would want me, anyway? And when she got tired of me, she'd go all *Nightmare on Elm Street* on me and slice me up into steaks and grind my bones to make her . . . porridge. I thought about all that as she was practically frog-marching me to the doorway. Only I didn't think it that calmly, or in words, exactly. I was pretty much one big ball of panic with a side of panic sauce, going OMG OMG OMG.

The skull in the door gaped, open-jawed, at me, as though it were surprised to see me going into the witch's house more or less of my own free will. Frankly, I was pretty astonished at that, too.

The teeth of the skull had been sharpened to points. When I saw that, my fear turned into one solid ball of sick in my stomach, but the kind that wouldn't even do me the favor of upchucking itself, that would just sit where it was, a lump of scary bad unhappy in my gut.

We stepped in through the door. It slammed shut behind us, and I heard the bolt in the skull lock slam home. We were locked in. At least, I was. And I wasn't going anywhere if the witch didn't want me to.

"Overstuffed" is the word I'd use to describe the decor inside Izbouchka. A plump love seat covered in intricate red and yellow embroidery, with fat matching cushions. Tiny shepherdess figurines on every surface. Punum would have a heart attack if she ever saw this place. Red and yellow rug. Red and yellow quilt on the bed. And I'd swear Izbouchka was bigger on the inside than on the outside.

The old lady let go of the back of my blouse. "Have a seat," she said. "Take the armchair. It's so comfortable you could fall asleep in it."

I boggled at her. She gave me a gentle push in the direction of the armchair. "Nu, go, sit. Don't worry. I'm not going to eat you this time."

Her smile was too menacing to be reassuring. But I stumbled over to the armchair. I couldn't sit down, though. "I'm all dirty," I said. "Plus I kinda drip."

She waved my objections away. "Oh, don't worry about that. When I tell the cushions to get clean, they get clean. If they know what's good for them."

"Then why do you need a maid?"

She frowned at me. "Because magic is hard work. It's just as exhausting as doing the labor with your own two hands. Why would I waste all that energy on cleaning a house? Begging your pardon, Izbouchka."

I didn't get her at all. But I sat down. It *was* comfortable.

"Now," she said. "What about a nice cup of tea?"

"Uh, okay."

She went over to the big cast-iron stove thing. It had no door, and there was a fire roaring inside it. I guess that was where Izbouchka had gotten the fire to burn the giant bird with. If I sat close enough, would some of this stuff melt off me? I went and stood near it, held my hands out to the warmth.

The old lady took a kettle out of a cupboard. "*Vada,*" she said to it.

"Hey, what does 'Oo blue duck' mean?"

She chuckled. She put the kettle onto the iron stovetop to boil. "Ублюдок" she said. "It means 'bastard.'"

"Yeah, that's what Spot is, all right," I replied, looking at my destroyed hands. I really wanted to touch my face. It was as though I couldn't believe what had happened so I kept needing to check. But I could feel my Koosh ball hair bouncing whenever I moved my head, and I could feel the weight of the false skin on me, like a rind covering the pretty fruit inside. I knew that my mouth was still a slit, my face a big ball of sticky. My feet were screaming from being jammed into my boots. I put my hands closer to the fire, to where the heat began to be uncomfortable.

"It won't help," said the witch. Her back was still turned to me, but she somehow knew what I was doing. "You would have to stand in the center of the flames. And then once the crust had burned away, well . . ." She shrugged.

Once the crust had burned away, the flames would burn my real body to ashes. I pulled my hands away from the stove.

The witch brought a tray with a funny-looking teapot on it, and two delicate china cups, decorated with a zigzag design in red and black. "Sit, sit," she said. I went back to the armchair. She put the tray down on a coffee table in front of me, and sat on the couch on the other side. The cups sat in matching saucers. Each saucer held two sugar cubes and a tiny silver teaspoon. She poured tea for both of us. The steam curled upward from the cups. It was the most normal thing in the world.

"Thanks." I picked up a sugar cube and dropped it into my tea.

"No, no, no. This is how you do it. Look." She put one of her sugar cubes onto her tongue. Then she picked her cup up and sipped from it. "You see? You drink the tea through the sugar cube until it dissolves. Or you can sweeten the tea with jam."

"Jam? Euw." I stared into my cup of tea. My tummy growled.

I was starving. "You don't happen to have any cling wrap, do you?"

"No, dear. This is a green household."

"Say what now?"

She cackled. "You think I was always like this? I used to be one of those old women you see in the shops trying to buy a week's worth of food with barely enough money to buy an egg to boil for dinner. Wearing those shapeless black skirts summer or winter and counting out her pennies, looking at the ground in shame." She sat back with a happy sigh. "But then I found Izbouchka wandering lost without her Baba. And now I have as much egg as I want, year round! And I don't look down at the ground anymore. I sail through the skies. These past years have been good ones."

"Wait a minute. The Chaos is only one day old. So how could you have had years of being who you are now?"

She shoved her face into mine. Startled, I jumped back. "BECAUSE, YOU FOOL, THIS HAPPENED TO ME YEARS AND YEARS AGO!"

She was sitting too far away from me to have gotten up in my face like that. Near as I could tell, she hadn't moved. I couldn't let myself forget that she was dangerous. But my curiosity was stronger than I was. "Not this weekend?" I asked.

She shook her head. "Long before that."

"So how come other people can see you now?"

"Perhaps I became real this weekend. Or they did. Either way, now everyone can see the madnesses we all carry around with us and try to hide from the rest of the world."

"And why are you being nice to me all of a sudden?" I whispered. "Is it because I'm ugly now?"

"You mean why am I not enslaving you?"

I nodded and sobbed. It didn't make any sense to be sad

because some horrid witch didn't want me to fetch and carry for her, but I still blubbered like a baby.

She slapped her knee and laughed. "Why, what a very odd question to ask, dyevuchka! You are a very entertaining young lady. And no, that's not why."

"Why, then?"

"It's because Izbouchka is broody."

"You don't want to make me work for you and then turn me into pot roast because your house is depressed?"

"Boje moi. I *should* do all that to you, just because it would be so much fun. But 'broody' doesn't mean that Izbouchka's depressed. It means she's sitting on her eggs to keep them warm. Thanks to you, Izbouchka has a mate!" The way her face lit up made her not look scary at all.

"How— Hang on. You mean that she and that giant bird—"

She nodded. "Yes! Isn't it wonderful? Two eggs she's laid over on side of the volcano there. And they are fertilized; I can see the shadows of the young ones inside them." She sighed happily. "I'm going to be a grandmother!"

"Yay. Listen; you're a witch, right?"

She narrowed her eyes. "Yes."

"Can you tell me how to get rid of a rolling calf? How to get back to my normal self?"

She looked confused. "But you are your normal self."

I felt Izbouchka stand. Then everything in the house lurched sideways. The old lady grabbed for the arm of the couch. Her legs flew up with the jolt, exposing about a mile of frilly white petticoat underneath her dowdy black skirt. My teacup landed in my lap and overturned. Hot tea soaked through my jeans, but with the false skin covering me, it barely felt warm.

"'Bouchka!" shouted the witch. "Dacha maya, kak dyela?"

Izbouchka gave an awful squawk. She jerked sideways

again, in the opposite direction. Her feet started pounding the ground. Izbouchka was on the run. It was like sitting on top of an earthquake.

"What's going on?" I asked the old lady.

"I don't know." She called out something in her language. She had to do it twice. A window appeared in a wall of the hut. She tottered over to it and looked out. "Oh, now, there's a fine pickle. You're in deep trouble, my girl, and you've dragged me and 'Bouchka into it with you."

I didn't point out that she was the one who'd dragged me into her egg ship. "What is it? What's wrong?"

She turned back to me. "It's catching up. You have to go, quickly!" She pointed to the stove. "In there, now!"

I stood up and backed away from her, dodging a plate that had gone airborne. "What are you, nuts? I'll burn up in there!"

She smiled that terrifying smile. "And wouldn't you make a fine dinner then? But it doesn't work like that."

With a crash of breaking glass and a rattling of chains, Spot leapt through the window, throwing the old lady onto the floor. And still, Izbouchka kept running.

Spot came for me. I fell more than dodged out of her way. The old lady lifted her head. The side of her face was bruised. "You have to trust me! Into the stove, or die!"

Spot snapped at me, got only the hem of my blouse. I pulled away, did a running crawl over to the stove. It was roaring full on. Either way, I was going to die.

I leapt in.

CHAPTER FIFTEEN

"So after that, Brer Fox was fed up with Brer Rabbit's prancing and capering, and he figured he'd get him some revenge."

"After what?" I asked Mom. I was in the bed I'd had as a little girl, with the covers pulled up to my chin, only I wasn't little. I was my sixteen-year-old self.

"Tell the thing the right way," muttered Dad. "Where I come from, is Brer Tiger and Brer 'Nansi, not Brer Fox and Brer Rabbit."

"I'm not from where you're from," Mom pointed out. It was true, too. She came from Chicago, from what she jokingly called "Up South" because of all the black people from the American South that had migrated there, looking for work. That's where her folks had come from.

Dad and Mom were sitting on the bed beside me. They didn't seem to notice that I was grown and my feet were hanging over the edge of the bed. My feet hurt, and for some reason I didn't *want to know what was hiding behind me, shielded by the pink composition board headboard.*

Dad scowled and massaged his knee.

"Does it hurt, Daddy?"

He looked at me as though he'd forgotten I was there. He smiled. "Little bit. The doctors say they will fix me up good as new." He'd balanced his cane on the wall where the head of my bed was. It had a black rubber tip, and a set of metal things like teeth you could clamp onto the tip, so the cane wouldn't slip when it was icy. I avoided looking at the toothy black rubber.

Mom brushed some hair back from my forehead. She'd braided my hair into two big plaits to keep it from getting tangled during the night. "Am I telling her this bedtime story or not?" she asked Dad.

"You don't hear the child asking you how the story begin?" he said irritably.

Mom was watching Dad's hand rubbing his knee. She took a breath and calmly replied, "I don't know that part. Did you take your painkiller?"

Dad pressed his lips together and stared at the ground. I actually did want to know what was behind me. I could sense it looming, getting closer. I needed to turn and look at it. But looking at it would make it real, and I wasn't sure I was ready for that.

Dad said, "Brer Tiger had a patch where he plant some peas. He tell Anansi to watch over them for him. But all the while Anansi was the watchman, it was him-one stealing the peas and eating them. Fulling up his belly with Brer Tiger's peas."

Mom smiled. "Every morning when Brer Fox—"

"Brer Tiger," said Dad.

". . . when Brer Fox came to the"—she gave Dad a questioning look—"peas patch?"

Dad nodded.

Mom continued, "Every morning, there were more peas missing. And that wicked old Brer Rabbit, he swore up and down that he'd watched over the peas all night but he hadn't seen a thing."

Dad said, "Brer Tiger—that is to say, Brer Fox—make up him mind him was going to catch that peas thief if is the last thing him do 'pon this earth."

Mom said, "Brer Fox, he sat himself down under a big old sycamore tree, and he thought and he thought. He thought till the sweat ran down his brow. And finally he came up with a plan. He got himself some tar—"

"And a stump."

Mom looked confused. Dad said, "A stump was sticking up out of the ground in him peas patch."

Mom nodded. "All right, then. A stump. Brer Fox smeared that tar all over that stump, and he carved it into—"

Together, Mom and Dad said, ". . . a tar baby!" They looked at each other and laughed. Ignoring the thing looming behind me, I snuggled uneasily down beneath the blankets. Looked like it was going to be a story after all, even if a mixed-up kind of story.

Dad took a turn. "So next morning, now—"

"Don't forget the hat," Mom told him.

"Hat?"

"Brer Fox put a big straw hat on that tar baby's head, so it wouldn't melt away in the sun."

Dad nodded. "Makes sense. So next morning, now, Brer Rabbit—"

"Brer Anansi," Mom cut in. "I think I like that better."

Dad chuckled. "Brer 'Nansi march himself over to Brer Fox peas patch, and him spy the tar baby."

"But Dad," I piped up, "wasn't Brer 'Nansi supposed to be in the peas patch already, watching the peas?"

Dad looked at Mom. Mom looked at Dad. They both shrugged.

"When you tell your version of the story," Dad said to me, "you can figure out that part."

"Okay." Was that a snuffing, snuffling sound from behind me? My parents were acting as though we were the only three in the room. I tried to turn my head to look behind me, but I couldn't make myself do it. My neck muscles refused to work.

"Now, Anansi is a liard son of a so-and-so, but him have manners. So when him see the tar baby, him say, 'Morning, Sister. How do?' But the tar baby never answer him."

Mom tucked the covers up under my chin. "Brer Anansi tried again. He said, 'Nice weather we're having.' But the tar baby said not one word. Now Brer Anansi was getting mad."

Dad straightened his leg out, grimaced, but continued, "Brer 'Nansi think say maybe a-deaf the tar baby deaf. So him shout, 'HOW DO, SISTER?' The tar baby never answer him."

"Brer Anansi had good and lost his temper now. He said, 'I just can't stand no-count, stuck-up people! You mind your manners and give me a decent Howdy-do or you're going to get such a licking!' But the tar baby just sat there."

"So Brer Anansi, he clap him one hand against the side of the tar baby face, braps! And him hand fasten."

"He hit a girl?" I asked. My mouth was moving, saying the right things. My face probably looked calm. But my skin was crawling with the need to turn around, to kneel and look over the headboard and confront the horror on the other side.

Mom cut in. "Brer Anansi said, 'Lemme go, or I'll hit you again!' The tar baby ignored him. So he took his other hand and smacked that tar baby upside the other side of its head. His other hand stuck fast."

"Anansi say, 'Oh, yes? I bet you I kick you!' Him kick the tar baby one time, two time, and both him feet fasten. Him say, 'You think because you fasten my hand and my foot, I can't teach you a lesson? I bet you I buck you!'"

"Brer Anansi," said Mom, "he butted that tar baby with his head as hard as he could. And what do you figure happened?"

"His head stuck, too!" I said, my mouth chortling with glee, my head straining to turn. I could ask my folks to look back there for me, to vanquish the thing, to save me. But only the expected words came out of my mouth.

Mom leaned over and kissed my forehead. "Exactly. So there he was, stuck fast to the tar baby, couldn't move any more than a snake can grow legs and walk. And nothing to do but wait there until Brer Fox came by."

Dad kissed me, too. "Good night, Sojourner. Sleep well." He leaned over and got his cane.

"But what happened to Brer Rab—I mean Brer Anansi? Did he get away before Brer Fox came back?" Or was it Brer Tiger, I wondered? Whatever. I needed them to stay with me, couldn't they see that?

Dad groaned to his feet. "That's a story for another day. We'll finish it tomorrow night."

I pouted, but said, "Oh, okay." I knew better than to argue with Mom or Dad.

Mom turned out the light as they left. Before they got out of earshot, I heard her say, "Cutty, why are you so stubborn? Why won't you take the damned painkillers?"

I never heard Dad's reply. I wanted to be in the story they were telling me. I wanted to be lying in the warm grass in the summer-sunny peas patch, watching Brer Anansi struggle to free himself from the tar baby.

I heard the smallest sound from behind the headboard, like

the rustle of a mouse. But something much, much bigger had made that sound. I took a deep breath in to scream

. . . and I hit the ground rolling. I came up coughing and spluttering. My mouth and nose were full of dust. I choked and gagged on it. A whooping sound came from my throat as I desperately tried to get air instead of dirt. It was hot dirt. It burned going down into my lungs. It *hurt*. I opened my eyes. Mistake. Grit flew into both eyes. I snapped them shut against the scraping sting of it. I sat up, still choking. With my fingers, I did my best to sweep dust out of my mouth. I spent the next few minutes hacking and spitting up dust, and blinking as much of it out of my eyes as I could. As far as I could see, Spot hadn't followed me. But I couldn't see much.

I was alive. No third-degree burns. Or would it be fourth-degree burns, now that I had an extra layer of skin? Whatever. There was fog all around me, so thick I couldn't see my own hand in front of my face. Just as well. I wasn't liking looking at me right now. It was like being completely wrapped in a flannel blanket. Cautiously, I put a hand onto the ground I was sitting on. It felt like soil, crumbly between my fingers. I swept my hands through the air all around me. Nothing. My heart was trying to slam through my chest wall; boom boomboom boom. I tried for deep breaths to calm it down, got more fine dirt for my trouble. I had to get the coughing under control. Didn't know what might come following the sound.

Where was I? The old witch had said I should trust her. Well, at least I wasn't crisping in her stove like bacon.

Except . . . that smell. Kinda smoky. It wasn't dirt getting everywhere, it was ash! Was I still in her stove? Had she magically instantly cooled it down so that I wouldn't burn? Who knew? Who knew anything for sure today?

The ash I'd kicked up was settling. It was getting a little easier to see. From the gentle breeze on my face, I figured I was outdoors. Vague shadows off in the distance, maybe buildings and trees. Was I back in High Park? If so, what had happened to it?

There came a soft hissing sound. Then a rumble I could feel in my bones, then a crack of thunder. Wherever I was, there was going to be a rainstorm, soon. The ground under me was pleasantly warm. It radiated heat that I could feel even through my new skin.

The cramped ache of my feet was getting to me. I leaned over and pulled my boots off. My feet were hideous, but I couldn't stand the burning pain from the too-small boots a second longer. OMG my toes felt so good not being bunched up anymore! Why hadn't I done that before now? I wiggled my toes on the warm ground. Ash sifted over them, dusting them to gray.

There was that rumble under my feet again. And more thunder. I stood. I was on an incline, a steep one. I looked up. An ash cloud bubbled above me, curling in on itself and expanding at the same time. It looked miles high. For a few seconds I just stared into the roiling mass of it, too awed to do anything else. The volcano cloud hadn't come this low over the city before.

Or maybe it hadn't sunk down lower. Maybe I was just up higher. My skin started to prickle with the awfulness of my approaching realization. I didn't want to know what I was about to know, but I had to find out. I had to turn all the way around to follow the pulsing mass of cloud back to its source, to the horrible thing I was sure I would see behind me—there. The spluttering mouth of the volcano Animikika, only about half a mile above me. It was spitting ash and the occasional plume of fire. Animikika; "it is thundering." I was standing on the slope of an active volcano. If everything weird in the world in the past couple of days was a manifestation of someone's madness, which rahtid insane so-and-so had been seeing Toronto Island as a live volcano?

As I watched, a red tongue of molten lava swelled up from Animikika and spilled over her top, into a channel already gouged by previous flows. For some reason, I'd thought that lava moved slowly, like heavy syrup. This came rushing down like a river. I was standing right in its path. You'd better believe I hot-footed it out of the way. Might have made it, too, if I hadn't tripped on a lump of rock hidden under the ash. I fell on my hands and knees right on the very edge of the river of lava as it hissed by me. The heat from it on my face was intense.

Yikes! The fingertips of one hand felt like I'd dipped them in hot water! I yelped, snatched my hand up and instinctively shook it off even as my eyes were seeing what had burned them. As I'd put my hands down to brace my fall, the tips of my fingers had landed in the lava flow. I was shaking liquid lava off my fingers. Holy crap. I blew on the scalded fingertips. Shouldn't they have burned right off, or something?

The new lava flow hit the lake water far below me. The water around it evaporated immediately into hissing steam. The fog around this place wasn't just floating ash, but steam from the lake.

A fish scuttled past my feet on four stumpy webbed legs. It said, "Whee!" as it leapt into the lava river. I watched its wavery shadow beneath the surface as it darted upstream. It'd looked like a salmon. All the way up and down the lava river, I could see other walking salmon taking the same leap. I tried to remember my bio lessons. Salmon changed a few times during their life cycle, right? Did they grow legs at some point and then lose them later? Whatever. I was pretty sure they never were able to swim in liquid rock.

I choked and coughed some more. I was breathing in ash and heaven knew what else. I could get buried in a lava flow any second. I needed to get off Animikika, like, yesterday.

The volcano rumbled again. I tensed myself and watched the mouth of it, ready to run. With a boom, Animikika spat out a jet of—what, exactly? Was that ash? Small rocks? Chunks of it started raining down on my head. I covered my head with my hands. The stuff didn't hurt as it fell on me, though. It was too light. The tiny pieces pockmarked the ash on the ground as they disappeared beneath it.

A bigger piece landed at my feet. It was beige, flattish, uneven, only about an inch or so around. It didn't sink into the ash. It had a strip of paper stuck to it. The paper caught the breeze and flew away before I could do anything.

More of those larger pieces were falling now. I crouched down and looked at one of them. I wasn't going to touch it until I knew what it was. Something about it looked familiar. And added to the smell of burning, there was also a sweetish smell in the air now. Not a good mix, let me tell you.

Something small bopped me lightly on the head. I put my arms up again to protect myself. My fingers touched the thing that had fallen into my hair. It was cool. It crumbled in my hand as I grasped it. I pulled it out of my hair. Apparently, I was smelling cookie dough baking. I was holding a crumbled fortune cookie. Whole bits of cookie were falling now from the volcano's last outburst. I unfolded the fortune in mine. It read, *Rhubarb, rhubarb, rhubarb.* I picked up a few more. They all read the same thing. I was still starving, so I ate a few of them, never mind that they had ash on them. They would have tasted better wrapped in cling wrap. My tummy grumbled. A few fortune cookies weren't going to be enough to satisfy it.

The breeze picked up, and the fog cleared a little more. The shadows in the distance looked like a couple of trees. On a volcano that a couple of days ago had been lava erupting from the bed of Lake Ontario? They weren't that far away, so I headed toward them. Maybe one of them would be a fruit tree, and I could have breakfast. Man, I was tired, too. Closest thing I'd had to sleep in nearly two days was being unconscious while a witch took me to her house. Oh, and I guess when Punum and I had had the joint dream, or adventure. That'd been a few hours. My body with its new coating was heavy, though. I was feeling it, dragging the weight of it around.

In the few minutes it took me to walk to where the trees were, the volcano spat out household smoke alarms (all beeping; go figure), a rain of clear plastic name tag holders (I ate a few of them; they were okay), more lava, and lightbulbs. That last one was messy; broken glass everywhere. My taint-thickened feet crunched through the glass as easily as if it were freshly fallen snow. There were some advantages to this new body.

I was almost at the trees. There were two of them. They were higher up on the hill, with only a small rise now between me and them. One of them was a fir. And was that other one a peach tree, complete with ripe peaches? I used to like peaches. But my new taste buds were sending me messages that the last thing they wanted was peaches. Great.

I clambered up over the rise. The roots of the two trees were hidden by low-lying fog. No. Fog didn't have a pearly glimmer like that. Fog didn't bulge out like a big balloon. It was the bubble I'd seen in Bar None! And lying facedown with one leg buried thigh-deep in it was—

"Tafari!" Fatigue forgotten, I sprinted in his direction, dreading the worst. "Tafari!"

My heart leapt when he lifted his head to squint at me through the gloom. He was alive! Or was he? "Tafari!"

He struggled awkwardly to prop himself up on one elbow. "Get away!" he yelled. "Shoo!" He picked up a branch that was lying nearby and swung it at me. He hit my leg. I barely felt it. I moved back a little.

"Taf, it's me. It's Scotch." Something smelled good, a mixture of molasses and new plastic.

"*Scotch?*" Tafari's eyes went wide. "You're Scotch? You're shittin' me."

"I'm not. It really is me." All I wanted to do was hug him. And maybe eat a little something. But he was ready to fight me off.

"What the hell happened to you?" He didn't put the branch down. "And how do I know it's really you?"

I remembered the fake Tafari I'd seen. "Yeah, I might say the same thing. Can you smell that?" My tummy rumbled again. I checked out Tafari's hands. One of them had fused fingers. It was him. "Are you okay?" I asked him. "Are you hurt?" I tried to get closer—for one thing, the delicious smell was somewhere around him—but he brandished the branch at me. "Get real," I said. "A little piece of wood can't stop me now."

I grabbed the end of the branch. He shouted as I yanked it out of his hand, but not in alarm; in pain. He held on to the thigh that was trapped in the bubble. He grimaced.

"Oh, crap!" I said. "Did I hurt you? Taf, I'm so sorry!" That smell was getting more and more distracting.

"I can't get out of this thing," Taf replied. "I've been trapped in here since—"

"Since Bar None the night before last. I know."

"What the hell is going on? What is this thing I landed on?"

"I don't know. Stuff is crazy all over." Mesmerized, I reached for the part of the bubble that was holding him.

Gently, he batted my hand away. "Don't touch it! It might suck you in, too. It's been getting tighter. I can't feel my leg anymore."

"Poor Taf." My hand was already sneaking back toward the bubble. I sniffed; it was what smelled so good.

"So, what happened to you really? Are you okay in there?" Taf asked.

"I'm seriously ugly now, I know." I was practically drooling, I was so hungry.

"That's not important. Are you hurt? Hey, what're you doing?"

I'd crouched down beside him. I was tearing at the bubble. It was stretchy, and tough, a bit like trying to get the cling wrap off a sandwich.

"Scotch, no! It's not safe!"

A strip of the bubble came away in my hands. Tafari gaped at it. "How'd you do that? I've been trying to get it off me for almost two days."

"Piece of cake," I replied dreamily. "And speaking of cake . . ." I held the strip of bubble up to my nose. I have no words for the glorious smell that rose from it. I put it into my mouth.

"Don't do that!"

But I was chewing it already. I stuffed it all into my mouth. "Don't be silly," I told him through the mouthful. "We have to get you free, right?"

He stared in amazement as I tore strip after strip of the bubble away. Soon I had his leg free. He cried out and started massaging the leg. "It's all pins and needles," he told me.

"That's the blood rushing back in." I crammed some more of the bubble into me.

"How's it taste?" Tafari asked.

I really didn't want to share, but this was Taf, after all. I held a strip out to him. "Here. Try it."

He grimaced. "No, thank you. Listen, we should get out of here. I'd say we both need to go to a hospital."

"Good luck trying to get in the door of one. Do you have any idea what's been going on in the rest of the world?"

He shook his head no. "My phone died yesterday morning."

The volcano erupted again. By the light of it, I finally noticed the burns on his face and hands. "Shit, I'm being so selfish! You're hurt bad!"

"And you're eating . . . What is that, anyway?"

"Breakfast."

"How'd you get here, Scotch? Did you come on the ferry?"

"No, I came through a witch's stove. Don't look at me like that. There is no ferry." I kept stuffing my face, but a thought was worming its way through my feeding frenzy. Rich had been able to call me, even though my phone was dead. Maybe it worked both ways? "Taf, get my phone out of my jeans pocket, will you? My fingers are too clumsy like this."

Hesitantly, he scooched closer to me and slid my phone out of my pocket.

"Now call Rich."

He punched in the numbers and put the phone to his ear. His face fell. "The phone's dead."

"I know." I held out my palm, and he gave me the phone. I put it to my ear and waited. Sure enough, Rich came on the line.

"Scotch! And you found Tafari! I just kept getting static when I tried to call him."

"And I see you got that whole surveillance camera thing worked out."

"Yeah. I can reach the telecommunications satellites. How cool is that? Holy shit! What's that thing beside Tafari?"

"It's me."

"Oh, my god!"

"I'm okay, Taf's okay, but this volcano could take us out any minute. I want you to practice saying something for me."

"How's that going to help? I'd send an ambulance helicopter or something, but most flights have been shut down."

"Just repeat it after me. I want you to send it out along the wires, or whatever you do, till someone answers. She's gonna be pissed. But tell her I solemnly pinkie swear never to use it again, and could she please send that fire bird over to the part of the volcano where we are?

"What? What're you talking about?"

"Just do it, please." I had him repeat the phrase for calling Izbouchka until I was certain he had it mostly right. And all the while, I kept snacking on the bubble. I'd eaten about half of it. The rest was beginning to look lumpy and deflated. When Rich rang off to try to get help for us, I said to Tafari, "We might have a lift out of here."

"Is Rich going to come for us, or something?"

"Or something, yes." I wanted to cry. "Taf, Rich isn't doing so well right now."

He replied, "Scotch, don't move."

"What?"

"Don't move, I said! There's something behind you."

I got the creepy-crawlies between my shoulder blades. I wanted to look behind me, but I didn't dare. "Is it black and blobby with a mouth like gears grinding in old oil and too many legs?"

"Six, or eight, or four. I can't exactly tell. I think it's black, but it's too covered in ash for me to be sure. What the hell is it?"

"Oh, no." Skin prickling, I turned to face the horror behind me, just as Spot leapt at me.

"So Brer Anansi, he clap him one hand against the side of the tar baby face, braps! *And him hand fasten."*

I slapped Spot. My hand held fast. Spot growled and snapped at me.

"He took his other hand and smacked that tar baby upside the other side of its head."

I slapped my other hand onto her. "Got you now!" I crowed at her. Spot was heavy. But I was the Queen of the Thunder-Thighed, and right now, I was pissed. I used my thighs and I pulled and pulled. Inch by inch I was dragging Spot along.

"Scotch, what're you doing!?" called Tafari. "You'll get killed!"

"Maybe, but I'm taking this bitch out with me!"

Spot did that nasty trick of swallowing her own face and then pooching it out somewhere else on her body; in this case, her snarling snout almost took my nose off.

"Oh, yeah?" I asked her.

"I bet you I buck you!"

I head-butted her as hard as I could, right in the snout. She yipped in pain. "Take that, you giant zit!"

Of course my head didn't come free. Being stuck like that made it harder for me to see where I was going. I had to kind of crank my neck, and I could only see out of one eye. The other eye was so close to Spot that it was seeing only black. I had to move kind of sideways. With each step I took farther up the hill, I stuck the landing, bent my knees, flexed my thighs, and dragged Spot a little farther. "How you like my one-two step now?" I growled at her. She was fighting to get away. Her legs scrabbled in the ashy powder dust, but couldn't get any purchase. And then we were at the roaring red mouth of Animikika. The volcano spat a red gout upward. Spot whinnied. She dragged me a few feet back down the mountain. I dragged back until we were at the mouth of it again. "Plenty power in these legs, sweetie. I could do this all day."

"There he was, stuck fast to the tar baby . . . and nothing to do but wait there until Brer Fox came by."

I looked down into the glowing heart of Animikika and tried to figure out what to do next.

"Can you tell me how to get rid of a rolling calf? How to get back to my normal self?"

I'd lied to Spot. I was getting tired. I don't know what I'd been thinking. That I'd be able to throw her into the volcano, at least stop her from turning other people into freaks like me. But I couldn't get unstuck. I sat down. Threw myself onto my butt, more like. I planted one foot on the ground. I set the other foot onto Spot's body and pushed, trying to pry her off me.

"Him kick the tar baby . . ."

It didn't work. And now, damn her, she had four of my five ends bound to her. Spot and I were both panting hard, from fatigue and because it was bloody hot up there. A limp black tongue hung out of Spot's mouth.

"Why can't you just leave me alone?" I asked her.

"But you are your normal self. You carry your taint around with you."

So I did the only thing I could do. Pushing with one leg, I dragged us right to the very edge of Animikika's blowhole. "Looks like you're stuck with me," I murmured to Spot, who was pulling wildly to get away. Then I leaned over the edge until I overbalanced us, and Spot and I fell into the heart of the volcano. I thought I heard Tafari shout as we tipped over.

It was freaking hot in there! The fall was short. For the umpteenth time this weekend I landed on something hard. I lay there, overheated but undamaged, waiting to burn up. It didn't happen. I opened my eyes. Everything was red and yellow, flames flaring upward, lava shooting out. And a sound like the biggest Bunsen burner in the whole universe.

Spot and I were on a ledge a few feet inside, just under Animikika's lip. Spot was whimpering. I lay there in the mouth of the fire and watched it turn my clothing to ash, and the only time it burned badly enough to injure me was when the metal button on the waistband of my jeans went red-hot and melted onto me. I screamed and thrashed and begged for someone to help me then. Couldn't thrash much; I was too stuck to Spot.

Slowly, the pain on my belly eased. I couldn't see the button anymore. Spot was smaller too! Was she melting away? Burning up? I raised my head. No flowing black runnels of Spot stuff. No flames on her. No ashes. She was just shrinking. And something was squeezing me all over, like I'd put on a woollen bodysuit and stepped into hot water. Like my skin was getting too small for me. Ow, ow, ow.

And eventually that feeling passed too, and there was no more Spot. I sat up and looked down at my body. I was back to my normal size! Something was weird about my skin, though. I couldn't tell for sure in the red light inside the volcano. It'd have to wait until I got back into the daylight.

I stood up and started climbing. I slipped a few times when handholds and footholds crumbled under me, and at one point I was stuck halfway. The nearest handhold was out of reach. I stayed there until I got up the courage to leap for it. Caught it! I made it right to the top, and clambered out.

I looked down at my skin. Yup, I was black all over. A for-real black, not brown. And gleaming. "Kind of like a Shrinky Dink," I muttered to myself. "Right on." I had a scrape on my shin. A little broken line of red. I guess I hadn't kept the magical healing powers. I so didn't care right then.

I felt my head. I was stone-cold bald. Crap. Just my luck.

Tafari was sitting where I'd left him, under the peach tree. Richard was lying beside him. I shrieked Richard's name and ran toward them both.

Taf's jaw dropped open when he saw me. "Scotch? Is that you?"

"Yeah. Where'd you find Rich?" I dropped to my knees beside them.

"He was inside that thing you were eating. When you were gone, it turned brown and kind of melted, and there he was."

Rich's skin had a sickly gray undertone. His eyes were closed. I didn't think I could take another blow. "Is he . . ."

"I'm here," whispered Rich. "Just barely." He didn't open his eyes. "Now I know how the roots of a plant feel when you pull it out of the ground."

I'd just come out of a volcano; I didn't dare touch him. "Oh, God; I thought you were lost forever."

"I thought I was lost forever, too. Listen, I'm really tired. Can't talk too much."

"Okay, but stay with us, all right? I couldn't bear to lose you again."

He nodded. He opened his eyes a little and looked at me. "Trust you to go changing into yet another outfit."

"Bite me." I don't think he heard me. He looked like he'd fallen asleep. "Rich?"

"He's okay," Taf told me. "He keeps drifting off like that."

Taf reached for me. "Careful," I said. "I think I'm still hot."

His smile was crooked. "You betcha you are. Still hot." He touched a pinky tip to my shoulder. "A little warm," he told me. "But I think I can handle it."

I went into his arms. I sighed, as though I'd been holding my breath for a very long time. And then we were both sobbing.

When we'd both calmed down a little, he said, "Is that thing gone?"

"Kinda, yeah. It won't be coming back to chase me anymore."

"You don't have any hair."

"I know, right? The volcano must have burned it away. I really hope it grows back in."

"And you're black and shiny all over, like somebody enameled you."

I swallowed. "Can you handle it?"

"Is it permanent?"

"How should I know?"

"It's kinda cool."

"Thank you."

"And you're naked."

I smiled. Trust Tafari. The first thing on his mind had been whether I was okay. Other guys would have been all like, *Ohmygod there's a totally naked shiny hottie in my arms; I must get with her.* "It's nothing you haven't seen before," I told him.

He held me away from him. "Oh, you're plenty I haven't seen before. You're amazing."

He was giving me a good looking at. "Stop it," I said. "You're making me feel shy."

"Here. Take my jacket. Sorry about the burn holes."

I put on the jacket, the one I'd given him. It smelt of him. It was like coming home. "Taf, this is so short it's almost worse than wearing nothing at all."

He leered at me. "Yeah."

I would have shoved his shoulder, but in his present condition that probably wasn't a good idea. Besides, all I could do was smile. "Hey," I said, "we need to get off this mountain. Rich?" Had he been able to get help for us before the bubble had released his body back to him?

He coughed weakly. "I'm on it." He sounded very pleased with himself. "Our ride should be showing up any minute now. That was some weird lady you sent me to."

"Tell me about it."

"Think she'll have room for one more?"

"Yeah, probably."

A loud caw split the air. Taf held his palms to his ears. I looked in the direction of the sound. Out of the cloud of smoke came the giant bird. Its gold and red plumage was the brightest thing in the sky. I smiled. "So Rocky's gonna be our ride. I guess it's Izbouchka's turn to sit on the eggs."

"Holy shit," said Tafari. "That thing's not coming here, is it?"

"It's okay. It owes me a favor. It's going to take us home."

Tafari stared at the bird and swallowed. "You're sure about all this?"

"No way am I sure."

"Scotch," said Rich hoarsely. I knelt close to him so I could hear him better. "Did you hear Dad? On the phone?"

"Dad? When?"

"When I put the call from him and Mom through to you in High Park."

"You bastard! You were eavesdropping."

"Yeah. And Dad cried because he thought I might be dead." His voice was weak, but he was smiling. He couldn't see it, but I smiled back.

"Guess the old man has a heart after all."

FIVE THINGS YOU THOUGHT WOULD
NEVER HAPPEN TO YOU

So here I am again, after all that excitement, sitting in school and filling out one of Mrs. Kuwabara's endless questionnaires. At least I have something interesting to write this time.

1. *The first, biggest thing is the Chaos. It came, it changed everything, it went, and the world more or less survived. Not all of us, obviously. Jimmy Tidwell lost his sister, his granddad, and his mom. I see him in class, and he looks as though he doesn't know what hit him. Panama won't talk about whether or not she lost anybody. In fact, she refuses to talk at all. The dance battle never happened; too many of the competitors were missing, injured, or dead. Besides, the hall where it was going to happen was now a pile of rubble. Every class I go to, there are more empty chairs than there used to be. I feel*

as though I've attended a million funerals. I've cried and cried, and I know there'll be more tears to come. There are people I will miss for a very long time. Our school has started doing grief counseling for students and staff. I've learned what the letters in "PTSD" stand for. There's still no explanation for what the Chaos was, what caused it, or what made it go away. Animikika sank, almost as quickly as it had risen. I don't know what happened to Izbouchka and Rocky and their eggs, or to the old lady. Sometimes I'm tempted to go outside and say, over and over again, "Dacha maya, idti syuda," just to see whether Izbouchka comes. But I promised the old lady I'd never do that again. I kinda hope she's okay, wherever she is. I thought she was scary at the time, but now that I think about it, she didn't do anything that scary.

2. *I became a hideous monster for a while. That was the thing I'd feared the most, and it happened. I still have nightmares about being attacked by Spot. In my dreams, when the rind covers my skin, it blocks up my nose and mouth, too, and I start to choke. A couple of times, I woke up screaming. Because my nightmares came true once before, so how do I know they won't this time? It's true that a lot of the symptoms of the Chaos are fading away. Mom says that it's as though the whole world suffered a flu epidemic, only the sickness we had was the Chaos. People on the news have been talking about whether we'll see successive waves of it, like we do with the flu. I hate to think about something like the Chaos happening ever again, but I hate to think about a lot of things. Doesn't stop those things from happening. When*

night terrors wake me up, Mom makes me hot cocoa. She lies on my bed beside me while I drink it. She tells me stories until I fall asleep again. Sometimes I get her to tell me the one about Brer 'Nansi and the tar baby.

3. *Speaking of my skin, it's faded from a shiny metallic black to a rich dark brown. It's turned back into plain old skin, except I'm darker than Mom! And I love it. Even though security guards follow me more often now when I go into stores. Even though some of the guys who used to be sniffing around me now look at me like I'm the help; which is to say, they don't see me at all. I love it, and I hope I stay this shade, because then no one will ever again tell me that I don't look black.*

4. *My friend Gloria is a lesbian! Even though Punum broke up with her, Glory still likes girls. Punum said Glory was too "ableist." I had to look that one up, but when I did, I understood. I couldn't date someone either who couldn't wrap their mind around the fact that even though we both live in the same world, my world is a different one from theirs. I think Gloria's beginning to figure out how that works. It was too late for her and Punum, though. Punum's dating Kathy from Bar None. When she and Kathy look at each other, they both go all goo-goo eyed. And the coolest thing; Punum's eyelashes are still gold. She got a steady gig working with the organization that's helping the Toronto Island dwellers rebuild their homes. She's got a new guitar on layaway.*

5. *I have a Horseless Head Man as a pet. I never thought I'd actually want one hanging around me. Horseless*

*Head Men were one of the things that didn't disappear
when the Chaos went away. Aunt Mryss still has her
two. But she doesn't play the "Out, Spot" game with me
anymore. Her Horseless Head Men are named Mickle
and Muckle. I named mine Charlie; get it? Charlie
Horse. Ben thinks it's the silliest joke he's ever heard.
Ben also says that his invisible friend, Junior, is still
hanging around. He's getting really good at not letting on. Only Glory and Stephen and I know about it.
Sometimes I think I can feel a slight breeze when Junior
walks by me, like a goose walking on my grave.*

6. *I think I can wait a couple more years before I move out
of my folks' place. Isn't that wild? Funny what a difference a couple days can make. Rich says he's no longer in
a big hurry to move out, either. For one thing, he'll need
a few more weeks to recover from having been inside that
bubble for nearly two days. Plus things are different at
home nowadays. Dad still tries to put Richard down
for every little thing, but now he does it like he's joking.
He hugs Rich a lot, too. Rich has started spitting some
of his rhymes for Dad; the ones he's polished to a shine
by rehearsing them on long-suffering Tafari and me.
And Dad listens! Sometimes he'll roll his eyes and say
something sarcastic about a particular line, but sometimes he'll nod at a line as though he agrees with it.
He's been boasting to his friends about his son the poet.*

*And yes, I told Mom and Dad that I was dating
Tafari. They seemed okay with it. They have their minds
on bigger things. Two of Dad's ten employees died during the Chaos. His brother back home in Jamaica is in
the hospital. They're not sure whether he'll survive. And*

no one's seen Mom's best friend here in Toronto, not since Animikika rose. I guess that compared with stuff like that, the news that your daughter wants to be a professional dancer and is dating a really nice guy doesn't seem so bad. So Taf and I are still together, and that's great. But lately, I've been thinking about it. Tafari's wonderful. He's nice and normal and he treats people well, and he has a car and he's hella cute. If his dad is anything to go by, he's going to stay cute for a long time. But as much as he can, he's going to do everything in his life exactly the way he's expected to. Finish high school. Go to university, major in something that looks really impressive on a resume. Use that resume to score a good job, and soon after that, find a wife and start having kids with her. He's already talking about how good-looking our children would be. Part of me thinks that's awesome, but part of me hungers for something different. I don't even know what it is yet, but I'm going to go find it. It'd be great if Tafari wanted to find it with me; in fact, I'll be a total wreck if he doesn't. But I've been a total wreck a couple of times already in my life, and I've learned that I can make it through to the other side.

Yeah, I know this is six and I was only supposed to list five. Bite me.